~ A ~
Question
of
Time

Tor books by Fred Saberhagen

The Beserker Series
The Berserker Wars
Berserker Base (with Poul Anderson, Ed Bryant, Stephen
Donaldson, Larry Niven, Connie Willis, and Roger Zelazny
Berserker: Blue Death
The Berserker Throne
Beserker's Planet
Berserker Lies
Berserker Man

The Dracula Series
The Dracula Tapes
The Holmes-Dracula Files
An Old Friend of the Family
Thorn
Dominion
A Matter of Taste

The Swords Series
The First Book of Swords
The Second Book of Swords
The Third Book of Swords
The First Book of Lost Swords: Woundhealer's Story
The Second Book of Lost Swords: Sightblinder's Story
The Third Book of Lost Swords: Stonecutter's Story
The Fourth Book of Lost Swords: Farslayer's Story
The Fifth Book of Lost Swords: Coinspinner's Story
The Sixth Book of Lost Swords: Mindsword's Story

Other Books
A Century of Progress
Coils (with Roger Zelazny)
Earth Descended
The Mask of the Sun
A Question of Time
Specimens
The Veils of Azlaroc
The Water of Thought

~A~
QUESTION
OF
TIME

T 19035

Fred Saberhagen

A TOM DOHERTY ASSOCIATES BOOK
NEW YORK

This is a work of fiction. All the characters and events portrayed in this book are fictitious, and any resemblance to real people or events is purely coincidental.

A QUESTION OF TIME

Copyright © 1992 by Fred Saberhagen

This book is printed on acid-free paper.

A Tor Book
Published by Tom Doherty Associates, Inc.
49 West 24th Street
New York, N.Y. 10010

TOR® is a registered trademark of Tom Doherty Associates, Inc.

Library of Congress Cataloging-in-Publication Data

Saberhagen, Fred
    A question of time / Fred Saberhagen.
      p.   cm.
    "A Tom Doherty Associates book."
    ISBN 0-312-85129-4
    I. Title.
    PS3569.A215Q47   1992
    813'.54—dc20   92-3602
                                        CIP

First edition: May 1992

Printed in the United States of America

0 9 8 7 6 5 4 3 2 1

~ A ~
Question
of
Time

~ 1 ~

1935

J ake Rezner had never owned a watch, but the lack
had rarely worried him, and he didn't mean to let it
bother him today. Squinting up at the first direct rays
of the morning sun, just coming clear of an eastern cliff,
he thought that today the sun would let him tell time well
enough. He might get back to camp too late for evening
chow, but that wouldn't really matter. All he really had
to worry about today was getting back before it got too
dark to walk the Canyon trails. If he should get caught
out overnight, or was so late returning that the camp
authorities started to organize a search for him, they
might begin to be uncomfortably curious about where
he'd been.

For Jake the seven days since last Sunday had
dragged almost as if he were in prison, or as if there could
be something wrong with all the clocks and watches in
the camp, and with the calendar that had spent this week,
like every other week, hanging on a pole in the orderly
tent.

Anyway, Sunday had at last come round again, and
right after morning chow Jake had got hold of a canteen
and come down here to the creek to fill it. At the moment
he was squatting on the rocky lip of Bright Angel Creek,
his right hand holding the two-quart vessel under water,

air bubbles coming up in a way that made it look like he might be drowning a small animal. The canteen was surplus military equipment, like Jake's khaki clothes, like his sturdy boots and his round-brimmed fatigue hat, all on loan from the army to help the Civilian Conservation Corps get going in these dark days of the Depression.

Early June sunlight, hot but not nearly as hot as it was going to be in a few hours, sparkled off the surface of the noisy creek, glinting in the small patches where the water wasn't too chopped up by turbulence to be anything but white froth. The dazzle of sunlight on rushing water suggested moving pictures, and was the kind of thing that on a dull Sunday might have tempted Jake to sit here for an hour and just watch—but today, whatever happened, was not going to be dull. Not for him.

Small rapids, both upstream and downstream, generated unending hollow noises that sounded to Jake like a murmuring of many voices. In camp you could hear the rapids of the creek all day and all night, and on workdays along one trail or another they were sometimes audible. Since coming west to work for the CCC Jake had discovered that he could never listen for long to the voices of this or any other creek before they started making words. Right now the rapids upstream were louder than those below; and that seemed only natural, because the water upstream had just come tumbling all the way down from its source up on the North Rim, a mile higher and maybe ten crow-flight miles from this spot. Downstream from Jake, not more than fifty yards away, Bright Angel Creek plunged in a final subdued roar to its union with the wide, swift, silent Colorado at the very bottom of the Grand Canyon.

All the rapids in the creek kept on shouting their imaginary words at Jake, but right now they sounded like people arguing in some foreign language. Only one of

those words was at all clear. It was a certain name, a
girl's name that he'd learned only two weeks ago.

The last remnant of air came bubbling up out of the
submerged canteen, and Jacob Rezner got to his feet,
screwing on the container's metal cap. Jake at twenty-
two was six feet tall and solidly built. His dark hair, kept
cut short ever since he'd joined the CCC, still retained a
tendency to curl. His greenish eyes had something in
them that most people found a little startling, though
very few could have said exactly why they were startled.
The mobility of his mouth seemed to be connected somehow, perhaps sharing a kind of energy, with the strangeness in his eyes.

Fastening the canteen to his webbed army belt, Jake
returned to camp by recrossing the creek, on a narrow
bridge that marked the foot of Kaibab Trail. Trudging a
few feet uphill from the bridge, Jake entered what the
army people called the company street of CCC Camp NP-
3-A. The street was basically two rows of khaki tents,
twenty-five of them in all, most of them housing four
enrollees each. Now that the hot weather was coming on
in earnest, at least a couple of each tent's canvas walls
were hiked up to let air circulate. Headquarters and officers' tents were grouped at the northeastern, upstream
end of the camp. Latrines, supply, and the mule corral
were scattered downstream along the creek. Today the
makeshift corral would more than likely remain empty;
generally no pack trains came down on Sunday. As a rule
the rest of the week saw fairly steady mule train traffic,
because all supplies except water had to be packed down
here from the South Rim.

The usual Sunday sounds of the camp surrounded
Jake. Laughter and swear words and arguments, and the
one ever-playing radio. The army chaplain hadn't made it
down today for Sunday services; most weeks he failed to
make it, because it was a seven-mile mule ride on switch-

back trails from the South Rim, and a lot more miles than that from the nearest place that even pretended to be a town.

Just below Camp NP-3-A, down on the cleared, relatively flat space of the creek's delta, some of the guys were starting a pickup softball game despite the growing heat. For most of the young enrollees this would be a day to play games, play cards, write letters, and just sack out. Here and there one of the guys would dig out a bottle he had secretly stashed away. Usually the officers and leaders looked the other way when that happened, unless someone showed up drunk for work, or too hung over to carve trails and haul rock.

With the filled canteen hooked securely on his GI belt, Jake approached his own tent, halfway down the company street, and stuck his head inside. Three of the four military bunks, including his own, were empty. Joe Spicci, short and wiry, looked up from the fourth sack, where he lay reading last Sunday's sports section.

Jake told him: "I'm going for a hike." He made the announcement reluctantly; but it made sense to let someone know he might not be back until late. He wouldn't want them starting a search if he missed evening chow.

"Where?" Spicci sounded interested.

"Just a hike." The answer was short; this was one hike on which Jake didn't want company. "See you at chow time. Or maybe even later."

"Too damn hot out there for me today." Joe raised the sports pages in front of his face again.

A hundred steps away from the tent, Jake had put the entire camp behind him. Hell, with a few more strides he was already practically out of sight of all the tents. The land down here at the bottom of the inner gorge was mostly barren rock, a real desert, but he was already around the nearest big outcropping shoulder. This formation, whose shape always put Jake in mind of a sheeted ghost, dwarfed the camp, even as it was dwarfed itself by the thousand-foot cliffs of the lower gorge. These cliffs mostly blocked out the view of the vastly greater and more colorful fantasies above. After living four months in a work camp at the very bottom of the Grand Canyon, Jake had learned his way around the place a little bit, but he still hadn't got used to it in his mind. Maybe you never could, at least not if you had any imagination.

But today, so far, he was hardly noticing the landscape. Because his mind was busy with something else. If any of the other men in camp had any idea . . . but none of them did. They couldn't, because Jake hadn't said a word to anyone.

His secret destination lay downstream, along the south bank of the broad Colorado. To reach the south bank he had to cross the Kaibab suspension bridge, just outside of camp. This bridge was somewhat longer than a football field, and just about wide enough to accommodate one loaded mule. It was the only span of any kind to cross the river for more than a hundred miles upstream or down.

The bridge sounded hollowly beneath Jake's boots. The river, here deep and smooth, rushed silently below. After Jake had crossed the bridge his way lay west, downstream along the newly constructed River Trail. He'd labored on this stretch of trail himself, worked hard, helping the experts set explosives here and there, digging and hauling broken rock.

Though water was a life-and-death necessity in this heat, he thought he might possibly have managed today without borrowing a canteen, because there was the river to drink from. But along these miles of uninhabited shoreline, more often than not the edge of the Colorado was too abrupt, too steep and sharp-rocked, to let a thirsty man get close enough to drink or scoop up water.

A man who fell in would be lucky to find a place where he could climb out again before the current knocked him against too many rocks. The mean and rugged riverbank was of a piece with the rest of the local landscape.

When Jake had made a few hundred yards down-stream he stopped at a bend in the trail. Pausing there, he looked back, to make sure that no one else was crossing the suspension bridge. He had no reason to think that anyone would be interested in where he went, or try to follow him, but just in case . . .

He could be sure now. No one was following him.

Jake moved on, briskly.

For once he was oblivious to all the giants' handi-work around him. All he could think of were the same questions that had been tormenting him all week: Two Sundays in a row she's been there. If only she's there again. And if only she's still interested . . .

When the time came to turn off the River Trail it was a matter of scrambling and climbing, finding his own way across rough landscape. There was not even a deer trail to follow here. But Jake had been this way enough times now to have worked out a passable route for himself through the harsh terrain.

An hour and a half after leaving camp he was several miles downstream, moving quickly despite the day's growing heat. Here he was still inside the lower gorge, a thousand feet deep and comparatively narrow. Still its high edges almost totally cut off his view of most of the vaster, deeper rocky wilderness of the upper canyon, and of both distant rims. At irregular intervals side canyons came slicing into the main one from both north and south. Some of these tributary gorges had names: Zo-roaster Canyon, Bright Angel Canyon, Travertine Canyon, among others. Most were dry most of the time, but in spring those on the north bank ran with snowmelt from the high North Rim. And the rangers who had been here for years said that summer rains would turn all of them on again. Greenery had established itself along certain of these watercourses, showing that their flow was continuous, fed by springs.

Jake's steps—and his pulse—quickened as he came at last to the familiar mouth of the particular side canyon that he wanted. If this one had a name, he didn't know it. Its entrance was a lovely, inviting place in contrast to the stark, dark, almost eternally shaded rock by which it was surrounded. From a narrow opening the ravine, its floor green with shady vegetation, went curving up into the towering south wall. The stream issuing from this side canyon was only a trickle, up to Jake's ankles when he splashed in, but steady, and felt as cold as the Colorado itself. Here at the entrance the bed of the stream, flowing between natural pillars that Jake's imagination could easily see as carven monsters, offered the only place to walk.

A few yards up the side canyon the footing became easier, and a little trail appeared, paralleling the stream. From here on Jake really had to climb, now and then mounting gigantic stair-steps of tumbled rock. His boots squelched water for a while but the dry heat quickly dried them.

Half an hour after entering the side canyon, Jake was clambering up the last—for a while—of the series of steps. Then, on an interval of almost level ground, he moved forward among cottonwoods and willows. Here the narrow canyon bulged out a little on both sides, having at this point ascended to a softer layer of light-colored rock that Jake had learned was sandstone. Suddenly he stopped in his tracks, letting out a silent sigh of great relief. Fifty yards away he could see and recognize a human figure, that of a young woman who wore jeans and a man's work shirt. Camilla was there, almost exactly where he'd pictured her, waiting for him.

Today she had perched herself on a handy ledge of sandstone, deep within the shadow of the enormous cliff, not far from where the creek came down over a series of ledges that made a waterfall. Even at this distance Jake could see the startling pallor of her skin; he'd mentioned that to her last Sunday, and she'd told him how badly she burned if the direct sun got at her.

Camilla's reddish hair, lovely, long, and curly, stirred in the breeze that today as usual was moving down the side canyon. Even though she was sitting in the shade, dark glasses shielded her eyes, and she had one hand raised to shade them further as she turned her head to look for him—as if, despite the waterfall, she might have heard Jake approaching.

Just as on the last two Sundays—could their first meeting have been only two weeks ago?—she had her easel set up in front of her, and her drawing tools and papers were scattered about on nearby rocks.

Jake waved an arm in greeting, got an answering wave, and moved forward, trotting now despite the heat. Camilla got up from her ledge of rock and came a little distance toward him, stopping just within the shadow of the cliff.

Despite the dark glasses, which pretty effectively concealed her eyes, he thought there was something odd in the way she looked at him today. Maybe it was the angle of her head. Whatever it was caused him a moment of uncertainty, of shyness. He stopped just close enough to Camilla to reach for and clasp her outstretched hands.

"Hello." To Jake's surprise his own voice sounded shy, as if this were the first time he had ever spoken to this girl, or touched her. Last week she'd kissed him for the first time—a single kiss, gentle and quick—as he said goodbye.

"Hello, yourself." Camilla's husky voice was just as he'd remembered it—almost, he thought, with a deep sense of the incongruous, like Mae West's. She was about six inches shorter than Jake, and yeah, she was really built as nicely as he remembered.

She added, with a wistful tone: "I was afraid you weren't going to make it."

"Hell, I'll make it. I always do, when I say I will. I was worried *you* wouldn't be here."

"And I told you I'd be here." She paused, and with the dark glasses it was hard to tell what she was thinking. "Didn't I?" She paused again. "Aren't you going to kiss me?"

Something was different about Camilla today, as if she'd come to some kind of a decision. The kiss was everything Jake had been imagining, hoping and praying for, for the last week. Ten seconds into it, his right hand moved up for her left breast.

She let him get far enough to discover that under the man's shirt there was nothing on her skin but a little sweat, before she broke off the kiss and pulled away. The rejection was not violent, but it was firm.

"No," she said, in a suddenly uncertain voice.

Jake turned away and looked around. He turned in a complete circle. He had the sudden feeling that every rock in the walls of the narrow canyon, and every plant along the stream, was somehow watching them.

Now he was facing Camilla again. "Why the hell not?" His objection came out rougher-sounding than he'd intended.

She shook her head, making her red hair bounce. "Not yet."

"Then when?"

Camilla said: "Maybe after I know some more about

you. Don't you want to know about me? You don't even know my last name."

"I don't care what your last name is. Tell me if you want."

She was quiet. Upset, maybe, though not at him. Still pretty much in control, of herself and of the situation. "You're right, names don't matter. Jake, I mean I have to be sure of you first. I have to be very sure."

"Sure of me? Sure of me how?"

"I have to know whether I can depend on you. Whether you want me enough to—take some chances for me."

Jake tried to think. All he could come up with at the moment was that this girl might be talking about getting married. It didn't really sound to him like she meant that, but what else could it be? He hesitated, making an effort without much success to see her eyes through the dark glasses.

He said uncertainly: "I tried to tell you last week what I'm like, what my situation is. If I had a real job, if I had any money, I wouldn't be here in the CCC."

"I know that. I understand about the CCC. If I'd had any money a year and a half ago, I wouldn't be here either." She paused, as if to contemplate her own situation, still mysterious to Jake. "That's not what I'm asking, whether you've got any money."

"What, then?"

"What I have to know, Jake, is can I depend on you? If I asked you to do something really hard, would you do it for me? Don't just blurt out yes. Take your time and think about it."

He took a little time. "I'd do it if I could. Anyway I'd break my ass trying."

Camilla seemed to be going through the various stages she needed to make her own decision final.

"All right," she said at last. It was almost as if she

were talking to herself, though the dark glasses looked at Jake. "Come here," she said. And she began to undo the buttons of her shirt.

Twenty minutes later, lying naked beside this woman he didn't know on a patch of soft, dry, shaded sand at the very foot of the side canyon's western wall, Jake was saying lazily: "I just can't figure it, is all. A girl like you, as good-looking as you are, smart and everything, why do you want to get hooked up with a guy like me?"

Their clothing was scattered around them. Along with everything else, Camilla had taken off her dark glasses, revealing a pair of greenish eyes much like those that Jake saw daily in his shaving mirror. Now she reached out for the glasses and put them on again.

Through the glasses she looked at him strangely. She asked: "What's wrong with you? I don't see anything wrong with you. I told you what I wanted, and you said okay."

Jake ran a possessive hand down her smooth side, along the ribs and down her hip. She was better looking, by far, than any other girl or woman he'd ever before managed to persuade to make love.

He said: "You didn't really tell me what you wanted. Not yet."

Suddenly she seemed tenderly uncertain. "Oh Jake. I'm not sure where to start."

"How about starting with where you live? You wouldn't even tell me that much last week."

Camilla hesitated, then gestured. "Right now I'm living a little way up this canyon."

Jake raised himself on one elbow, squinting in that direction. He saw no sign of habitation. "You mean up on the South Rim?"

"No, not quite that far. Just a little way from where we are. Half a mile maybe."

"Jeez, the Rim is a lot farther than that. And I didn't know anyone lived *in* the Canyon. Except us poor slobs in the camp. Live with your parents?"

That made Camilla smile. "No. Where'd you get that idea?"

"A lot of girls live with their parents. Hey, you're not married, are you?"

"No."

Jake, somewhat reassured, lazily wondering what to ask next, reached out again with a large, sun-darkened, calloused hand. This time he just extended a forefinger and traced patterns on Camilla's marvelous, taut white belly. At the touch her belly contracted slightly with some kind of tickle reflex. So white and smooth . . .

"Got a cigarette?" she asked him, with a sudden, wistful yearning.

"Poverty got me out of the habit."

Whatever else was worrying her didn't let her fret about cigarettes for long. She was framing another question for Jake: "Would you still help me, if I was married? Not that I am."

"Sure. Damn right I would."

Camilla lay there in silence, letting him tickle her belly.

"So, you're not married . . . what's the story, then? You live alone?"

Camilla heaved a deep sigh. "No, not that either, I'm afraid."

I was beginning to figure something like this, thought Jake. Otherwise this would have been too simple. His right hand kept on exploring, testing the fact that he was now allowed to put his hand anywhere he wanted. Anywhere at all. Wonderful.

When Camilla spoke again, she seemed to want Jake's full attention on her words, and so she first reached down her own hand and caught his exploring fingers in a grip of surprising strength. Then from behind her dark glasses she asked, "Did you ever hear of a man named Edgar Tyrrell?"

"No, can't say I have. Should I?"

"No special reason why you should. He's a sculptor. A man who carves statues."

"I know what a sculptor is."

"Sorry. Edgar's pretty well known, among people who study art. Not really famous."

"All right. So you live with Edgar Tyrrell. I bet he's used you for a model."

Camilla had nothing to say about modeling. She extended her right arm gracefully, turning her body a little, pointing almost vertically up behind her. "He used to live up there on the Rim, near Grand Canyon Village, in a little house built right on the edge. He was there for something like thirty years. And then one day he left his house and his family and disappeared from human society. That was before I met him. He says he just walked down into the Canyon one day and never went back."

Camilla fell silent, looking at Jake. It was hard for him to tell with the dark glasses still covering her eyes, but he got the feeling she was hoping he would understand—something, whatever it was—without her having to spell it out for him.

But he wanted to hear her spell everything out, tell him just what she wanted from him. "So this fella disappeared from human society."

"That's how he puts it."

"And when was this?"

"I don't know exactly." Camilla hesitated. "A few months before I met him. That's what he tells me."

"Maybe he disappeared, but he still socialized enough to get acquainted with you."

"I let him pick me up." Camilla gave a sudden, nervous little laugh. She released Jake's hand and sat up abruptly. "I don't know how to tell it. Let's get dressed. It's a long story. I'll take you to see where I live. Maybe that'll make it all easier to explain."

So far, it didn't sound so awfully complicated to Jake. He said: "I'd rather look at everything you're showing me right now." But Camilla was already on her feet, brushing sand from her sweaty skin, picking up her clothes. Jake sighed and went along.

By the time he was dressed again, Camilla was already busy packing up her easel and stuff. "Give me a hand," she pleaded. The down-canyon breeze was freshening, trying to make off with some of her sketches, though she had them weighted down with small black rocks.

"Sure." Jake corralled the sheets of drawing paper that were on the brink of making an escape, and stuffed them under his arm, trying not to crinkle the papers too much. Now that he really thought about it, she couldn't be living all the way up on the Rim, and carry all this junk up and down with her on a fourteen-mile round trip every time she wanted to go sketching.

They had Camilla's art materials bundled up when, as if struck by a sudden thought, she demanded of Jake: "You didn't tell anyone you were meeting me today, did you?"

"Hell, no. Tell those guys there's a good-looking girl down here? Think I want an expedition following me out from camp?"

"No, I didn't think you'd want that . . . Jake, the creek water's safe." He had started to drink from his canteen.

He shrugged and drank from the canteen anyway. "I can refill before I head back."

"Oh my God. You know what? I packed you a lunch and then forgot all about it!"

Suddenly it was as if Camilla at the last minute wanted to delay taking Jake up to where she lived, and was thinking up ways to delay that trip. As if she was getting cold feet about something.

Jake had also forgotten about food, but at the mention of it he was suddenly hungry. If Camilla wanted to postpone his tour of her living quarters, it was all right with him.

Or maybe, Jake thought, she wanted him to be a thoroughly contented man before she took him there. From somewhere she brought out a metal lunch box with flowers on it, like something a little girl might have carried to school, and opened it to reveal sandwiches neatly wrapped in waxed paper, and fruit, and a vacuum bottle she said held lemonade.

The bread turned out to be home-made, the sandwich filling cheese and ham. Sitting on a rock Jake ate and drank with a good appetite. All the better, because by now he had thoroughly resigned himself to missing evening chow. Not that he would have minded missing a few more meals, in a cause as good as that of getting laid by this girl.

"You're not eating anything," Jake commented, chewing. "Want one of these?" He held out a wax paper packet.

Camilla shook her head. "I'm not hungry."

Jake shrugged. He thought vaguely that maybe she was dieting—though with a figure like hers he didn't see any need for it.

He asked: "So, how long have you been living in this mysterious place up-canyon?" Being diplomatic, as he thought, he didn't say with this mysterious guy.

Camilla started an answer, but broke it off. Then with seeming irrelevance she asked, "Have you ever been up on the South Rim?"

He nodded. "Sure. When I first came to the Canyon, four months ago, they drove us in that far in a bus from Flagstaff, then marched us down the trail on foot—ever see our camp, upriver at the foot of Kaibab Trail?" Jake took another bite of sandwich.

Camilla shook her head.

Jake went on: "Maybe I'll show you some time. In four months I only been up out of the Canyon a couple of times, for a weekend. You have to ride a mule up Bright Angel trail, or else hike up. And each time we passed through the little village on the rim." As he recalled, there had been about half a dozen buildings in view, including the railroad station where the Santa Fe spur line ended. And of course the big log hotel, with a few more structures scattered back among the trees. "What about it?"

"I came in that way, too. With Edgar, after he picked me up in a bar in Flagstaff." Camilla looked at Jake from behind her dark glasses as if she were daring him to comment on this admission. He didn't.

She went on: "One of those houses up there on the Rim is the one he used to live in. He used to have different models all the time, until he finally married one of them. You have to get over a little west of the head of Bright Angel Trail to see the house, and you might easily miss it even from there."

She was, Jake decided, harping on Edgar Tyrrell and his house because she was having a hard time deciding how to approach whatever it was she really wanted to explain. This decision was harder for her than the decision she had made when she took off her clothes.

She added wistfully, "I've never seen that Rim again."

Then, shaking her head as if to clear it, she asked Jake: "Are you finished eating?"

"Sure." He was definitely getting curious.

He closed up the lunch box, leaving the crumbs and remnants for the chipmunks and coyotes, and Camilla took the little box with the other stuff she was carrying,

and started to lead the way along the little trail upstream. Jake followed her, carrying a couple of her
things.

Before they had gone more than a hundred feet or so,
she stopped and turned to Jake to say, in a voice that was
growing strained: "See, there's too much time down here,
near the bottom of the Canyon."

"What?" He blinked and squinted at her in the bright
sunlight. "Too much time? You mean you've got nothing
to do?"

"No. That's not what I mean. Too much time is what
Edgar says when I ask him about—about some funny
things that happen down here. At first I didn't know what
he meant by too much time. But lately I can understand—I think. He says the river cuts open the earth, and
the deep time comes spilling out of it like blood." Then
she smiled nervously at the expression that must have
been growing on Jake's face. "I'm not crazy, lover. You'll
see what I mean."

"Okay. I don't think you're crazy." Actually the suspicion had very recently been born. But he wasn't really
worried about it yet.

"Thank God," said Camilla, and once more turned to
lead the way up along the trail beside the creek.

Jake, staying close behind her, was nagged by the
feeling that the voices of the nearby stream were trying
to tell him something. But he was distracted from pursuing that thought by the movement of Camilla's hips. Even
if her jeans were a loose fit.

"So," he said, raising his voice a little to be heard
above the sound of rushing water, "you live with Edgar?"

"I don't sleep with him. Not any more." Camilla
paused, glancing back. "He's a—strange man."

"Yeah? He must be pretty old now if he lived up on
the Rim for thirty years."

"He's pretty old."

They climbed on. Jake couldn't see the sun from down here in the narrow canyon, but judging by the angle of the shadow on the east wall they still had a good many hours to go before sunset.

Camilla led Jake on, up along what was no longer really a trail at all. Glancing to right and left, Jake noted that the steep and winding walls of this little side canyon displayed basically the same strata of rock as those in the tremendous walls of the big one; there was no other way it could be, he supposed. That pale layer was limestone and the somewhat darker one just below was shale. For the last couple of months he had been picking up some knowledge of geology from the rock experts back at camp.

Presently he called again to Camilla: "You and old Edgar live in a pretty isolated place back here."

For some reason that made her turn, to study him through her dark glasses. Then she emphatically agreed with what he'd said and went beyond it. "Not one in a thousand people hiking downriver the way you did could find this canyon."

"Well, it's not *that* hard to find. I didn't have much trouble."

"Only because you're something special. It *is* that hard to find." For some reason her voice quavered. "Not one in a thousand. Maybe not one in a million. How many other hikers and boaters do you suppose have gone right past the entrance to this canyon where you turned in, and never seen it there?"

Jake blinked at her, wondering. "That's easy. Not very damned many. There wouldn't be a hundred people hike or boat past the mouth of your little canyon in ten years. This place is not exactly populated like a city park, you know."

Camilla smiled at him, as if she wanted to be reassuring—or perhaps be reassured—and then turned back to her climb.

Jake went back to watching the hypnotic movement of her hips.

Another minute or so of staring at that movement, and Jake caught up with her and tugged gently on her belt.

Camilla stopped and turned and held out her arms. A moment later he was kissing her, and feeling up under her shirt again. How marvelous when there was no resistance!

Afterward they sat naked in the chill shallow water of the creek, letting it rush over their bodies, splashing each other.

Jake said: "In a way it's funny, your talk about how hard this canyon is to find."

Camilla, who had been laughing at something else he'd said, stopped suddenly. "Why is it funny?" she asked. At the moment they were in shade, and she'd left her dark glasses off.

"Because yesterday I looked at the big map back at camp. And I couldn't see this canyon on it anywhere. This isn't Pipe Creek we're sitting in, and it isn't Horn Creek, right? Because there are rapids in the Colorado where Horn Creek comes in. And there's not supposed to be any side canyon with a permanent water flow between those two. But here we are." Jake gestured at the steep enclosing walls.

Camilla didn't seem surprised to hear about the map. Instead she just looked melancholy and thoughtful. All she said was: "I bet there are a lot of things your map doesn't show."

* * *

When they were dressed again, they climbed on, while the canyon that had swallowed them turned this way and that like a great snake. The bends were getting sharper. Jake could no longer see farther than about fifty yards ahead at any point.

Once Camilla paused to tell him, as if in after-thought: "Edgar calls this place Deep Canyon."

Rounding the next turn, they came to a place where the canyon straightened out and expanded into a steep-sided amphitheater, the size of a small football stadium. The land inside was relatively level, half-overgrown with typical canyon bush and a few trees. At the far end of the amphitheater the creek fell into it in a high waterfall. Jake saw to his surprise that someone had neatly built a tall, narrow waterwheel into this cataract. And at the foot of the drop, getting splashed a little by the spray, stood a little stone building that looked like it ought to house a generator. Sure enough, wires ran on poles from the generator housing to another small building. This one was constructed of neatly trimmed logs, and actually appeared to be a house.

For the time being Jake took less notice of a kind of grotto, or cave, opening into the base of the western cliff, at the level of another layer of rock that Jake could recognize. The camp geologist had called this one Ta-peats Sandstone, and had said it lay just over what he called the Great Unconformity, a term whose meaning Jake had never grasped.

At first sight the cave was only a shallow concavity, with a low, rather inconspicuous entrance; at second glance it looked deeper.

But right now Jake was paying attention mainly to the neatly constructed little house, which was sited high enough above the creek to avoid floods. No prospector's cabin, certainly. Not a shack or a hut, but a real house, boasting stone walls, glass windows, and a real shingled roof.

Camilla was standing right beside Jake, looking at him as if judging his reaction.

He asked her: "You live here?"

Camilla said: "I do."

"With Edgar."

"Yes." She cast a nervous look around, and lowered her voice. "But I don't want to live with him any longer."

"Leave."

She shook her head. "It's not that easy. You'll see."

"He hasn't got you locked up."

Camilla said nothing.

Jake squinted at the layout before him. All was quiet, not even a dog barking. "Where is he now?"

"Resting. He usually works at night. Digging out the kind of rocks he likes, carving them . . ."

"Can't blame him for resting, in this heat."

The path leading to the cottage brought them closer to the grotto. Jake, getting a better look as he passed, saw that it was really a cave, considerably deeper than it had first appeared. The hole was too dark inside for him to see much more.

Camilla observed his interest. "Want to go in and take a look? We can, Edgar won't mind."

"I don't care," said Jake. But he followed Camilla when she went in.

The relative coolness was welcome. Once Jake's eyes were out of the glare of sunlight he could see the interior fairly well. A ghost of the glow of sunset was reflecting in from the light limestone wall on the other side of the amphitheater.

"It's sunset now," said Camilla. "Now's the time when—"

Then she fell abruptly silent.

It took Jake another minute to realize that the two of

them were no longer alone. The figure of a man was now standing at the dark mouth of the lightless inner regions of the cave. Just standing there and looking out at Jake.

Jake peeked as best he could into the zone of greater dimness. The spare figure might have been almost as tall as Jake if it hadn't been hunched over. The man was dressed in overalls, some kind of boots, and a work shirt, and his hair and skin and clothing were all gray with what looked like rock-dust. He was holding an inhumanly motionless pose; he might almost have been a statue.

In the gnarled fingers of one evidently powerful hand, the man was clutching a sizable chunk of rock. After a moment he opened his hand and let the chunk fall, to strike the rock floor with a dull sound.

In the next moment the same hand reached out to a large switch bolted to the rocky wall, and a battery of electric lights sprang into life. The half-dozen fixtures, mounted on tall metal stands around the cave, were streamlined, looking very modern. In fact they looked somehow more than modern, they looked like no lights that Jake had ever seen before.

Under their radiance the whole inner cave, which had been deeply shadowed, burst into full visibility. The lights were positioned on every side, some high, some low, and they almost abolished shadow. The glowing, peculiar bulbs revealed that the floor and walls of the cave were pockmarked with holes, places where sizable blocks might have been dug out. A long workbench, crudely built but sturdy, littered with tools and chunks of pale stone, ran along one wall. The walls and floor and overhead of the cave were mostly dark, formed of a material Jake had heard the rock-and-blasting experts call Vishnu schist. It was commonly found in the lowest layer of the Canyon's walls just below the mysterious Great Unconformity. The whitish intrusions here and there in the cave's walls were new to Jake.

But none of this, interesting as it was, could hold Jake's attention for more than a moment or two. Not in the presence of the man who now stood before him.

The dust-covered figure suddenly turned his gaze on Camilla, and rasped a comment. "So, you've caught another one."

She answered timidly. "Don't say that, Edgar. He's a friend of mine."

"Oh, I don't doubt that. Most men would be delighted to be your friend. But have you told him yet?"

Camilla, looking from one man to the other, seemed to be afraid to say anything more.

"Told me what?" Jake demanded.

Suddenly Edgar caught sight of the lunch box, which Camilla had put down on a ledge of rock. With some muttering that sounded vaguely like a curse, he snatched up the little container at the same time raising his other hand as if he were about to strike the girl.

Jake, starting to shout something angry, took a step forward. But Camilla, cowering back from the blow that never fell, yelled at Jake to stop. It was a scream of such sudden heartfelt terror that he unthinkingly obeyed.

Then he looked back at Edgar. "Told me what?" he repeated, harshly.

"Nothing of real importance." Wicked eyes gleamed at him out of the old man's dusty face. "Just that, today, the silly business that you have called your life is over."

~ 2 ~

1991

Bill Burdon and Maria Torres, who both worked for a big agency in Phoenix, had driven up to the Grand Canyon together. Neither of the two young people had ever been to the Canyon before, so they had both initially welcomed the assignment as offering the chance of doing a little sightseeing.

Recreational possibilities faded from their thoughts as they learned a little more about the case. The problem, as Bill's and Maria's boss in Phoenix had explained to them before they left, was a missing girl. Seventeen-year-old Cathy Brainard had vanished into the Canyon almost a month ago. No ransom demand had ever been presented, kidnapping was no longer regarded as a good possibility, and the feds had retired from the investigation. A wealthy relative of the girl was taking a strong interest, and private investigators were now on the job.

Missing teenagers were common enough, but there seemed to be something about this case that had caused the wealthy relative to bring in a specialist from out of state. Either the boss in Phoenix didn't know what the exotic details were, or he had chosen to be reticent about them. He had told Torres and Burdon they would be given all the details they needed by Mr. Joseph Keogh, who ran his own investigative agency out of Chicago and had been hired to take charge of the case. They were to report to Keogh as soon as they reached El Tovar hotel, which was situated just a few yards from the South Rim, inside Grand Canyon National Park.

Someone high up in the administration of the big Phoenix agency evidently owed Keogh a favor. Anyway, Bill's and Maria's boss was ready to loan out a couple of his best young people.

The job specs called for a man and a woman, both athletic as well as intelligent, able to deal diplomatically with clients, and also capable of functioning at a high level in a non-urban environment, as the boss had put it.

The week between Christmas and the New Year was a time of high tourist activity at the Canyon. Getting the two newly assigned operatives a room, let alone two rooms, in any of the park lodges presented a problem, so Bill and Maria had been instructed to bring their sleeping bags. Most likely they would be able to sack out, when either of them had time to sleep, in Keogh's room or suite in El Tovar, a lodging presumably also shared by anyone else who might have come out from Chicago. Well, Bill had graduated from the marines and Maria from the army, where among her other duties she had taught survival for a while. Sacking out on a couch or floor inside a luxury hotel did not seem likely to give either one of them a problem.

Maria and Bill had yet to work together, and were no more than vaguely acquainted colleagues when they began the five-hour drive up from Phoenix. But by the time they turned off Interstate 40 at Flagstaff, and were heading straight north on a smaller highway, they had begun to be on good terms, at least professionally. On a number of subjects they thought alike.

Morning sunlight and springlike warmth had been left behind hours ago, in the low-altitude desert of southern Arizona. Passing Flagstaff in Bill Burdon's car, they were at seven thousand feet above sea level, on a dull, cloudy, winter afternoon. Patches of snow were visible among the trunks of the pine forest surrounding the small city, and, to judge from the leaden sky, more snow might well be on the way.

The Grand Canyon and its surrounding thousand square miles of national park lay still some eighty miles farther north, reachable by good but narrow roads through partially wooded flatland.

The eighty miles were uneventful. Once Bill had paid their way into the park, the traffic, both foot and vehicular, on the winding narrow roads quickly became even brisker than he had expected, notwithstanding the warnings about tourist crowds. The two-lane road and its traffic wound on for a mile or so, flanked by rustic signs indicating the way to Pima Point, the Tusayan Museum, and widely scattered tourist lodges called Yavapai, Maswik, Thunderbird, and Kachina.

Among some lesser buildings largely concealed by trees, El Tovar Hotel soon loomed up, stone and shingles and dark brown siding, a generous three stories high. El Tovar's several wings extended widely enough to accommodate more than a hundred guest rooms. According to a map in the brochure handed to the new arrivals at the gate, the brink of the South Rim ought to be only a stone's toss to the north. But the intervening slice of ground sloped upward just enough to keep the Canyon itself totally invisible from roads and parking lot.

Bill, who was taking the last shift behind the wheel, carefully negotiated the small parking lot nearest El Tovar, where several other vehicles were simultaneously seeking space. Maria swore under her breath when someone beat them to a slot; she was dark-haired, attractive, and compactly built, looking younger than her twenty-five years. Bill was two years older, lighter of complexion and considerably larger. The jockeying and delays of parking did not interfere with his whistling softly a small cheerful tune.

At last a space became available.

Getting out of the car in their ski jackets and hiking boots, standard tourist garb for here and now, Bill and Maria stretched their bodies after the long ride, worked their shoulders into backpack harnesses, and checked their watches. They had a few minutes to spare before Mr. Joseph Keogh would actually begin to expect them.

"Shall we take a look at the view?" Maria asked. "Looks foggy, but we can give it a try."

"I guess it would be a shame not to. Familiarize ourselves with the location, and all that."

From where they were standing in the parking lot, there was a subtle oddity about the view, having really nothing to do with fog. Just a few yards past the massive old hotel, the world came to an end. Or at least Bill and Maria were given that impression, because at that distance to the north the landscape abruptly terminated, the boundary being delineated by a stone parapet not three feet high. Beyond that modest fence there existed no horizon, and thus apparently no earth, only a lowering continuation of the leaden sky.

Walking past the hotel, Bill and Maria steadily approached the parapet, which was already defended on the near side by a handful of Japanese tourists, garbed for cold and armed with cameras. Standing among these foreign visitors, the two Americans looked out with them. Vision plunged out and down, losing itself in an infinite depth of colorlessness—with one exception. In one place, more downward than outward, at a slant range of a hundred yards or so, a dim rocky promontory rose from unguessable depths to become intermittently visible through slowly marching mist. Around that one fragment of solidity, decorated with a couple of small evergreens, nothing but drifting grayness was perceptible. Right now even the finest cameras were not going to be of much use.

Maria Torres was ahead of Bill in observing that someone else had joined them.

While Bill, momentarily lost in contemplation, was still assessing the view, a moderately tall man, dark-haired and bearded, had come up just behind him, moving in total silence. The newcomer, as Maria observed, stood waiting at Bill's elbow for many seconds, an embarrassingly long time for an investigator, before Bill became aware of his presence.

Alerted at last by a certain tenseness in Maria's attitude, Bill turned his head sharply. The bearded man, standing close enough to touch him, was only gazing at him mildly.

There followed an interval in which the three of them stood regarding one another. They were ignored by the Japanese, and by other tourists who, despite the poor viewing conditions at the moment, kept drifting to and fro along the rim, singly and in small groups.

"Can I help you?" Bill finally asked the man.

The newcomer spoke up smoothly, as if he had only been waiting to be prompted. "Let me introduce myself," he said in a deep quiet voice. "My name is Strangeways, and it seems that we are likely to be working together for the next day or two."

"I think you must have the wrong—"

"No, I think not."

Bill looked blank. He did an excellent job of it, thought Maria, who felt sure that she herself was having no trouble appearing puzzled.

"Sorry," Bill told the man, firmly, at last. "You must be mixing us up with two other people."

Strangeways permitted himself a faint smile, as of mild approval. "In that case I trust you will pardon my impertinence," he murmured. Turning half away, he gazed out into the murk that filled the Canyon, as if he might indeed be capable of seeing something through it. Maria noticed vaguely, without giving the matter any particular thought, that his breath, unlike her own and Bill's, was not steaming in the chill air.

After they had all three stood there for another half-minute, Bill nudged Maria, and the two of them turned away from the brink and moved toward the hotel. Glancing back when they had gone a few yards, Maria saw Mr. Strangeways still intent on his viewing, apparently taking no interest in where they went.

"What the hell do you suppose that was all about?" she whispered to Bill when she judged that they were safely out of earshot.

"Either he's a stray loony or we're being checked out. Whether by friend or foe . . ."

The sprawling, three-story hotel, all shingles and age-darkened logs and stone, was looming over them. In another moment Bill and Maria were striding up onto a deep wooden porch which led to the front entrance. Seen at close range, the building had even more of a settled, established look. Carved in wood over the entrance Maria read an unpunctuated fragment of a sentence, or perhaps of verse:

DREAMS OF MOUNTAINS AS IN THEIR SLEEP THEY BROOD ON THINGS ETERNAL

The images evoked in Maria's mind by those words were incomplete but somehow disturbing. She wondered vaguely where the phrase had come from. Her brief sojourn in college had been as an English major; sometimes she was bothered by hearing or reading a quotation and being unable to trace its source.

With Bill leading the way, they entered the lobby

through a double door, a spacious airlock whose purpose was no doubt to minimize the effect of wintry blasts.

The lobby of El Tovar was a large room—actually two large rooms, Maria saw—each two stories high. The peaked ceiling of the first room was supported by log beams and posts, rough-hewn but smoothed by some mellowing effect of age. Despite the modern gift shops on both sides of the lobby, and the modern lighting, the walls and ceiling had a dark settled solidity that confirmed their tenure here for very nearly a century. Holiday poinsettias on shelves and tables everywhere in the lobby outnumbered the thronging, ski-jacketed, pack- and camera-carrying people. Wreaths and chains of real evergreen twigs and branches, some dotted with miniature lights, festooned the rugged beams and posts. Stuffed animal heads, some antlered, some snarling to expose dead fangs, looked down from the high walls with an air of disapproval.

A two-story Christmas tree occupied the center of the inner lobby, its upper branches surrounded by a log-railed mezzanine where people sat at tables. The hotel desk was on the tree's left as the travelers approached.

While Bill paused at the desk to ask a question, Maria turned swiftly to scan the crowd, on the chance that Mr. Strangeways had followed them inside. But she could discover no sign of him.

Playing tourist, Maria grabbed up a brochure before she left the desk. A moment later she was following Bill down one of the ground-floor hallways that branched from the lobby. Glancing at her brochure, she read something about the hotel having been built in 1905. Having seen the dark log walls of the lobby from inside, she could readily believe that date, though obviously the heating and lighting—and, she hoped and presumed, the plumbing—were quite acceptably modern.

Having passed the doors of half a dozen rooms, Bill stopped at the next one and knocked.

A cautious voice within called something. When Bill responded, the door was opened from inside, by a wiry, middle-sized, fortyish man wearing a ski sweater. His sandy hair was beginning to be flecked with gray. He sized up his visitors quickly and said, "Come in, I'm Joe Keogh."

Keogh's room was actually a suite including a small bedroom and sitting room, casually furnished in a kind of pseudo-Victorian style. In the sitting room four unmatching chairs had been drawn up around a table. A man was sitting in one of them.

The new arrivals were quickly introduced to Keogh's brother-in-law John Southerland, who had come with him from Chicago. Southerland was about twenty-eight, the same height as his boss—a little under six feet—and solidly built. His light brown hair still retained a tendency to curl. At the moment he was either starting a beard or badly in need of a shave.

Maria, studying Joe Keogh's impressively tough-looking face, decided that his looks did him no harm in his business. She'd already learned that he had been a Chicago cop before marrying Southerland money.

"Have a seat." Keogh indicated the chairs around the table. His voice was mild, almost nondescript. "Glad you guys made it up here. They tell me the weather might be getting worse any time now."

An exchange of comments on the weather was interrupted by a tap at the door. John Southerland opened it to admit, as a trusted colleague, Mr. Strangeways.

Brief introductions were performed. Another small chair was brought from somewhere, and presently five were seated around the table.

A pause ensued. It seemed to Maria as if Keogh, now

that he had his two reinforcements from Phoenix, wasn't
sure of how to go about explaining the job to them.

"What we've got here is—has the possibility of
being—a strange case," he said at last, and paused,
frowning, shooting a quick glance at Strangeways, who
gazed back at him impassively.

Wind, beginning to pick up velocity in late afternoon, moaned at the window.

Bill cleared his throat. "Who's the client?" he asked
Keogh directly.

When Keogh seemed to hesitate, Maria put in: "They
told us down in Phoenix that this was a missing person,
a seventeen-year-old girl—and that the case had what
they described as possibly interesting complications."

Strangeways sat with his arms folded, attentive but
unmoving.

Keogh looked at Southerland. "You tell 'em."

The younger man cleared his throat and began, "Client's name is Mrs. Sarah Tyrrell. She's about eighty years
old, give or take a few. Her late husband, Edgar Tyrrell,
was a fairly well-known sculptor back in the early
nineteen-hundreds. He was born in England, but spent
his most productive years here. His stuff is enjoying
something of a revival now, I understand, and the old
lady is well off financially.

"The missing girl is Sarah Tyrrell's niece, or rather
grandniece, if that's the proper word."

"It is," said Strangeways shortly. Everyone glanced
at him.

John resumed: "Cathy's father—adoptive father,
whatever that might signify—is Mr. G. C. Brainard, a
lawyer who deals in art. I don't know that he's too happy
about our being called in at this late date to investigate
his daughter's disappearance—anyway something's both-
ering him. Anyway someone recommended us to the old
lady, and she insisted on calling us in, and he tends to

humor her, as I suppose is usual among people with wealthy aunts. Is that a fair way to put the situation, Joe?"

Keogh only squinted, in a way that Maria Torres took to mean he wasn't entirely sure. He glanced at Strangeways, who gave him a moody look in return, but no comment.

"Mrs. Tyrrell is staying here?" Bill asked, when no one else seemed eager to talk.

"Not in any of the hotels," Joe Keogh explained. "There's a building called the Tyrrell House, a little bit west of here, right on the rim. It was her husband's studio in the early thirties, and it's the house where the two of them lived together. It belongs to the Park Service now, of course, but part of the agreement when the government took it over was that Mrs. Tyrrell would have the right to use the place whenever she wanted during her lifetime. She and Brainard are staying there."

"Was Cathy staying in that house," asked Maria, "when she disappeared?"

"No," Keogh shook his head. "It's more complicated than that. She was in one of the regular lodges—not this one—with a small group of her friends from boarding school. Everyone agrees that Cathy had never been anywhere near the Grand Canyon before her visit at Thanksgiving.

"The kids did some of the usual tourist things, hiked around, took pictures. They had camping equipment with them, and they debated whether to take a mule ride down to Phantom Ranch—that's an overnight trip to the bottom of the Canyon and back—but decided not to. Then, on the second day of their visit, for some reason, Cathy began acting strangely. Or so her companions thought later. She left them suddenly, saying something about going for a walk. They assumed she meant that she was going to the Visitor Center or the general store. But a few minutes later, a disinterested witness saw a girl who looked like Cathy Brainard, and was dressed like her, carrying a pack and equipment as if for an overnight hike, starting down Bright Angel Trail alone.

"As far as we know, that witness was the last person to see Cathy Brainard anywhere."

Bill said slowly: "I'm no expert, but that doesn't sound to me like a planned kidnapping. Maybe some lunatic encountered her and—"

Joe nodded. "I agree. There've been no demands. Kidnapping's a federal offense, of course, and the feds did come here and look around. But they pretty quickly decided that the girl had most likely just walked off on her own, a deliberate runaway. And a fatal accident wouldn't be too surprising; that kind of thing happens to someone in the Park practically every year. By all reports she's a good hiker, or an energetic walker anyway, and in a few hours she could have gone all the way down to the river at the bottom of the canyon, and drowned. The Colorado's deep and swift, and very cold. It wouldn't be surprising if a body was never found.

"Or she could have simply got off the trails, perhaps got herself lost, and fallen into a hole or off a cliff somewhere—you'll see how very possible that is, once you get a close look at the terrain. Have either of you had a chance to do that, by the way?"

Bill and Maria shook their heads. "Never been here before," Bill said. "We tried today, but it was too foggy."

Maria said: "I presume none of the girl's schoolmates are here at the Canyon now?"

"No reason to think they are. I haven't had the chance to talk to any of them yet, and it's one of the things I want to do, of course, eventually."

Bill asked: "And the witness at the head of Bright Angel Trail? Who was that?"

"Good question. A middle-aged lady schoolteacher,

long since gone home to Ohio. No reason to doubt her story."

"How'd she happen to notice Cathy, among what I suppose was the usual throng of tourists?"

"Cathy came up to her and asked her where it might be possible to get a map of the trails in the Canyon. The teacher remembered the girl who spoke to her, because she thought the youngster seemed worried or disturbed. Later she could describe what Cathy looked like, how she was dressed. I don't doubt it was our girl."

Maria nodded, eyes gleaming faintly. "I wonder what disturbed her suddenly?"

Strangeways gave her a sidelong glance of interest, but did not comment.

Joe Keogh continued the briefing. "Some more information, possibly relevant. I get the feeling that young Cathy is likely to inherit old Aunt Sarah's money one day—if Cathy is still alive. There seem to be no other close relatives, except Cathy's father, of course. Old Sarah gives nephew Brainard a hard time, from what I've seen. And sometimes vice versa. They have a business relationship now but that's about it. Whereas the old lady was—is—much attached to Cathy."

"A possible conflict of interest," commented Strangeways, "between this Brainard and his adopted daughter."

Maria decided that this unexplained colleague had a commanding air about him, despite the fact that he seldom spoke. He might be thirty-five at the most, she thought. His dark hair and beard were full and short, and he wore a dark turtleneck shirt or sweater under a brown jacket that in the arrangement of its pockets suggested to her vaguely that it had been designed for a hunter rather than a skier to wear. The more she looked at Strangeways the more certainly she felt him to be in some way truly out of the ordinary. It wasn't easy, try as she might, to pin the feeling down any more specifically than that.

"You think he made her vanish?" Joe Keogh asked him, somewhat deferentially.

"Stranger things have happened, Joseph."

"That's for damn sure." Keogh sighed, ran fingers through his sandy hair, and looked as if he wanted to ask Strangeways another question or two. But perhaps the presence of his new recruits constrained him. Turning to them, he began questioning them on mundane matters. Maria and Bill quickly ran through their qualifications and experience.

Apparently satisfied on that score, for the time being at least, Joe returned to the main business at hand. "There are reasons, reasons I'm not going into right now, to think this case is likely to have unusual aspects. And I want the people who work for me to be able to deal with the unusual in a level-headed way." He stopped, waiting for a reaction from the recruits.

"Unusual how?" Bill Burdon asked.

"How would you react if I told you there could be— psychic factors, involved in this case?"

Having asked that question, Keogh paused again, waiting for a reaction from his two loaners. "Neither of you look especially surprised," he commented, as if that fact surprised him.

"We're not getting paid to be surprised," Maria said.

"Psychic?" asked Bill. "Meaning like in spiritualism? I don't believe in that stuff."

"I'm not asking you to believe in anything," said Keogh. "As long as you follow orders."

Bill shrugged. "That's what I'm being paid for."

Maria agreed in a businesslike way. "A missing person is a missing person. Whether the causes are psychic or whatever. So our job is to get this girl back, or at least find out what happened to her." She added: "Actually, my own grandmother was fleeced by a fake medium out in LA. I'd like to get my hands on one of those people."

"Yes, naturally." Keogh sighed faintly. "Well, I doubt there's any fake medium involved in this."

"What do you suspect?" Maria asked.

"I don't want to suspect anything, until I've talked to the client face to face. So far I've only spoken to her briefly, on the phone." He looked toward Strangeways, as if in a silent appeal for help.

"I concur," said Mr. Strangeways, in a voice that despite its softness had nothing tentative or deferential about it. Maria, still trying to place him, suddenly wondered if he was supposed to be some kind of a medium or psychic. The trouble was he didn't at all match her notion of what one of those people, genuine or fake, ought to look like.

There were still a few items that needed to be carried in from Bill's car, including some small two-way radios and some cameras he and Maria had brought with them from Phoenix. Also Joe Keogh wanted someone to check at the desk on the chance that another room in the hotel might have become available.

As soon as the two young investigators had been sent out of the room to accomplish these errands, conversation among the three men who remained became somewhat less guarded.

"Mr. Strangeways," said Keogh, in a speculative tone. It was a comment, almost a question.

Strangeways leaned back in his chair and raised an eyebrow. "Do you see any reason, Joseph, why I should not use that name?"

"No. No, none at all. A change of names doesn't surprise me. It's just your being here that does. When you walked in on us this afternoon I was—surprised." He hesitated. "So, is it a fair guess that some of your people are involved in Cathy Brainard's disappearance? And how did you know John and I were here?"

The man who was now calling himself Strangeways nodded slowly. His answer ignored the second question. "At least one of my people, as you call them, is concerned. I fear not innocently. I mean Tyrrell."

"Tyrrell? *Edgar* Tyrrell, the one who—?"

"The artist, who disappeared approximately half a century ago. Yes, he is *nosferatu*. Oh, there are indeed complications." Strangeways stood up slowly, staring in the direction of the window, where clouded daylight had not yet entirely died. "A thought occurs to me. I am going outside, Joseph. I take it you are soon going to visit the Tyrrell House?"

"That's my plan."

"Then I shall probably meet you on the way." Strangeways turned to leave. Joe was vaguely relieved to see that he opened the door and passed out of the room in mundane breather's fashion. Of course the day's clouded sun was not yet down.

"Vampires," John Southerland said meditatively, as soon as the door had closed behind one of them. "Okay, Joe. Where are we now? What are our two new helpers going to say if we start briefing them about vampires?"

Joe turned to him. "I don't really want to undertake that chore. How about you?"

"No thanks."

"So, we're not going to tell Burdon and Torres any more than absolutely necessary about the nature of Mr. Tyrrell and Mr. Strangeways. That means we have to be careful how we use them."

"And how will we?"

"They can certainly help us search the Canyon. If I understood Mrs. Tyrrell properly on the phone, that's basically what she wants. Okay. Maybe she has reason to think we can do better than the hundred or so people who searched a month ago—I'll know better after I've talked to her face to face."

" 'Strangeways'?" John managed to sound the quotation marks.

"God, John, I don't know any more than you do about why he's here. But evidently our client isn't exactly a widow after all."

"I wonder if she knows?"

"Well. If old Sarah's husband is still around as a vampire, I wouldn't be surprised if she knew about it. That's why she wanted Keogh and Company, the famous discreet psychic specialists. As for her nephew, he gives me the impression of a man who has never heard of vampires in his life. Not even fictional ones. Outside of that, he's somewhat haggard and worn, as you might expect of a man whose only daughter has been missing for a month. The police have been no help to him."

John tilted his chair back so it balanced on its hind legs. "Is there a Mrs. Brainard around? The girl's adoptive mother?"

"There was, but she died three or four years ago. Since then Cathy's been spending a lot of time in boarding schools."

There came a tap at the door, and John got up to answer. The two young helpers were returning together, laden with the hardware from the car, and bringing confirmation of the fact that no additional hotel rooms were available.

When all four were seated at the table again, Joe began to share with Maria and Bill his meager stock of information on Cathy Brainard. John got out several photographs of the missing girl and passed them around, along with a terse typed description. When last seen she had been dressed for hiking, carrying a pack and camping gear.

While his assistants were contemplating this material, Joe looked at his watch. Getting up from the table, he went to peer out around the edge of the window curtain, into the slowly darkening afternoon. The next step would be to introduce his crew—with, he thought, the probable exception of Mr. Strangeways—to Mrs. Tyrrell and her nephew.

He decided it was time to set out for the Tyrrell House.

Before ushering his colleagues out of his hotel room he opened the last suitcase Bill had brought in from his car, and handed out two-way radios to everyone. Each radio was small enough to fit easily into a winter jacket pocket.

There was some other hardware in the suitcase, tools loaned by the Phoenix agency at Joe's request. After a moment's hesitation Joe decided to let it stay where it was for the time being.

Thus equipped, Joe and his colleagues put on their coats and left El Tovar by the west entrance, bypassing the lobby. Gathering darkness had begun to diminish the number of tourists on the broad, paved walk that closely followed the rim through most of Canyon Village. Joe led his people west, past Kachina Lodge, Thunderbird Lodge, and Bright Angel Lodge; all of these auxiliary hotels were decades more modern than El Tovar, built of more conventional twentieth-century materials, lower to the ground and on a less ambitious scale.

Before the crew of investigators had gone very far, they found Mr. Strangeways waiting for them, standing in the gathering gloom with the hood of his jacket pulled up. He joined them wordlessly.

Modest streetlights, widely spaced, now suddenly came to life along the esplanade, giving the area the look almost of a city park. Late daylight was fading steadily behind persistent clouds, though still the sun was not quite down.

As the investigators walked west along the esplanade, the low stone barrier was on their right. Beyond that, the Canyon fell away from a brink as abrupt as the shoreline of an ocean. Still fog-filled and all but totally invisible, this gigantic vacancy began to dominate Maria's awareness as a brooding presence, surreal as a dream.

"They say," said Bill conversationally at her side, "that it's a mile deep and about ten miles wide. Wish we could see it—what's this building, now?"

Maria was able to pass on information gleaned from her brochure: this had to be the Lookout Studio, constructed (in 1914, by the Fred Harvey Company) of unfinished limestone that blended with the cliff on which it stood.

A few paces farther west they passed the Kolb Studio. According to the brochures, Maria recalled, this structure had been put up early in the century, by a pair of brothers who were both explorers and photographers. Their studio stood empty now, preserved by the Park Service.

And then, a little past Bright Angel trailhead and its mule corral, which stood a few yards in from the brink, the four at last came in sight of the Tyrrell House.

Mr. Strangeways excused himself at this point. After a few murmured words to Joe Keogh, he seemed to fade away along the dim walk leading back toward the corral. Maria, quietly curious, watched him go.

And now the remaining four investigators had very nearly reached their goal. Actually little more than the roof of the Tyrrell House was visible from where they were now standing on the broad paved walk. Most of the Tyrrell House, like most of Kolb's Studio, was down out of sight below the rim.

Joe led his colleagues to the door of the Tyrrell House, where he knocked briskly.

Almost at once the door was opened, by an elderly

lady who, Maria thought, could only be Mrs. Tyrrell herself. It was as if she had been waiting expectantly just inside. She was slender and silver-haired, her body beginning to be bowed under the weight of eighty years and more, her movements slow but still authoritative. She wore a Navajo necklace of turquoise and silver, over a purple dress.

"Mr. Keogh?" The old woman's voice, at least, was still strong.

"That's me, ma'am. These are some people who are going to be working with me. And you must be Mrs. Tyrrell." Even as Joe spoke, he could recognize his client's nephew, Gerald Brainard, hovering just inside the house. Old Sarah's nephew was fiftyish, of stocky build and pale complexion, with a neatly trimmed dark mustache. He was wearing a Pendleton wool sweater over a shirt and tie.

"Come in, then," said the old lady, with a kind of tired eagerness. She looked with interest at the people who had come with Joe. "Come in, all of you."

The entryway, of logs and stone, reminded Maria strongly of the lobby of El Tovar, though naturally on a vastly reduced scale.

Joe performed quick, businesslike introductions. The old lady shook hands with the people she had not already met; Brainard contented himself with a nod in their general direction.

The old lady's eyes rested briefly on Bill Burdon, moved on and then came back to him. It was, Bill thought, as if he might have been recognized, or perhaps was in danger of being mistaken for someone else.

The old woman turned her attention back to Joe. "Mr. Keogh, you are almost too late. I heard our Cathy's voice just now."

~ 3 ~

Standing inside the mouth of the cave, in the glare of those electric floods, which were like no lights that twenty-two-year-old Jake Rezner had ever seen before, he managed to control his temper. He was certain now that the man before him was old, despite his violent behavior, and despite the fact that his hair, under its powdering of rock-dust, was still mostly dark.

Jake asked the old man, mildly enough considering, just what the hell the old man thought he knew about how long Jake's life was going to last.

The old man grinned. "I'll have more to say on that subject than you think, young fellow. What's your name?" The voice coming from the figure white with rock-dust was a powerful rasp, and to Jake's surprise it sounded British. His only experience with British voices was from the movies, but still he didn't think he could be mistaken.

"My name's Jake Rezner. I work for the CCC."

The other blinked at him almost benevolently. "Ah yes, you're in the thirties."

Jake blinked. "In the what?"

"In the decade of the thirties—that's all right. You're the people who put in trails and bridges." The tone of the last sentence was contemptuous.

"We put in only one bridge," Jake said, momentarily unable to think of any better comeback.

The old man was surveying Jake with what appeared to be increasing disdain. "And now you've come to stay with us, have you?"

Jake almost laughed. "*Stay* with you? No, I'm not planning to move in."

The other really did laugh at that, and the sound was harsh. "If you still don't know, having been enticed along this far . . ."

"If I still don't know what?"

Instead of answering that question, the old man, with the child's lunch box still tucked under his arm, shook his head pityingly and turned to Camilla.

"So," he remarked to her, "you've not told this one very much as yet. I suppose he's just now arrived?"

Camilla, somewhat to Jake's surprise, was just standing there with her arms down at her sides, her small fists clenched. Without looking directly at either man, she nodded fiercely in reply, as if for some reason she did not trust herself to speak.

Jake, turning back to the old man, trying to put him at ease so it wouldn't become necessary to punch him out, said tolerantly: "Don't worry, I'm not staying."

"I'm not worried." The other, irritated rather than soothed by tolerance, glared at Jake from under bushy, white-dusted brows. "Of course you're *staying*." It was a statement of fact, not hospitality. "On that point you no longer have a choice. What I'm interested in right now is whether you're going to be worth anything as a worker."

"I tell you I'm not . . . a worker?" Jake's tone changed in the middle of the sentence. It actually sounded like the old guy was offering him a job.

The elder once more emitted his harsh chuckle. "I said *worker*. There's a lot of work to be done here, important jobs, some of them too heavy for a girl—for this one at any rate—and I don't have time to do them all myself. I'm much too busy." His eyes judged Jake's physique. "A strong young man who's been building trails and bridges ought to be good with rocks. Ought to be able to break them as instructed, and to move them carefully."

The suggestion of a real job changed everything. Jake, like everyone else he knew in the CCC, would have stopped whatever else he was doing, at almost any time, to listen to a job offer. Had there been regular jobs available instead of a Depression, none of them would have been living in tents, breaking rocks and building roads on a make-work government project a thousand miles from home and at least a hundred from civilization. And thank God, the CCC wasn't quite like the army; if a better offer came along you could put down your tools and quit and walk away without being arrested.

"I'm a good worker," Jake said after a pause. His voice now had a different tone, serious and respectful. Still, with his food and shelter already being taken care of by Uncle Sam, he could afford to be a little choosy. "What's the job, and what does it pay?"

The old man looked from Jake to Camilla, leered at her, and then repeated his coarse laugh. Somehow to Jake it did not seem to go with his British voice. "You want money as well?"

Jake could feel his face getting red. "Money, of course I want money. I don't work without pay."

"Oh, do you not? And if I were to pay you money, where do you think you'd spend it?"

Jake, supposing the old man was trying to make some kind of joke, shook his head, and gave a puzzled little laugh. "Even if I did stay here for a while, I figure I'd get into town eventually."

"It's not a matter of 'if,' young fellow. You're here and here you'll stay. Unless and until I decide that you're not worth your keep."

"Until *you* decide?"

Edgar Tyrrell made soothing noises, as if to a child or an animal, and calming motions with the hand that did not hold the lunch box. "I'll pay you, I'll pay you, never fear. What would you say to—five dollars a day?"

Jake relaxed a little. "That's all right."

"And some day before you die I may even let you go . . . but that isn't likely, now you've seen my operation." Folding his arms, the elder stared at him judicially.

"What do you mean, you may let me go? What the hell are you talking about?"

No answer.

Jake locked eyes with the old man for a few moments; it was a grim and confident glare that Jake faced, and if he hadn't been two or three sizes bigger and maybe forty years younger, it might have frightened him. Yes, the old guy was crazy. No use talking to a crazy man. Too bad, five dollars a day would have been good pay—but Jake wasn't going to try working for a lunatic. No job here. No wonder Camilla wanted out.

Jake sighed, and stood up a little straighter. He looked at Camilla, feeling sorry for her. She avoided his gaze. Yes, no wonder she was frightened, and wanted to get away.

He said: "I'm going, then. You coming with me, kid? I think you'd better."

She still looked timid. Standing in the shade, she held her hat in front of her in both hands, and kept turning it round and round. Her voice when she finally spoke was small. "Jake? I'm sorry, you *can't* go. You really can't."

"Who says I can't?"

No one answered him. "Watch and see," Jake added. "I think you better come with me," he told the girl in a softer voice. Only now did he start to think about the complications that would result if Camilla did come with him. There was nowhere to take her but the camp, and Jake couldn't really predict what would happen at camp tomorrow if he showed up with a good-looking redhead in tow, after being AWOL all night—but it would be interesting. She sure as hell wasn't going to be allowed to move into camp with him. His days with the CCC would probably be over, and he'd have no job at all. But right now he thought it would be worth it.

Camilla hesitated only for a moment, then, rather to Jake's surprise, she said: "All right." Somehow, given her sudden timidity as soon as the old man appeared, he'd expected her to choose staying here with a sure meal ticket, even if Mr. Tyrrell was more than somewhat cracked.

Jake looked at the old man to see how he was taking this defection. There seemed to be no need to worry. The rock-dusty figure stood with its arms folded, regarding the two young people with a gaze rather more amused than angry.

So it didn't look like there was going to be any real trouble. Jake relaxed a little. "Hey," he asked the old man, gesturing: "Where'd you get these lights?" The lamps on their poles really looked like something out of Buck Rogers, or almost. When Jake listened for the sound of the generator, he thought maybe he could hear it droning in the background, barely audible above the steady noise of waterfall and rapids.

"Somewhere beyond the nineties," the old man said. "I couldn't be quite sure."

"Huh?"

The old guy didn't bother trying to explain. Instead he turned back into his quarry-cave, returning his attention to whatever strange tasks he needed the lights to help him with. Standing among the strange white shapes that his tools had called forth from the deep rocks, the old man picked up a steel chisel and a hammer, and looked ready to carve away some more.

Camilla, talking to Jake and sounding resigned rather than eager, repeated: "I'm ready."

Tyrrell turned to look at her over his shoulder. "Better take a gun," he suggested. "Just in case."

Jake, not sure that he had heard correctly, gave the old man an intent look.

But Camilla only nodded and turned away. She walked over to the little house, went in, and a few seconds later came out again, carrying a shotgun, but nothing else. She held the weapon casually on her shoulder, as if she were familiar with it.

"I'm ready," she said to Jake. "Let's go." It was as if she had no real intention of taking leave of the old man at all, or he of her. It was just as if she expected to be back here in ten minutes.

Jake looked from her to the shotgun, to the old man. Tyrrell was once again busy with his own tasks, ignoring the young people.

Looking back at his girl, Jake nodded.

Moments later Jake, with Camilla silently keeping close behind him, was descending the side-canyon trail, going back toward the river, following the little creek whose name he had never learned. Behind him, for a little while, Jake could still hear the faint clink of the old man's tools on rock; he was ignoring their departure.

Fifty yards downstream, Jake, puzzled and unsatisfied, stopped and turned to ask his companion: "Why did he suggest you ought to take the gun?"

Camilla stopped too. "For protection."

"Against what? There's no animals in the Canyon that'll hurt a person. Except a rattlesnake, and you don't need a gun for them. Mountain lions stay clear."

She didn't answer.

"Not protection against *me*, for God's sake?"

"Oh, Jake. No, no, not against you. Not against any person."

Jake shrugged, turned, and resumed his walk. Trudging downslope amid deepening shadows, descending now and then a natural step or two of rock, he pictured how he and Camilla were going to be spending the night without bed or blankets, under the stars. He grinned at the prospect; tonight two were going to sleep a hell of a lot warmer than one, whatever might happen to them tomorrow.

They'd followed the side canyon back down toward the river for perhaps half a mile, Camilla keeping silently just behind him all the way, until they passed the place where he'd always found Camilla waiting for him. Immediately after that, Jake Rezner realized that neither the trail nor the canyon itself looked as familiar as they ought to, considering that he'd climbed up the same identical path this morning. It wasn't a question of possibly having got onto the wrong trail; no way in the world they could have done that. There was only one side canyon coming up from the river to the old man's house and workplace, and only one path running down the middle of that canyon, right beside the single tumbling, babbling stream.

Only now Jake could not escape the feeling—more than a feeling, it was a certainty—that the path had changed. So had everything around him.

Jake kept moving, listening to the rushing water. But for once a stream's voice made no words in his mind.

Five minutes after Jake first began to sense a wrongness about the trail, he found himself emerging from the mouth of the little canyon, his steps slowing to a halt on the shore of the broad racing river. There was only one big river within five hundred miles, so this had to be the Colorado. But at the same time it couldn't be. In this river, vicious rapids frothed and raged, extending at least fifty yards upstream and down from the inflow of the creek.

On both shores of the river the mighty buttes and walls of the big canyon towered over Jake, just as he had seen them before—

No, not like he had ever seen them. Now something was wrong with the walls and mesas and promontories of the big canyon too. Even its overall shape was indefinably wrong. Maybe it wasn't really deep enough. And the rocks and the soil were the wrong color. The sun was lowering now and the light had changed, sure—but what had happened went far beyond any possible effect of changing light.

Jake turned around uncertainly. "Wait. This—"

Camilla was still holding the shotgun casually on her shoulder, like someone who had experience with weapons. She stood watching him and waiting.

Jake let his verbal protest die away. He had to. Because there was no way to express in words the full extent of the wrongness that surrounded him. The shapes of the cliffs were all false, and though they were still high, they were no longer nearly high enough. And how had he ever managed to follow the Colorado downstream from camp to this point? He'd done that. Of course he had. But now, the way upstream on this side of the river was completely blocked.

Night was approaching quickly now. Jake had the feeling that even the sun was sinking faster than it ought. But there was still light enough for him to see the landscape. It wasn't the onset of dusk that was making everything look crazy. The whole landscape had really altered, so much that he thought he was going mad.

Again, this time wordlessly, he looked to Camilla for

help. She had nothing to say either, but only stood gazing at him calmly and sadly, as if these weird changes in the world, and his reaction to them, were no more than she'd expected.

Then Jake's head jerked around. "What in the hell was *that?*" It had been a howl, loud and not far away, like nothing he'd ever heard in the months he'd spent here living in a tent.

"Just an animal," Camilla assured him, in her recently acquired apologetic voice. Looking alert but not particularly excited, she shifted her grip on the shotgun slightly, and stood scanning the wilderness of rocks and scanty brush behind him.

There was no help to be had from her. A moment later Jake had started trying to make his way upstream along the roaring Colorado's bank, despite the absence in this version of the world of anything like a path along the shore. Before he'd gone ten yards he had to stop, blocked by sheer slick walls of rock. There just *wasn't* any trail here. No way to get through, unless maybe if you were a mountain climber. Although, of course, there had to be a way. Because he'd come downriver this way, somehow, no more than a few hours ago . . .

Again he had to ask himself: Could he now be standing on the bank of a whole different goddammed *river?* Hell no, no way that could happen. There were a great many miles between big rivers, in this southwestern country.

This whole situation, this series of incomprehensible changes, just couldn't be happening. But it was happening. Therefore—

Therefore what?

Presently Jake found himself retreating up into the mouth of the side canyon again. He moved in this direction without any conscious plan, only because this had become the most familiar part of an almost completely unfamiliar world.

The creek, one seemingly constant factor amid a multitude of changes, still gurgled down among the broken rocks to pour itself into the altered river. In Jake's mind the voices of the creek were making only nonsense words.

Fair-skinned, red-haired Camilla looked more comfortable now that the sun was down, and she had taken off her dark glasses. She carried her shotgun with nonchalance and continued to watch Jake patiently, as if she felt sorry for him—and perhaps, he thought, responsible.

Finally he gave up, for the time being anyway, trying to figure out for himself what the hell was going on. He asked her humbly: "What's happening? Why am I lost?"

"I'm sorry, Jake." Her voice was still quiet, but a little louder than before. "I can't explain it very well. I wish I could . . ."

There was a rustling noise behind Jake, a scrambling that moved low among dry brush and over loose rock. He turned to see a striped bear the size of a dairy cow, a monster that looked capable of swallowing a large dog. Black stripes ran fore-and-aft over a brown background, with one dark line passing right between the eyes. The teeth, a brilliant white, looked somehow not quite the right shape to belong to any animal or monster that Jake had ever seen, even in a picture. The red mouth distended itself, the shaggy form came lumbering toward them, not too fast but utterly unafraid.

Camilla muttered something. She raised her shotgun, at the same time sidestepping to get Jake out of her line of fire. A moment later the twelve-gauge blasted, twice in quick succession.

Jake saw, or thought he saw, small fragments of dark fur, white bone, and bloody brains go flying. The hulking shape had crumpled and was crashing about in the sparse brush, twisting and straightening. Camilla broke the

double-barrelled weapon open and loaded the chambers
for a third shot and a fourth, but held her fire. Jake, who
had scrambled to one side, giving her more shooting
room, turned back and cautiously approached the creature she'd hit.

He stood and stared in disbelief. The bear—he didn't
know what else to call it—was obviously dead now, its
most peculiar head a bloody mess, white bits of skull
protruding, almost detached from the body by the double
impact. Either buckshot, thought Jake, or else a load of
rifled slugs. The heavy limbs still twitched.

Jake took a couple of uncertain strides closer to the
body, and stood there marveling.

He turned his head to Camilla. "What—?"

She shook her head. "I call 'em canyon bears. I know
you don't have 'em round your CCC camp, but here
there's quite a few. No fear of human beings, they'll walk
right up and eat you if you let 'em. Except they've learned
to keep clear of our house; Edgar scares them off somehow. Most aren't this big, but I've seen a few bigger.
Edgar says we might as well kill 'em when we have a
chance. That's why he said to take the shotgun."

"But—I never saw anything like it. Where'd it come
from?" Jake once again walked closer to the dead creature, giving his eyes a chance to confirm what they
thought they had seen the first time. Camilla stood by in
silence, patiently letting him look his fill.

For a time that Jake could not have judged as either
long or short, he stood there looking. Then, slowly, in
some kind of wordless agreement, he and Camilla
resumed their walk back up the side canyon. This time he
let her lead the way.

Swiftly night was becoming established, darkness
oozing up and out of the deeply shaded crevices and small
ravines that marked the canyon's walls. Jake searched
the strip of sky above. Now stars were appearing, faster

than you could count them, but when Jake sought the familiar in the sky he could recognize none of the constellations that he knew. The North Star, which he'd always been able to locate winter or summer, ever since he was a boy, wasn't to be found at all.

He stopped and turned to his companion. "Camilla, where are we? What's happening?"

"Poor Jake." Shifting her grip on the shotgun, she reached up with her free hand to stroke his hair. "But I don't know what to tell you. Except what I said before, that the rocks down here are full of time. In here, what we call the Deep Canyon, days and years get all mixed up. Edgar can find his way in and out through them, but most people can't. You found your way in—with a little help. But now you can't get out again. Edgar's right about that. I can't either."

Jake made an inarticulate sound.

"Unless—" she said, and paused.

To Jake it sounded like now she was telling him the plain truth, as best she knew how, and she wanted to make sure he understood it. "You won't be able to get out, unless Edgar dies, or decides to let you out some day. And I can tell you he's not going to do either one."

Camilla looked over her shoulder, up the Deep Canyon toward the house and cave. Then she added in a whisper: "Unless between us—now that there's two of us—we can find a way to make him."

~ *4* ~

Standing just inside the front door of the Tyrrell House, Joe asked the old woman quietly: "You say you heard Cathy's voice just now, Mrs. Tyrrell?"

She nodded. "I did." Her tone was challenging, ready to deal with skepticism.

"But you didn't see her?"

"No. I heard her, though. Almost as if in a dream—but I was wide awake."

Joe nodded, noncommittally. Brainard, standing a little behind his aunt, smiled nervously. Maria thought there was hostility, strangely mingled with relief, in the glance he directed at the strangers crowding the stone entryway.

Joe looked around, and asked: "What room were you in when you heard Cathy speaking to you, Mrs. Tyrrell?"

"I was lying down, in my bedroom—I presume all these people are experienced?" Mrs. Tyrrell had obviously decided to change the subject.

"They are." Joe let the matter of Cathy's voice drop for the time being.

In the course of the introductions, everyone had moved into the living room from the entryway. Maria noticed that Brainard kept glancing at the windows.

Following his gaze, she noted that the very sky

looked bitterly cold out there as the daylight faded steadily, and the temperature in the house was certainly low
enough to justify a good sweater. The only heat, in this
room at least, seemed to be coming from a small blaze in
the fireplace beside the entry.

"Have you planned your search for my daughter?"
Brainard was asking Joe.

"Not yet, sir; not really."

Brainard shook his head and would have had more to
say, but the actual client had no intention of letting her
nephew take over. Sarah interrupted briskly, inviting Joe
into another room to have a private talk. Maria got the
impression that the old lady and her nephew were at odds
over something, perhaps over a number of things. Perhaps chronically. It also seemed evident that Brainard
didn't quite dare to argue openly with his aunt.

Joe paused before following his client into the next
room. He said to his colleagues: "Why don't you three
wait outside—take a little look around while you have
the chance."

As if on impulse, Sarah interrupted, speaking to
Maria: "Why don't you wait in here, my dear? Not outside." Maria thought the sharpness of the old woman's
gaze mellowed as it came to rest on her.

Maria looked at her boss, who nodded. John and Bill
nodded in turn, and retreated out through the front door.

"Do you speak Spanish, my dear?" Aunt Sarah
asked, as soon as the door was closed. "I used to try to
practice that language, a great many years ago."

Maria decided that now would not be the best time to
put that practice to the test. Staying with English for the
moment, she murmured something intended to be non-
commital.

With a vague, distracted smile, Sarah turned away.
"If you would come this way, Mr. Keogh?"

"Certainly." Joe followed Aunt Sarah into an adjoining room—Maria caught a glimpse of mellow lamplight, and booklined shelves—and the old lady closed the door.

The entrance at the level of the rim walk had brought the visitors into the house on its highest floor. What little Maria had seen of the interior so far seemed fitting for the dwelling's location. The log walls and stone fireplace were decked by a number of animal trophies, fossils, and what appeared to be Indian artifacts, along with a few small sculptures. In this large room, a couple of electric table lamps were dim enough to allow the firelight to make a pleasant show. Under other circumstances, Maria thought, the room would have been quite cheerful.

At the moment Maria found herself left alone with Brainard, who was watching her suspiciously, as if he thought she might pocket a souvenir as soon as his attention flagged.

Not easily perturbed by what she considered boorish behavior, she might have rather enjoyed a stare-down. But in the interests of peace Maria decided on the diplomatic course instead, and turned away to stroll about and study the interesting furnishings without touching them. And promptly discovered that the furnishings, or some of them at least, really were of interest. The sculptures she had noted earlier, little carven stone animals, perched on some of the rough wood shelves and tables, reminded her of something similar she had seen very recently—yes, in the window of a gift shop in El Tovar.

Turning to Brainard, she gestured—from a safe distance—at a carving. "This must be a Tyrrell?"

He seemed somewhat mollified. "Yes. A reproduction, of course. The insurance company wouldn't let us keep any of the originals in here. The house is unoccupied most of the time."

"I saw some others in the gift shop."

Brainard nodded, his mind obviously already drifting elsewhere. He took out a cigarette and lit it absently, neither offering Maria the pack nor asking if smoke bothered her. Well, it was his house—at least it certainly wasn't hers.

Maria didn't ask, either, for permission to pick up the next carving, the shape of a beaverish-looking animal, which sat waiting invitingly on a small table. Something about it seemed to draw her, and it felt—right—in her hands.

Brainard didn't object. Perhaps he didn't notice. He was staring at the windows again, listening to the wind, paying Maria little or no attention.

So, this gray, authentic-feeling and -looking object was actually only a reproduction . . .

In the next room, Mrs. Tyrrell had turned from closing the door to say to Joe: "Mr. Keogh, I have been given to understand that you have—some considerable experience investigating matters that lie beyond—shall we say, beyond the normal?"

Joe, who approved of getting right down to business, looked at her attentively. "Who gave you to understand that, ma'am?"

"Someone you have helped. Does it matter?"

"Maybe not. To answer your question, yes, in the course of business, over the last few years, I have been asked to look at some peculiar things. I'm convinced that not everyone who reports an experience beyond the normal is a crackpot. Because I'd have to count myself as crazy if I said that."

The old lady considered him. Evidently she saw something comforting. "I am reassured, Mr. Keogh. Please, sit down."

They both took chairs. Then Joe said: "Let's get back to a moment ago, when you say you heard young Cathy's voice. Did it just seem to come out of the air, or what?"

Aunt Sarah's smile was almost sheepish. "I might possibly have been mistaken about her voice."

"Oh?"

"Mr. Keogh, I shall pay you the compliment of speaking openly. The point I *do* want to make is that I *am* sure she is near to us as we speak. Very well, I heard no voice. Yet I feel I must convince you that Cathy is somewhere near, though not accessible to any ordinary search."

"Where is she, then?"

"That is a long story. I will tell it, but the telling will take time. Can you, for the time being, accept as a fact that she is near?"

Joe thought, then answered carefully. "All right, I can accept, at least provisionally, that you have reason to think she is somewhere nearby. Is she being held against her will, do you think?"

Old Sarah nodded solemnly. "I fear she may be. I want her found, and brought back to me safely. The police had no chance of even finding her, let alone—enabling her to return. I would like to think that your chances are much better."

"Let's hope so. Cathy's father seems to have less confidence in me than you do."

The old lady sighed faintly. "My nephew is fond, in his way, of his adopted daughter. And he is really frightened lest harm should come to her. But—I fear that Gerald is currently even more afraid of other things."

"Other things such as what?"

"Mr. Keogh, I fear we are digressing." Old Sarah paused, ruminating. Then she asked: "What do you know of my late husband?"

Joe took his time, then spoke carefully. "Did you say 'late,' Mrs. Tyrrell?"

The old lady, with wariness and hope blended in her expression, had already been gazing almost steadily at Joe's face. But now the scrutiny became even more intense. The silence in the room stretched out. Only the voice of wind sounded, whining in the fireplace, and around some exterior angle of the rough log walls.

At last the eyes of the old woman gleamed. "Then you do know. You understand."

He nodded slightly. "I know of the *nosferatu*. Yes. And I understand a little of their ways. And that your husband is still very much alive, as one of them."

The keen eyes closed, briefly. "Thank God," the old woman whispered. "Thank God, for sending me someone I can talk to in this matter. This matter of the undead." Sarah's eyes opened. "There has been almost no one to talk to, on this subject, for more than fifty years."

Joe said, almost lightly: "Sometimes they find it amusing, when you call them that. Undead." Wind whined again, making him glance at the windows. "The sun is setting, Mrs. Tyrrell. Are you expecting your husband to visit this house tonight?"

She shook her head. "How often he may come here, stand in this room, or in his old studio downstairs, I do not know. But I doubt very much that he will pay a visit while I am present. I have not seen Edgar for many years, nor do I think that he wants to see me. But I do fear that he may be involved in Cathy's disappearance."

"Why do you fear that?"

Aunt Sarah drew a shawl more firmly around her shoulders. "I know my husband, Mr. Keogh. He is near us as we speak, even as Cathy is—and I warn you that he is deadly dangerous—no doubt, if you understand as much as you say you do, you have some appreciation of how dangerous one of them can be. And even of his kind, he is not ordinary."

"I can believe that."

"Can you? Then are you ready to try to deal with him?" When Joe was slow in answering, she demanded fiercely: "You are a simple, mortal, human being, like me.

Tell me, what help have you to count on, besides those innocent young people who came with you to my door? What powers?"

Joe did not answer directly. "First I'd like you to tell me more about your husband, Mrs. Tyrrell. When did you last see him?"

"Mr. Keogh, I have not seen or spoken with my husband in more than half a century." She looked up at the exposed logs that braced the roof. "Not since I lived with him, here. And in another house—nearby."

"You separated over fifty years ago. And you've never tried to contact him in all that time?"

"I have not. We parted under conditions of bitter recrimination."

"And has he ever tried to make contact with you, during the past half century?"

"My husband is a vampire, Mr. Keogh."

"I understand that."

"Then surely, you must understand that I could not have hidden from him had he really wanted to find me. Therefore he has never tried."

Joe shook his head. "Vampires, thank God, are not all powerful, any more than the rest of us are. Thank God also for our limitations. Now tell me—the absolute truth this time—about your last contact with Cathy."

Again old Sarah sighed. "I had a postcard from her, when she was here at Thanksgiving. A routine message, mailed the day before she disappeared. There was nothing in it, no hint, to suggest that she was about to vanish voluntarily."

"And where were you when she disappeared?"

"In the hospital, back in Boston. Only recently have I recovered sufficiently to come here and begin a real search for her. None of those who searched earlier had the vaguest idea of how to go about it."

Joe nodded. Then he said: "I understand that Cathy

and several of her friends from school were staying here at the Park. But not in this house."

"That is correct. Gerald stays overnight in this building from time to time, when he comes here to the Park on business having to do with my husband's estate—of course Edgar was declared legally dead a great many years ago."

"I see—or maybe I don't, exactly. What kind of business brings Gerald here?"

Sarah chose the words of her explanation carefully. "In the art world, Mr. Keogh, it is rumored and commonly believed that Gerald and I have hidden a number of original works by my husband, works executed decades ago, and that we place one or two of these on the market every year. I believe opinion is divided as to whether the hiding place of this treasure trove is really here—somewhere in the vicinity of this house—or whether my nephew's occasional visits are only misdirection.

"Actually, of course, he comes here to meet Edgar." The old lady paused, looking at Joe as if defying him to prove himself after all incapable of understanding.

Joe only nodded. "Your nephew periodically meets your husband. Go on, please."

Sarah relaxed somewhat. "Generally, in the course of the meeting, Gerald receives from Edgar a new carving or two—you'll have to speak to Gerald if you want to know the details of their arrangement. He may, of course, try to deny the whole thing as preposterous, and insist that Edgar has been dead for fifty years."

"I'll have to talk to him. Gerald, I mean."

A log cracked in the fireplace; Joe tried to keep himself from starting at the noise. He knew too much about the *nosferatu* to stay calm when he dealt with them.

"A question on another subject, Mrs. Tyrrell."

"Yes?"

"What are the terms of your will?"

"There's no secret about that. The bulk of my wealth will go to Cathy when I die."

"Not to her father."

"No. Gerald is—not a responsible person when it comes to money. And I am fond of the girl."

"Of course. And if Cathy should die, or be declared dead, before you die?"

"At the moment, Gerald would inherit everything. Mr. Keogh, I am now seriously thinking of altering that provision of my will."

"Does Gerald know that?"

"He probably suspects it. Mr. Keogh, my nephew is not an evil man, and I cannot imagine that he would harm his own daughter—though she is, as I believe I have mentioned, adopted. But Gerald is under great pressure at the moment. Will it be possible for you to guard this house tonight?"

"Guard it? Mrs. Tyrrell, if your husband should decide to visit, there's nothing I can do to prevent him. Not tonight, anyway—you understand that?"

She shook her head impatiently. "I understand that. The people Gerald fears are much more common creatures than my Edgar. My nephew will feel better if the house is watched."

"Certainly, we can keep an eye on things, if that's what you want. Who is he afraid of?"

"He has not told me exactly. But I believe it is a matter of gambling debts."

"I see."

"Then I suggest you make your arrangements now, to have some people watch the house. First things first. Later you and I can talk about my husband. And about Cathy."

"All right." Joe got up from his chair and went back into the living room, where with a nod he indicated to Maria that she should now attach herself to the client.

Brainard was standing on the far side of the living room, chewing absently on an unlit cigar.

Joe asked him: "Want to give me a guided tour? Your aunt would like us to keep watch over the place tonight."

The stocky man relaxed a trifle. "Gladly."

The house was of a unique design, partially due to its situation on and beyond the very brink, and partially by what had evidently been the builder's whim. The design was part Western and part fantastic, three stories high. Two bedrooms occupied most of the middle level. The two upper stories were of log construction. Steep interior stairways connected all three floors. The lowest level, mainly of stone, was partially supported by a rocky ledge a few yards below the rim. Here Joe and his guide looked into a large room, lighted by large northern windows, which Brainard said had served as Tyrrell's studio.

Back in the main part of the house, Brainard kicked aside an Indian rug, revealing a trapdoor. Unlatching and raising this door exposed darkness underfoot, and timber piers on which the building was supported. Attached to one of these log columns, a wooden ladder went down twelve or fifteen feet to a worn spot on the rocky ground, from which a barely visible trail descended the steep slope.

"It'd be easy," Brainard muttered, "for someone to come up this way, and set fire to the place."

"I'll put at least one man down here," Joe assured him. "Don't worry."

In five minutes, Joe had some people posted. John Southerland was out on the paved and civilized walk along the rim. Expecting that diplomacy would be at least as important as athletic ability in dealing with anyone who approached the house openly, from this direction, Joe put his most experienced and trusted man here. John was standing in a strategically chosen place where he remained shadowed from the streetlights, and from which he could see anyone who approached the house from the front.

Joe himself went down with Bill to the slope just below the house. "Let's figure," said Joe in a low voice, "that the hour after sunset may be the most dangerous."

"Why?" asked Bill, with interest.

Joe ignored the question. "So we'll set a double guard for an hour or so. You on one side of the path, me on the other."

Bill quietly told Joe that he wished he had had a chance to scout the terrain out in daylight. But there just hadn't been time.

Joe, earlier in the day, had had the opportunity to look over the steep slope. Now he did what he could to describe the lay of the land to Bill.

"Main thing to remember is that it's a long way down, and that it's steep. The trails going down all switchback, and there are some really sheer dropoffs."

"I can believe all that," Bill responded. What little he could see now of the terrain strongly suggested that the spot of level ground where they were standing was only a small ledge.

Neither man had used his flashlight yet. With the lingering traces of daylight baffled by persistent clouds of mist, the awesome dimensions of the Canyon remained concealed—though the mist was now beginning to sink into the depths.

Joe pointed. "I'll be right over there, about thirty yards. The tree with a long branch that looks like an arm?"

"Right."

"Got your radio?"

"Check."

"Flashlight?"

"Check. Also camera, though I don't know what good that's going to do."

Hardly had Joe taken up his own position on the fast-darkening mountainside below the house, on the other side of the almost non-existent trail, when he gave a nervous start, and then relaxed. The man calling himself Strangeways had suddenly materialized, almost at Joe's side and seemingly out of nothing but the dusk itself.

By way of greeting, Joe said in a low voice: "I thought you'd want me to invite you into the Tyrrell House. Just in case you feel you have to get in there later."

The other shook his head. There was tension, and an uncharacteristic suggestion of unease in the way he stood, first with arms folded, then with hands clasped behind his back.

"My presence on the scene just now would be disruptive, Joseph. And once in the house, I would leave traces of my presence there, a spoor some unfriendly agent could detect . . . were you given a warm welcome by the family?"

"I'd say a mixed welcome. If you can call those two people a family." Tersely Joe recounted the main points of his conversation with Sarah Tyrrell and his impressions of her and her nephew.

Strangeways heard him out with interest. Then he said: "I am in general agreement with what the lady told you about her husband. And after a preliminary investigation I think it highly probable that the missing girl is still alive—somewhere. But where I do not know. Perhaps nearby, as the great-aunt says. I very much doubt whether the young lady is capable of returning to her relatives at will."

"I have grave doubts of that myself."

"Then can we agree on this as well: that perhaps

others besides the girl are in grave, though probably not immediate, danger?"

"You mean besides Brainard with his gambling debts?" Joe asked. "No, I don't have any reason to think so. But if you do . . ."

"I do. And I am beginning to think," Strangeways added after a pause, "that the search for a true solution must begin far away from the Grand Canyon—yes, far indeed."

"How far?" Joe asked in surprise.

"In England."

Joe scowled into the thickening dusk, wishing again that it had been possible to give all his people a look at the real Canyon in the daylight before they went on guard. Even he himself felt unprepared, though at least he had been here once before, as an innocent tourist, many years ago.

Then, almost unwillingly, he looked back at his companion. "What does England have to do with this?"

"For one thing, it is the birthplace of Edgar Tyrrell. According to my informants, his birthplace in each phase of his life, if you take my meaning. There he drew his first breath, I believe some time around the middle of the nineteenth century—and it was in the same land, some two or three decades later, that he drew his last. I hope to be able to tell you much more on that subject, Joseph, when I return."

"Wait a minute—" Joe paused. He had been about to say You can't just leave—but he had caught himself in time; he really didn't want to give this man the impression that he, Joe, was trying to forbid him to do anything.

"What do you expect is going to happen here tonight?" Joe finally asked instead.

Strangeways shrugged, as if he did not consider the question of paramount importance. "Probably nothing that is beyond your competence to deal with." Then, with an elegant gesture, he added: "I can assure you that no one of those now present in the house is *nosferatu*. But you have undoubtedly been able to see that for yourself."

Joe nodded. "But it seems that old Tyrrell definitely is." Whistling silently between his teeth, Joe tried to ponder the implications. He wasn't sure that he could see all of them.

His companion nodded. "But I doubt that he is going to visit the house tonight . . . so far, I have deliberately avoided contact with his wife. Most likely I will talk to her when I return from England."

Joe went on: "You think young Catherine may have somehow become the victim of her great-uncle? Her great-uncle by adoption. A pretty distant relationship."

The other let out a faintly reptilian sigh. "I fear the girl may indeed be a victim. But under what circumstances I do not know."

"Has she been . . . will she be *nosferatu* too?"

Strangeways shook his head. "When we find her, we will know what she is. What she may have become. And Joseph . . ."

"Yeah."

"I sense that somewhere, not far from where we stand, at least one presence even more intriguing than Mr. Tyrrell is waiting to be discovered . . . however, my instincts warn me to approach this whole problem cautiously. This is a time for subtlety."

On that note Strangeways turned to leave, then turned back with an afterthought. "Joseph, I am not abandoning you."

Joe raised his eyebrows. "I didn't think you were," he answered truthfully. "But you are leaving me in a hell of a state of ignorance."

Strangeways shrugged, a businesslike gesture. "Regrettably I must, being still in that state myself. But I foresee no disaster here tonight. No problem, as I say, beyond your considerable competence to handle. I do advise you to exercise restraint and caution until I return, which will be in as few days as I can manage it. In the meantime, commit no rash acts. In particular I advise against your attempting to track this particular vampire to his earth—not that I really think you mean to do so, or that you would find it possible."

Joe nodded. Then he blinked. The path beside him was suddenly empty of any human presence, emptied in a way that had nothing directly to do with gathering darkness, or with fog. He had seen *nosferatu* come and go in similar fashion often enough so that it was no longer really a surprise; but even so it was always something of a shock.

Meanwhile, up in the house, Maria was telling Mrs. Tyrrell, truthfully, what a lovely place she thought the house was, how wonderful it must have been to be able to live here.

Old Sarah smiled understandingly, and thanked Maria, but it was plain that the old lady did not completely agree. Although she admitted it was a lovely house, and had cost Edgar a great amount of work to build.

"Each room has its own fireplace, and these are still the only means of heating. The Park Service has made a few changes; they put in basic plumbing decades ago."

According to Mrs. Tyrrell, much of the furniture in the house dated from the thirties. Some of the simple chairs, tables, and benches were fairly valuable, she told Maria, because Tyrrell had built them with his own hands.

A minute or two after his extraordinary colleague had disappeared—Joe thought it highly likely that the man calling himself Strangeways was already on his way,

by one mode of transportation or another, to England—
Joe cautiously made his way over to where Bill Burdon
was posted, just to see how Bill was doing.

"Everything under control, chief. Did I hear you
talking to someone else just now?"

"Strangeways. He's gone now."

Bill shook his head, impressed. "He can sure move
quietly."

Joe let that pass without comment. "I'm going back
into the house now. Someone will be out to relieve you in
an hour or so."

"Check."

Moving as quietly as he could, Joe climbed the trail
leading up under the house. He had more questions to
ask, and Bill had so far given every indication of being
steady and reliable.

As Joe approached the house from below, he murmured into his radio. Moments later, looking up from the
foot of the ladder, he saw Maria open the trapdoor for
him. On the level above her a door was standing slightly
open inside the house, letting enough light through from
the upper floors for Joe to see to climb.

"Anything new?" he asked Maria, as she closed and
latched the trapdoor behind him.

"Only that this house contains about a thousand fossils, and a million Indian arrowheads and things. When
you look at it closely, it's quite a museum, though I guess
none of the stuff that's left here is really valuable."

"Must have been here for decades."

"Joe?"

"Yeah?"

Maria looked around as if to make sure that they
were quite alone. "About your brother-in-law?"

"What about him?"

"Just that I noticed both of his little fingers are missing."

"You're observant."

"Well, it's none of my business, of course, but I was just wondering how that happened."

Joe gave the young woman a level, thoughtful look. "A vampire pulled them off," he told her at last. "When John was sixteen."

Maria's lip curled slightly. "All right, Boss, just asking. I admitted it was none of my business."

"Ask John if you don't believe me."

Following a silent Maria back upstairs, Joe noticed a few trophy heads of big game, deer and mountain lion primarily, like those decorating the lobby at El Tovar.

In a small room on the middle level of the house they encountered another scattering of Indian artifacts, pottery and arrowheads and little figures woven of twists of bark.

Sarah joined them here. "Well, Mr. Keogh?"

"We're watching the house, front and rear, Mrs. Tyrrell."

"My nephew will be relieved. Now, I think, we can begin to discuss the matter of my grandniece."

"Yes, I think we'd better." Joe leaned against a log wall, watching the old lady carefully. "Mrs. Tyrrell, did you leave your husband or did he leave you, back in the thirties?"

"I left him," Sarah answered after a moment.

"Why?"

"You should ask, rather, why I stayed with him so long."

"All right, why did you?"

"I loved him, I suppose. Do you know, Mr. Keogh, the age of the oldest rocks in the bottom of the Canyon?"

"I have no idea."

Maria, obviously not understanding any of this, was still watching and listening carefully.

Sarah Tyrrell said: "Some of the oldest exposed rocks on earth are down there—notably the Vishnu schist, almost two billion years old, metamorphosed from ocean sediments. That intrigued Edgar from the start, you see; something that had been made an infinity of ages before there ever was a Canyon."

"Mrs. Tyrrell, does this have something to do with—?"

"Yes, it does, Mr. Keogh. The whole matter is a question of time, you see, and of the efforts people make to deal with time and to control it. In that Edgar is far more successful than most."

Maria was squinting at the old woman in total incomprehension.

Sarah went on: "Down there is also something called the Great Unconformity—not a layer of rock, but rather an absence of layers, somewhat more than half a billion years old, that might be expected to be present. In among those absent strata, somehow, is where Edgar built another house—and in that house I refused to live."

Joe was nodding, as if he understood at least partially. "Did you have any children?"

"What does that matter now?"

Joe stared at her a moment, and then gave up. "I don't know. Just curious. Let's get back to Cathy. You told me you think she's in a place nearby."

Sarah nodded.

"Where is that place, Mrs. Tyrrell?"

"To reach it, Mr. Keogh, I think you must be capable of finding it for yourself. I cannot tell you how—nor can I any longer show you. I am too old, and my heart too tired and my legs too weak for canyon trails."

Several hours after sunset, all was quiet in the Tyrrell House and its immediate vicinity. Maria, established in a comfortable chair near one of the bedroom fireplaces, found herself having to fight to keep from nodding off after a long day.

Sarah had made no objection to Maria's sitting in that chair. From there Maria found it easy to keep an eye on Sarah while the old lady, in the next room with the door open, tried to get some sleep.

"Shall I stay in the room with you, Mrs. Tyrrell?"

"There's no need for that, girl. I'm not the one in danger."

And Maria, on the verge of sleep, saw, or at last thought she saw, in firelight or candlelight, movement from one of Tyrrell's carvings.

The impression became a dream, a dream in which the horror was still too remote to cause her to awaken . . .

Joe, downstairs in the studio and looking out of a window, observed that night had by now almost completely darkened the mist-filled Canyon.

He thought to himself: No use in a breather trying to look for someone, anyone, down there tonight.

Not that he had any intention of doing that.

~ 5 ~

Bill Burdon was standing just where he had been posted, close beside a gnarled juniper, just a few yards down into the Canyon from the lowest level of the Tyrrell House. In his carefully chosen position the small tree shadowed him from the moon as well as from the nearer lights up on the Rim, while a long section of the nearby trail lay exposed in moonlight for his inspection. He doubted very much that anyone approaching the Tyrrell House from below by any route would be able to see him, or get past him without being seen.

Bill, who considered himself good at this kind of thing, had no trouble remaining patient and keeping quiet. At intervals he changed position. When he went so far as to sit down, very carefully, on the ground, he congratulated himself on managing the movement without making a sound.

It looked like he was in for a long, dull night, with no reason to really expect any action. Joe had told him he'd be relieved in a few hours, but Bill was already beginning to wonder if he was going to find it a problem to keep awake.

To keep alert, Bill turned over in his mind the distinguishing features of the case. He had to admit that perhaps number one was that here was an old lady with lots of money, one of her relatives missing and another one nervous, and if she wanted to spend some of her wealth hiring detectives, it wasn't the detectives' business to discourage her.

Distinguishing feature number two might be that old Sarah Tyrrell really seemed to think that some kind of psychic connection existed between her and her grand-niece, and that young Cathy stood in some kind of occult peril. That led Bill to wonder why anyone should accept ordinary-looking Joe Keogh from Chicago as an expert in the field of solving psychic mysteries. It was more than Bill could understand. Joe didn't seem at all the type—

Bill heard a faint sound. Some thirty yards down-slope from where he sat, something of roughly human size was moving. Bill's right arm raised his dark flashlight, thumb resting on the switch that would turn it on. Presently a middle-sized mule deer came far enough out into the moonlight to let Bill see its big ears cupped in his direction. A moment later, the animal was gone down-slope again, even more quietly than it had come.

Bill lowered the light, still unused. All right, back to the case. Another of its peculiarities, at least in Bill Burdon's admittedly inexperienced opinion, was Mr. Strangeways, who certainly had something odd about him. This peculiarity was hard to define, but Bill wouldn't have especially related it to the occult. Well, Keogh had given his temporary employees fair warning that he wasn't necessarily going to tell them everything about how he ran his business. And in the business of security and investigations, Bill had already learned, you had to expect to meet odd people.

There was another faint sound, this time from the direction of the house. A moment later, Bill saw and heard Joe reemerge from his conference, descending the wooden ladder. After waving silently in the direction of

Bill, whose shadowed and motionless form was probably invisible to him, Joe Keogh returned to his own post on the other side of the faint descending path.

A minute later, another faint noise came, downslope somewhere—to Bill this one sounded like an owl. Trying to pierce the darkness with his vision, Bill noticed that the fog had now sunk deeper into the Canyon, so that an eerie moonlit landscape fell away from him on a steep overall descent. The moonlight was just bright enough to suggest the overall outline of the fantastic terrain, while leaving almost everything but the largest features to the imagination. Bill had identified the deer at a distance of thirty yards, but much beyond that he thought it would be impossible to distinguish animal from human.

He hoped that the remaining high clouds were going to let the moon—tonight not quite half full—show him a good deal more of the Canyon. But so far the visibility hadn't yet improved enough to give grounds for real hope along those lines.

Time passed.

Bill was wearing a watch, but he couldn't see the dial in the dark, and he wasn't about to use his flashlight for that purpose. The movement of the moon across the sky would let him estimate time's passage accurately enough to satisfy his own curiosity.

Another hour or so had passed, and it was beginning to seem to Bill, at least, that things were likely to remain quiet all night, when the next sound came. This time it came from the direction of the house, and this time there was no doubt that it meant trouble.

A crash of glass was blended with yells in several different voices. Then Bill heard heavier impacts, like a hammer pounding on boards or logs. Additional shouts and bangings followed.

In the midst of the uproar there sounded a single gunshot.

Looking toward the house, shrouded as it was in gloom except for faint lamplight at a couple of windows, Bill could see nothing out of the ordinary.

For the moment, not seeing anything else to do, he stood his ground.

Maria, who had been still faithfully keeping the client company, saw a moving light behind the window curtain. Then in the next moment the light—it had to be only some kind of strange reflection—was actually in the room with her.

Old Sarah, who a moment ago had been asleep, was sitting bolt upright in her bed.

Maria saw—and then forgot that she had seen—the figure of a man, standing close in front of her. And then, for the time being, she saw and heard no more.

Joe Keogh, when the uproar broke upon the quiet night, started to rush for the ladder to get back up into the house, but then remembered that the trapdoor should still be locked or latched on the inside. Slowly he retreated to his original position, watching and listening.

Bill stood for a long moment indecisive, half in and half out of moonlight now, on the verge of charging back up to the house, in the name of doing something. But then the thought of the locked trapdoor passed through Bill's mind as it had through Joe's. Following it was the sudden suspicion that all this noise might be meant as a distraction, to draw him away from the place where he had been posted.

But before this state of indecision had endured for more than a second or two, Bill's attention was drawn from the house, by the sight of first one strange figure and then another, striding downhill as if they had just come from Tyrrell's old dwelling. Both figures were moving so swiftly and unexpectedly that both were past Bill before he could react in any purposeful way.

A moment later Bill, reacting instinctively, had started in pursuit. Pulling out his flashlight, he turned it on, and in the same instant cried out for the two to halt. His shout had no visible effect.

Even in the excitement of the moment it struck him as unsettling that his quarry, the figures of someone—or something—at least generally, vaguely human—were eerily not really running, but rather striding away from him, moving at the speed of runners, gliding downhill, departing untouched into the invisible depths of the Canyon.

They were escaping, scot-free, after making a mockery of Bill's and his colleagues' efforts to protect their client.

Worse than defeat was insult. There was something indefinably daunting about the figures Bill had glimpsed—about that first one in particular—but he was a brave young man and did not hesitate, at least not more than momentarily, to pursue.

His flashlight now failed to reveal anything of the foremost figure that fled from him down the slope—that appeared to have already vanished—but the beam afforded him one fairly clear look at the rearmost, who had paused momentarily. In Bill's sight this took the form of a man, a total stranger as far as he could tell—grayhaired, and dressed in gray work clothing. Bill yelled at this man to halt.

The gray-haired man paid not the least attention, but strode on, resuming his effortless Olympic pace.

Bill, running now at something like full speed, started to give chase in earnest.

*   *   *

Joe Keogh had been able to catch only a fleeting glimpse of the same two figures. To him they were extremely ominous, but in the next moment he saw something that scared him more—Bill, plunging heedlessly down the trail after them.

Joe yelled for Bill to stop.

If Bill heard Joe's command, he paid no more attention to it than Bill's quarry had to his.

Joe, drawing in breath to yell again, started in full-speed pursuit also.

But before he could shout Bill's name a second time, or run more than a few yards, Joe tripped and stumbled on the rough and unfamiliar trail. A numbing shock shot through his ankle, sudden forewarning of agony about to come. Joe fell, hardly aware of the impact of rock and dirt beneath his hands, scraping palms and fingers painfully on tough brush and unyielding rock.

Heedlessly wasting what little breath he still retained on useless oaths, Joe struggled to his feet and tried to resume his run. One attempted step on his right leg was all he needed to convince him that he was through running for the night. He collapsed again, with a groan of pain.

Meanwhile John Southerland, dutifully holding his assigned post at the front of the house, heard some disturbance inside, or, as he thought, at the rear. There was a crash of glass and other violent noise, accompanied by yells in several voices.

John crouched slightly, alternating his attention between the house and the approaches to it, from which the last tourist had disappeared more than an hour ago. He refused to let himself be drawn away from his post. The disturbance was quite possibly a planned distraction.

* * *

Gradually Maria became aware that Gerald Brainard, trembling and muttering, carrying a heavy revolver in hand, was standing beside her chair, in the room next to where old Sarah was still sitting upright in the bed.

"They're gone now. It's all over," said Brainard in a husky voice. Maria thought that he looked curiously relieved.

Maria's radio was buzzing on the little table beside her chair, and she groped to answer it.

Outside, Joe, sitting helplessly on the ground, was using his own radio to call for help.

John Southerland, getting the call, at last did leave his post, moving decisively. With flashlight in hand he went running around the house and downhill to the place from which Joe was calling for help.

John relaxed somewhat when the beam of his flashlight showed him his brother-in-law sitting on a rock, swearing too loudly for a man with a mortal injury.

"Help me up, goddam it!"

"Where you hurt?"

"My ankle."

John grabbed the older man under the arms and hoisted. "Where's Bill?" he asked, looking around.

"Went chasing off downhill like a damn fool." Joe balanced on one foot, leaning half his weight on John's shoulder. "After those . . . I tried to stop him—no, don't you go running after him."

"He went chasing after . . . ?" John didn't complete the question; he could already read the answer in Joe's frightened eyes.

For the next couple of minutes they both tried, with no success, to get Bill on the radio.

"Help me back to the house," Joe growled at last. "What's going on in there?"

"I haven't looked. Maria sounded like she had things under control—still there, Maria?"

"Still here," her voice responded after a moment. "If you guys are coming in, I'll open the trapdoor."

Getting the injured man up the ladder was difficult, but with Maria tugging from above and John pushing from below the task proved not impossible. Joe's adrenaline was up, and his arms were strong enough to hoist his weight repeatedly.

Brainard and Sarah came to meet the investigators in the lowest level of the house.

Of those present, no one but Joe had been hurt.

"Did I hear shots?" he demanded.

No one answered that directly.

"I thought I heard one," said Maria. "And Mr. Brainard here was carrying a pistol. Also there's a small hole in one of the windows."

"All right, we'll deal with that later." For a moment Joe stared at Brainard, who looked back numbly. "Maria, try again to get Bill on the radio. John, get me up the stairway to the main floor, can you?"

While John was helping the boss upstairs, Maria tried her radio. "This is the house," she kept saying. "Bill, is that you? Come in."

Only noise responded.

Joe, hobbling now through the middle level of the house, leaning on furniture, muttered something to the effect that the radios were expensive junk.

"They always worked great before," John commented.

And then, suddenly, unexpectedly, Bill's voice was coming clearly through the little unit in Maria's hand. Some of the words were unclear, half-drowned in noise, but the burden of Bill's message seemed to be that he had managed to get himself lost, or at least bewildered; he was going to have to sit tight until daylight.

Joe, at the head of a stairway, looking down at Maria at the foot, let out a sigh of relief. He nodded at her.

"Sit tight, then," she told Bill. "Anything you need?"
Bill did not answer. Joe shook his head and muttered.

Maria was left with the puzzling feeling that she had fainted during the excitement; but no, she couldn't have done that. She had been sleeping when it started, that was it. Noise had awakened her, and lights at the windows, and then . . . Brainard, standing over her with gun in hand.

She had the nagging feeling that there had been something else. But just exactly what . . .

Neither the client nor her nephew, thought Maria, puzzling, were as outraged as she would have expected clients to be under the circumstances. At first old Sarah had been, naturally enough, somewhat stunned by the intrusion, but now she appeared much calmer. Neither she nor Brainard wanted to call in the Park Rangers, who served as the police here on this federal land. She, Maria, would certainly have been outraged if she had hired a private security force at great expense, and her new employees had failed her dismally within a few hours of going on the job.

Joe established himself for the time being in a chair on the highest level of the house. Maria suggested tentatively that she and John try searching downhill for Bill in darkness; or they could at least try shining flashlights in that direction, so their missing colleague might have a beacon that could guide him home.

Joe fiercely forbade any attempt to search, and proclaimed that shining lights anywhere would be a waste of time.

"But there's no use his just sitting there on a rock all night if he doesn't have to. If we could just show a bright light—"

"Sit down and shut up." Joe Keogh's gaze for once

was icy. "I know what I'm doing. I'm not sending any more people down that hill tonight. Our client is up here."

"Okay." Maria wondered silently why the boss was so vehement. Well, some people got that way after they had screwed things up.

All of them gradually became aware that Brainard seemed much more at ease now than he had been before the mysterious visitation. Now he was going out of his way to be friendly with the hired investigators, offering to get them coffee or hot chocolate from the kitchen.

Sarah Tyrrell on the other hand, after a few minutes of apparently peaceful contemplation, had resumed worrying. She had retreated to her bedroom, where she sat in a rocker, tense, staring into space, saying little. The old lady seemed still to welcome the presence of Maria, who tried to comfort her.

John and Joe also remained in the Tyrrell House for another couple of hours. The two men took turns, one dozing in a chair while the other remained awake, listening for any further radio communication from Bill. A light was kept burning in one of the northern windows of the house.

But Bill's radio remained silent, despite the fact that they tried several times to call him back.

~ 6 ~

Numbly Jake followed Camilla uphill through heavily gathering darkness, treading the path beside the nameless little stream whose voices chanted only nonsense. She was leading him back, Jake knew, to the place where the side canyon widened into a kind of amphitheater. Back to the neat little house standing not far from the strange cave.

Jake's companion led the way in silence, now and then pausing to look over her shoulder at him, as if she wanted to make sure he was still with her.

In a few minutes they were standing once again in front of the small log house, whose windows showed no lights behind their curtains. There was plenty of light in another place, forty or fifty yards away, at the foot of one of the surrounding cliffs. An electric glare poured from the cave's low entrance, as wide as a garage door. The glare was growing steadily brighter and brighter against the coming night. The generator, whose housing was now invisible in the background dusk, droned on as before, making noise that was barely perceptible through the voice of the waterfall. Nearer at hand, intermittent clinking and hammering sounds from the direction of the cave indicated that the old man must be still at his labors, though for the moment at least he was out of sight.

Jake jerked his head in that direction. "You say old Edgar is to blame for my troubles. He's the one who can show me the way out of here. The one who can let me go."

Camilla bobbed her head, and whispered, as if she feared old Edgar might hear her even against the noises of the generator, and the stream, and the racket he himself was making. "He can. He could. But—"

Jake had already turned his back on her, starting toward the place where the old man banged fanatically on rock. Camilla grabbed Jake by the arm.

"No!" she whispered fiercely. "Don't mess with him tonight. Not while he's working. Stay with me tonight, and—and get some rest. You don't want to try to walk back to your camp tonight anyway. Tomorrow you can talk to Edgar. That'll be plenty time enough."

Jake hesitated. The truth was that he did feel as if he'd hiked a hundred miles today. He was almost swaying on his feet.

"Come get some rest," Camilla coaxed him again. "And I'll fix you something to eat."

Giving up for the time being on the idea of a confrontation, Jake let her lead him to the little house, where she held open the neat screen door for him to enter. Despite all the strangeness that engulfed him, and his weariness, Jake retained enough capacity for surprise to notice how nicely the place was fixed up inside. He thought it could almost be in the middle of a suburb somewhere instead of here in the wilderness.

It was really a small house, not a shack. Camilla after opening a couple of windows clicked a wall switch and an electric lamp came on, revealing the main room, furnished with rustic chairs and tables. A large, new-looking rug covered much of the floor of broad planks. Under the windows at one side was a kitchen sink, complete with faucets—indoor plumbing was more than anyone had back at the CCC camp.

Crossing this main chamber, Camilla led Jake to a door that opened into what seemed to be the only bedroom. There she gestured for him to sit down on the only bed. Another door on the far side of the bedroom remained closed. Maybe, he wondered, a real bathroom?

Sitting on the bed, which softly squeaked beneath his weight, Jake looked around him. An ordinary dresser, with drawers. No mirror on the dresser, or anywhere else. Several pictures decorated the whitewashed walls.

He asked: "Where's the old man sleep? What time does he turn in?"

"Don't worry about him," Camilla assured him positively. Bustling about almost maternally, she fluffed pillows and turned down covers. "He won't turn in till dawn, and he never comes in the house."

"He doesn't?"

"No. You can go to sleep."

Sleep was tempting, but for the moment Jake just sat stupidly, watching a mouse scamper along the neat baseboard right in front of him. He felt too tired to think.

Camilla had retreated briskly to the main room, where she struck a match and was now kindling some kind of brighter flame with it. In a few moments she re-entered the bedroom and set down a lighted kerosene lamp on the small table.

"No electric light in this room," she explained apologetically. Now, with more light, Jake could see stains on the neat whitewashing of one wall, up near the ceiling, as if a roof leak had been neglected.

"Are you hungry?" Camilla was asking him.

"Not any more." Then Jake burst out, pleading, demanding help: "Tell me, what's going on?"

"Right now," said Camilla, "this is." She turned away to close the bedroom door firmly, and then turned back. Then, standing right in front of him, she began to undress.

* * *

Jake woke up several times during the night. On each occasion he alternated between wondering whether he was going mad, and deriving considerable comfort from the warm presence of Camilla sleeping at his side. Once Jake got out of bed and wandered naked from one dark room to another of the small house, looking for the shotgun. For some reason it was preying on his mind. He found the weapon at last where Camilla must have left it, in the main room, leaning casually in a corner. Jake put his fingers on the cool metal of the double barrel, and then decided to leave the shotgun where it was.

He checked the door leading outside, and discovered that it was unlocked. In fact, as Jake now discovered, there appeared to be no way to lock it.

Holding the door open, looking out, Jake could see a steady glow of electric light from the direction of the quarry. Faintly he could hear the metallic sounds of the workman at his unceasing labor.

Despite Jake's weariness, hours passed before he was able to sleep soundly.

On waking to broad daylight, with a sharp start, from some dream that vanished even as he tried to grasp it, he found himself alone in the neat little bedroom. The sun was coming in around the edges of flowered window curtains. Now he could see more plainly the colors and the decoration of the room, and now he was no longer too stunned and tired to think about them. This was a woman's room, all right. There were no man's clothes or things about.

Sitting naked on the edge of the bed and doing his best to take stock of his surroundings, Jake confirmed last night's impression that the little house boasted real glass windows. There were even window screens, though they fit poorly. The interior walls were formed of the flat sides of split logs, neatly smoothed and whitewashed. There were two pictures hanging on the walls, one was of flowers in a basket, another small boats in a harbor. They were in the same style as sketches he had seen Camilla make. Small shelves attached to the walls held knick-knacks. There was even a good carpet, looking practically new, on the plank floor. But the clothing Camilla had dropped on the floor last night was gone. Jake opened the door of a small closet. Some men's clothes here, shirts and pants, but he recognized one of the shirts; Camilla had worn it on their second meeting. There was also a single dress, light blue, hanging by itself. The shelves and the floor in the closet were dusty. On one shelf stood an alarm clock, hands stuck at five minutes to twelve. Jake picked up and shook the timepiece, but it remained silent.

Somebody had put in a hell of a lot of work, building this place and fixing it up. But now Jake had the impression that it was starting to run down.

Hoping to find a bathroom, Jake tried the unopened door in the bedroom wall. Instead, to his surprise, he found an even smaller bedroom, as neatly fixed up as the room where he had slept, but furnished with a child's bed instead of a regular sized one. There was a child-sized rocking chair as well. This room was even wallpapered, in a pattern of teddy bears and clowns, and a lone, forlorn toy animal sat on a shelf. The stuffed rabbit looked as if it might have been there for a long time.

On a small table stood the child's lunch box that had so aroused Edgar's anger.

Jake found the bathroom just off the main room, the logical site from the point of view of whoever had done the plumbing, where pipes could be economically coupled to those of the sink in the kitchen area. Water had been piped in from the creek. And someone must have gone to the trouble of putting in some kind of septic tank.

On coming back into the main room he also took note of the small electric refrigerator and even a tiny electric stove. Neat. But on the wall, as Jake now noticed for the first time, hung a calendar, just three years wrong, informing him that this was June of 1932.

Camilla wasn't here, or anywhere in the house.

Jake got into his clothes and went exploring outdoors, taking note in passing of how a couple of cottonwoods had been strategically planted where they would shade the house on summer afternoons. There was still no sign of Camilla. Fortunately or not, there was no sign of the old man either.

Jake walked closer to the mouth of the cave. He had to duck his head a little to see inside, but past the entrance the height opened up. The space inside, or what Jake could see of it, was now silent and dark except for what sunlight got in past the overhang. Evidently old Edgar had tired himself out at last and gone to his rest somewhere. He certainly wasn't anywhere in the house.

Standing just inside the entrance to the cave, confronted by invisible depths of shadow, Jake thought of calling for Edgar, but decided against that course for the time being. Peering into the dimness, he was unable to see anything that gave him any help.

He didn't know where else to look for either Camilla or Edgar. But he swore to himself that he was going to demand some answers from the old man as soon as he got the opportunity.

Returning to the little house, Jake noticed something he must have somehow missed the first time through this morning. A note was lying on the large table in the main room.

The message was very short, printed in pencil on the back of an old envelope:

Jake: I've gone fishing.
Love,
Cammy

Love, huh? Jake thought about that word, and then he thought about all the other words of the message individually. Then he let the paper fall back on the table. Suddenly he was hungry. He opened the door of the electric refrigerator and was glad to find some food available.

There were tired-looking apples and a couple of oranges, and some other less interesting things wrapped up in wax paper. Two unopened quart bottles of beer, and a few six-ounce nickel bottles of Coke. Cheese and ham and bread, leftovers from the making of yesterday's sandwiches. There were also some eggs in a cardboard carton, but Jake didn't feel like trying to cook.

He made himself a breakfast sandwich of ham and cheese, adding a little mustard, and continued to look around. So far this morning he was quite successfully keeping his big problem, the fact that he was lost, in the back of his mind. Without thinking very much about the problem directly he had almost convinced himself that once he set about getting back to camp in daylight, when he was rested, he'd have no trouble finding the right route.

In kitchen cabinets Jake discovered cloth bags of rice and beans, heavy paper bags of flour, a small bin of potatoes. Higher up, three or four shelves were packed with cans containing what looked to him like just about everything edible.

The smell of coffee led him to a pot, keeping warm on the stove, and he found cups on a shelf and sugar in a jar. Things were looking up. At last, having eaten and dosed himself with caffeine, he took a deep breath and went outside.

Now when Jake, fed and rested, looked around him

calmly and rationally in full daylight, the little canyon appeared to have nothing particularly remarkable about it. Not as scenery in the Grand Canyon went. There was no reason why a man shouldn't be able to get home from here. Puzzled more than ever, now unable to fully credit his disorientation of the night before, Jake once more started downstream along the faint riparian path.

In morning brightness, with birds singing, the side canyon held no surprises. The only trouble was, he couldn't distinguish his memory of the canyon as he'd come up it looking eagerly for Camilla, from that of the twilight canyon he'd hiked up and down during his abortive attempt to leave.

At least Jake was soon able to confirm that the changes had not been only in his imagination. Consistent with his experience at twilight, Jake this morning needed only a few minutes to walk down to within sight of the Colorado. If this river was indeed the one he'd known for four months by that name. This was last night's transformed torrent complete with unexpected rapids, not the Colorado he'd followed down here yesterday from camp.

Detouring slightly, he stopped to look at the place where he seemed to remember Camilla shooting the peculiar bear. The remains of the beast were still there, and something had been chewing on it during the night. What was left was starting to draw flies and ants.

Jake stood there for some time looking at the mess. When he closed his eyes and opened them again, it was still there.

In broad daylight the peculiar landscape along the big river was no less strange than it had been at nightfall—in a way it was even stranger now, because now Jake could see the unfamiliar formations all too plainly.

Still gazing at these geographical impossibilities, his mind a numbed blank, he heard a sound, and saw

Camilla, dressed mostly in yesterday's clothes, approaching him from a little way downstream along the riverbank. Against the morning sunlight she was wearing a woman's broad-brimmed gardening hat. She really had been fishing, and was carrying the proof, a rod and line, and three fair-sized trout by a willow twig threaded expertly through their gills. The fish still had enough life left in them to twitch their tails.

"Good morning," Camilla said tentatively, as if she and Jake were two people who barely knew each other. And maybe, he thought, that was the truth.

" 'Morning," he responded.

"I caught some fish for breakfast."

"I've had mine. Thanks for the coffee. I'm going home. Back to camp. Come with me if you want. I expect I can find the way in daylight. If not, you can show me."

Her face fell and her voice became hushed. "I wish to God I could do that, Jake."

He stood looking at her, not knowing what to do or think or say.

"Jake?" She put a hand on his arm, almost timidly. "Walk me back to the house, sweetie, before you go. I have to talk to you."

Again he let her lead him. The thought crossed his mind that it wasn't any good pretending that he could do anything else right now.

Back at the house, Camilla immediately got to work cleaning the fish, working outdoors, on a rough wooden table just outside the kitchen window. A calico house cat, acting about halfway tame, appeared from somewhere and took a keen interest in the proceedings.

Wielding a small cleaver, Camilla expertly whacked off a fish head. Then she took up a sharp thin-bladed knife and began to gut the slippery body. Her face looked grim, but Jake didn't think it was because of the messy work.

Jake said: "Go ahead and talk."

"I'm sorry . . ." she began, then didn't know how to continue.

Before she could say anything more Camilla began to cry. With the fish in one hand and knife in the other, she couldn't deal with her tears very well, and wound up wiping her eyes on the sleeve and then the shoulder of her man's shirt.

Jake's heart sank, feeling sorry for her. Whatever that old bastard had done, he had done now to both of them . . .

The cat, its interest now concentrated in the fish guts Camilla had thrown to the ground, was getting itself entangled in pink and yellow strings.

All these tears weren't doing Jake any good. To get Camilla talking rationally again he asked her: "What'll happen if I hike upstream along the creek instead of down?"

"Same thing. I mean you won't be able to get nowhere." As Camilla got more upset, Jake noticed, her grammar deteriorated.

He said: "Eat your fish for breakfast if you want. Then I want you to come away from here with me. Or anyway we'll give it a good try."

She hesitated. Then she said: "All right," in a defeated tone, and resumed her work.

When the trout were cleaned Camilla took them into the house and dipped them in flour, then fried them with a touch of bacon grease.

She tried to persuade Jake to eat at least one of the fish; presently he gave in, thinking he didn't know when his next meal might be. No doubt about it, the fresh-caught trout was good.

Still there was no sign of Edgar, in or around the house. Neither Camilla or Jake had mentioned him.

When breakfast was over, Camilla started to scrub out the frying pan.

"What do you want to do that for? Let the old fart clean up after you for once."

Again, as if she were only humoring Jake, she said: "All right." She ran some water in the pan and left it soaking in the sink.

Then the two of them went outside again, Camilla carrying the shotgun with her as before.

This time Jake led the way, upstream along the creek, in silence. There were places, away from the creek, where the little cliff down which the waterfall came tumbling didn't look too difficult to climb. Before he left the creek to start climbing he remembered to refill his canteen.

Climbing after Jake, Camilla, on reaching a difficult place, handed up the shotgun for him to hold.

Jake accepted the weapon and looked it over. Everything seemed in order. "Edgar won't care if I have a shotgun, huh?" He reached down with his free hand to pull Camilla up beside him.

"He won't mind that, no." Her voice was sweet and soothing.

Jake stared at her and shook his head.

Soon they had reached the top of the small cliff. There were no more cliffs in sight above this one, no more big climbs, only a jumble of rocks, all sizes up to that of a small house, stretching away in every direction, across terrain that on the large scale was generally level.

He wanted to go east, of course, but still the way was practically blocked.

Jake persisted, and a few minutes' additional clambering brought him all the way atop a minor rise that had to be the absolute rim. But this rugged height was as impossibly close to the house as the river was close to the house in the opposite direction. As if the great depth of the Canyon had not yet been established, and the rim were no more than a few hundred feet above the Colorado.

Standing here on this version of the South Rim, and looking in the general direction of the morning sun, Jake could see for miles. It wasn't very much like the South Rim he'd known for the past four months, and there was no sign of Canyon Village in the distance. For all he could tell from here, this strange and unnatural landscape before him was totally uninhabited.

He made a tentative attempt to do some exploring, at least, to the east. But the tilted slabs of rock that so obviously blocked his path simply continued to do so, and no hidden pathway became apparent. He was effectively prevented from travelling in that direction. The creek had disappeared—it must, thought Jake, have its source under some of these slabs. He could try looking for that source. But he was going to get some answers first.

He considered trying to go west instead, then circling around. But going west across this field of jagged rocks was no more feasible than going east. There had to be some better way.

Carefully Jake descended from the little rise, and made his way with difficulty, climbing over tilted slabs, back to the top of the waterfall-cliff.

Camilla was waiting for him there, just where he'd left her.

He set down the shotgun and took her by both arms—not a hard grip, just firm. Very firm. "All right, tell me. You knew that once I came up Deep Canyon I'd—I'd get stuck here, in this—this place. That's when it happened, isn't it?"

Camilla tried to pull away, but Jake wasn't letting her do that. So she relaxed and said: "That's when it happened, when you came up the canyon with me. Jake, I'm sorry—but I couldn't help myself. I had to do something."

His breakfast was turning to lead in the pit of his stomach. "You mean you knew once you brought me here, I couldn't get out?"

"I *had* to bring you, Jake. Because I needed you."

"Needed me for what?"

Her voice dropped. "To get out. To get away from Edgar. He thinks I brought you here to be his helper, because he told me he needed a helper. But that wasn't why I did it. The real reason was, with two of us here, I figured we could find some way to get out."

He kept on staring at her, in silence.

Camilla tried to smile brightly. "Besides, now I love you, Jake, I couldn't let you go. You know you can have me anytime you want. It's great. I like it when you do it to me." She did her best to give her hips a sprightly wriggle.

"That's what you need me for?"

"No, but I like it. Do it to me now. We can go in the house, or do it right here. There's nobody to see. Nobody anywhere—" Camilla's voice broke on the last word, and she was weeping again.

Jake stared at her for what felt like a long time. He had an impulse to take her in his arms and comfort her, but the thought of what she'd done to him, trapping him here, kept him from doing that.

At last he said: "Right now there's a couple of other things I want to do first."

At Jake's request Camilla took him on a tour of the cave where the old man worked at night. He had her turn on the bright lights in the cave, convincing himself that Tyrrell wasn't sleeping in there somewhere.

Then Jake's interest centered briefly on the lamps themselves. "Where'd these electric lights come from? I never saw anything like 'em."

"Edgar says . . ."

"What?"

"He told me once he got them from 'sometime past 1990.' Those were the words he used. I told you time runs funny down here."

"He was just sayin' that," said Jake without conviction. "Making up a story to have a little joke."

"Maybe," said Camilla, after a pause. "You know where he says we are now? Where all the canyons are not as deep as they ought to be, and with all the peculiar animals?"

"Where?"

"Edgar says: 'About one million BC.' And then he laughs." Her voice caught. "I don't know if he means it or not."

Maybe, thought Jake, that idea about being a million years in the past was something that needed thinking about. Well, if so, he wasn't up to the task right now. Instead he went into the cave again and wandered the several chambers and alcoves, which took up at least as much room as a small house. He stared at everything by Edgar's bright electric lights, but being able to see clearly did nothing to clear up the mystery. Trying to get a better idea of what the old man was up to here, Jake looked at the long workbench, the pits in the floor, the fragmentary carvings, so many of the latter that some must have been started and abandoned.

Camilla had come back into the cave too and was following him around in silence.

"Where's old Edgar now?" Jake demanded of her at last.

"Sleeping."

"You told me that a couple of times already. What I'm asking now is where he sleeps."

Camilla did not reply.

"You think I'm just going to stay here—wherever

this is—and work for that bastard because I can't find my way out? And every time you shake your little ass at me, I'll forget everything else?"

"No, Jake. Like I told you, I brought you here because I was desperate, I needed you to help me. I want out of this as much as you do. More, I've been here longer." Again Camilla seemed to be on the edge of breaking down.

"Old Edgar thinks I'm going to work for him, because I don't have any choice?"

After another pause Camilla said: "You want to know the truth? I don't think old Edgar really cares much if you ever do any work or not. But he'll make you work, to keep you busy, so you won't spend your time thinking up ways to give him trouble. And he doesn't need me as a model anymore. Not really. But still h-he won't let me go."

"Why not? If he doesn't need us, what's he keeping us here for?"

She wouldn't, or couldn't, answer.

"What's he want us for?"

Answering appeared to cost Camilla a great effort. It was as if she were putting her deepest fear into words. "I think he wants—our lives. In some way."

Jake felt a chill. "What do you mean, our lives? For what?"

"I don't know. It's just a feeling. But for now we're all right. So you can just make up your mind to stay here for a while. With me. The old man won't ever bother us during the day. You can work for him a while. I've worked for him, he's not that bad." Her voice dropped to a whisper. "Then together you and I have to figure out something. Find a way for both of us to get out of here."

"A way? Like what?"

"That's what we've got to figure."

"I want to talk to him."

"Not now, he's sleeping. Believe me, you're not going to talk to him now."

"At least you can show me where he sleeps."

Camilla sighed heavily. "All right. You're not gonna believe me, but all right."

~ 7 ~

Bill Burdon, leaping recklessly downhill along a barely perceptible trail, intent upon pursuing into darkness what had appeared to him as two striding figures, managed to stay creditably close to his quarry, the rearmost of those figures, for the first sixty yards or so. At the start Bill had confidently expected to be able to gain ground, but this hope proved embarrassingly futile.

Summoning up his best authoritative sergeant's voice, he cried for his quarry to stop.

But if his command to halt had any effect at all, it was the very opposite of what had been intended. The single speeding form still visible ahead of Bill did not look back, but seemed to accelerate. Now Bill was definitely losing ground.

Some twenty seconds into the pursuit, that pacing figure reached the level of the lowering mist and vanished completely. Bill could still hear brush crackling and rocks sliding under his quarry's feet; a few moments later he plunged into the fog himself, and was forced to reduce his own speed, as even the ground immediately ahead of him became almost invisible.

Bill flicked on his flashlight. The beam set a small volume of fog aglow, and revealed something of the slanted earth just before his feet, but was of no help to him in locating his quarry.

And now the sounds of the other's passage had faded completely away.

Bill slowed to a fast walk. Examining the ground carefully with the help of his flashlight, he was able to identify and follow a faintly visible path, winding downhill among rocks, blackbrush, and prickly pear. Here and there traces of snow persisted from the last fall, evidently several days ago. Looking for individual tracks, of course, trying to find anything like a footprint on a surface composed almost entirely of hard rock, would have been foolish, especially in darkness.

For a few more minutes he continued down this trail, pausing several times to listen for movement in the darkness ahead. He disliked having to use the flashlight at all, but there hadn't been any real choice.

At last, when even with the light he could no longer convince himself he had a trail to follow, Bill came to a halt. He snapped off the flash.

Whoever he had been chasing might very well have managed to get away, he decided, but he wasn't quite ready to give up. Again he started downslope, moving more slowly and cautiously now, alert for any sound or spark of light in the murky depths ahead.

Whatever human presence had vanished in that direction was remaining neatly concealed, or else was by now so far ahead that Bill might as well give up. As far as he could tell, he might be entirely alone on the whole damned canyon wall. Again he regretted not having been able to get a good look in daylight at the lay of the land. Well, he hadn't had the chance to look around, and that was that.

His little two-way radio was buzzing in his jacket pocket.

Sighing, Bill pulled out the device. Speaking into it in a low voice, he tried to make contact with home base but, for the moment, failed.

Stuffing the useless device back into his pocket, he dejectedly reversed course and started back uphill—only to come to a halt before he had climbed ten yards, his way blocked by a mass of boulders. Now it seemed that he was going to have trouble even finding the trail, or faint imitation of a trail, on which he had just come down.

That he should have become confused was, in the circumstances, easy enough to understand. But he didn't consider that that gave him an excuse for doing so. Well, as long as he kept climbing, whether on a trail or not, he had to be going in at least approximately the right direction.

Detouring around the immediate obstruction, Bill ascended patiently, one step after another. But soon he got into difficulties again. Sidestepping again, he climbed some more—only to come to a halt, looking warily about him and turning on his light. Now, in a place where he seemed to remember a steep but smoothly rising slope, a minor precipice dropped off. His light revealed the tips of tall pine trees, yards below his boots.

Mentally rerunning the brief sequence of his headlong pursuit downhill, Bill couldn't convince himself that it had lasted more than a couple of minutes. And now, only now, he became aware that something else was wrong. The lights of Canyon Village ought to be bright and fairly close above him. He could see no lights at all up there.

Frowning and muttering to himself, he began to use his flashlight steadily. The beam was thoroughly spoiling whatever night vision he might have left, but he'd given up the chase now anyway. Right now he'd have to be content with finding his way home.

He was now making his way along what seemed to be a kind of minor ridge, gradually getting higher. Following this spine up until it ran into a more sharply ascending mass of rock, Bill resigned himself to finding his way through completely unfamiliar territory. His hopes were raised when he encountered what appeared to be another faint trail, and followed it uphill for a short distance. But again, suddenly, there was no more trail.

By now Bill had climbed enough to be once more well above the depth where the fog still held sway. But somehow his surroundings were not in the least familiar. That dark mass above him, discouragingly remote, making a sharp line of demarcation against the stars, naturally had to be the rim. But, incredibly, this rim still bore no sign of the clustered lights of Grand Canyon Village.

Were they suffering some kind of power failure up there? What next?

Sighing, Bill doggedly resumed his effort to get up the hill down which he had so briskly run. All right, it wasn't quite the same hill. He could no longer even find that one. For some reason, this slope was vastly, incredibly different. Now barriers of rock loomed where he could swear none had existed only a few minutes earlier.

Soon he came to a halt again, this time swearing under his breath. Unfamiliar terrain or not, he *couldn't* have gotten lost as stupidly as this. He never had, not since he was six years old. It would have made him angry had anyone even suspected that he was capable of such a failure.

And again he climbed.

Having gained a little altitude, and, as he thought, perhaps surmounted some interfering wrinkle in the landscape, he tried his two-way radio once more. Again the device brought him at first only a little noise—and then, at last, the noise was followed by a half-familiar voice.

"This is the house," Maria was saying, speaking very distinctly in an evident effort to make herself understood at all costs. "Bill, is that you? Come in."

Pressing a key, Bill reluctantly described his problems. He told Maria it looked like he was going to have to sit tight until daylight.

"Sit tight, then," said her small, distorted voice, sounding relieved. "Anything you need?"

He told her that there was not, but he couldn't be sure that he was getting through. All he got back was some more static.

Switching off, he stuck the radio back into his jacket pocket. Partially unzipping the jacket, still muttering and swearing, he told himself that at least the air was notably warmer down here than up on the rim. Maybe his chase *had* lasted longer than he'd thought. Hell, that must be the explanation. Though that didn't explain why he could no longer see even a glow from the Village lights . . .

Despite what he'd told Maria, he kept trying. Making very slow progress uphill, Bill at last admitted to himself (in some embarrassment, not lessened by being so far private) that it looked like he was going to have to wait until morning to find his way back to the Tyrrell House and the hotel.

Admitting that he seemed to be lost was bad, but not as bad as stepping over a cliff would be. For a little while he sat on a comfortably placed ledge, and thought. Then for a longer time he stalked around in a safely explored little space, waving his arms, and with half his mind considered building a fire. But really, the air wasn't that cold, not any longer, and there was very little wind. Alternating periods of movement and resting, Bill even got a little sleep, sitting on one rock and leaning against another, hoping any rattlesnakes in the area would keep their distance.

*   *   *

Something roused him from an uncomfortable doze. Rubbing his stiff neck, he got to his feet. The stars were fading, which meant that dawn was coming at last. Stretching, moving about a little to keep warm, he watched the process. The eastern sky was now remotely gray, instead of nothing but a mass of sheer dull darkness. Then, forming itself by indefinable gradations, there appeared a broad line of pale light, following the almost flat horizon for a long way. Now, all around Bill, vast shapes of land, vaster extensions of sheer airy space, were beginning to take form out of mist and darkness . . .

Dawn brought lighter grayness and then the beginnings of color in the sky, as you might see the sky almost anywhere on earth. But here the land being drawn gradually into existence by the dawn did not look like any known earthly territory. Bill pondered the remoteness of a butte, slowly turning redder and redder, even as the crimson faded from the sky. Was that particular upthrusting of the earth, surely shaped like no other portion of the planet, half a mile away, or a mile? Or perhaps two miles, or five?

Moment by moment the complexity of the scene before Bill became clearer, and at the same time more incredible. He had seen pictures of the Canyon, of course, everybody had. But no picture, no model, could show this, or come close to showing it. This was genesis. The creation of the world.

At last, reluctantly, he forced his thoughts back to business. In all this scenery there was no sign of the people he had been pursuing last night—or of anyone else.

For all the indications that this view showed to the contrary, he, Bill, might well be the last person—or the first—on the planet.

Awesome sights surrounded him, towering, grandly colored rock formations. He knew the Canyon was roughly ten miles across at this point, a broken, inhospitable, magnificent land, barely fringed here and there with vegetation, carved up into countless side canyons, looking utterly impossible to cross on foot, even though he knew that there were trails.

The river, which Bill had more or less expected to become visible far below with daylight, remained concealed within the deepest part of the gorge. The upper edges of that final abyss, Bill estimated, lay at least a thousand feet below the ledge from which he was observing. At that depth a broad bench of land, studded with what looked like sagebrush, declined slowly to the lip of the ultimate split in the earth. Again, all heights and distances were hard to judge.

Bill climbed again, for half an hour, and paused to look around him. As far as he could tell from any shifting of the more distant portions of the scenery during his climb, he might not have changed his position at all.

Bill resumed climbing, then stopped, staring downward at a broad shelf of land, dotted with vegetation, that stretched perhaps a thousand feet below him. He had the distinct impression that he had just seen an elephant down there—had at least seen *something,* with an elephant-style trunk, stripping or at least tugging at a tree-limb. He had rubbed his eyes and questioned his own sanity when he saw the thing again, or another creature very like the first. This time he watched the dark peculiar shape for several seconds, until it moved out of sight behind a fold of land.

He moved on.

Presently he got a look, a good enough look to really shake him up, at another creature, almost on his own level. The single-humped camel calmly returned his gaze, and moved along.

It was then, trying to remember what might have happened to drive him mad, and having unconsciously given up the idea or hope of meeting anyone, he topped a small ridge and found himself looking at a girl who was sitting in front of a small modern tent with her back to him, gazing out over the depths.

Beside the girl was a small fire, and it was plain that she had established a kind of camp. On the other side of her was a small cave, big enough to shelter one person in a pinch, whose entrance the fire guarded.

The girl was dressed much as any well-to-do young camper might be dressed in the world to which Bill was trying to return. Both her jacket and her scarf fitted the description of clothing worn by Cathy Brainard. The wind toyed with her dark hair as she sat facing out over the Canyon, and something in her pose suggested to Bill that she was, or recently had been, weeping.

Bill let one of his boots scrape on rock, and the girl's head whirled round. Blue-gray eyes under dark brows, filled with—anger? Fear? Shock?—confronted Bill.

He said: "It's all right, Cathy. Your friends have found you."

~ 8 ~

As Camilla left the cave with Jake, she tried to keep stalling him, but Jake was no longer to be put off.

"Where is he now, and when'll he be back?"

Camilla sighed. "Right now he's resting, I keep telling you. He'll be back soon as it gets dark; maybe a little before."

"I know you keep telling me that, but resting where?"

"I don't think now's the time to—"

"Where?"

Camilla slumped, giving up. "There's another cave, a smaller one. In the cliff on the other side of this canyon."

"Well then, show me."

With a sigh Camilla took him by the hand. As if she were a child, Jake thought, who needed to hold someone's hand for support. She led Jake across the creek and a little way up the slope on the opposite side.

When she had brought Jake to the new cave where Tyrrell was supposed to sleep, and pointed it out to him, he said nothing for a moment. He looked carefully at Camilla, who seemed perfectly serious. Jake felt his scalp creep. It looked like he might have to face it: maybe she was really crazier even than the old man.

The shallow cave she was pointing out might be big enough to house a sleeping man; but the entrance was almost completely blocked by a single huge block of limestone, a slab weighing tons. A cat might have squeezed past this barrier, but it was obvious that no human being could have done so.

Jake made his voice quiet and reasonable. "No one could get in or out through that little crack. I could hardly put my foot in there. What're you telling me?"

Camilla was unshaken. "I know it looks that way, but he's back there now. Really. He has room enough to get in and out, while the sun is down. The shape of his body changes. I've seen him do it. In daylight he can't get in or out."

"There's another entrance, you mean."

"No, I mean what I said. He comes in and out this way."

Jake paused again, this time for a longer interval, and then he asked: "Look, Camilla, tell me again—how long have you been here with old Edgar?"

She swallowed. "I've lost track. I know it's more'n a year."

"And you haven't been out, away from this place, anywhere, in all that time?"

Starting to weep, she shook her head. "I know how crazy it sounds. I'm about going crazy. But I'm not crazy yet. I'm just trying to tell you the truth about him. You'll see."

The way Camilla was talking at the moment did little to dispel Jake's impression that she was really insane.

"I'm not crazy," she repeated, as if she might be reading his thoughts. "You're the one who's acting loony, if you really want to know. You keep saying you're going to walk back to where you came from, when you know you can't."

Jake swallowed. He said nothing.

Camilla pursued him. "Edgar's right, you are going to stay here." It wasn't at all a question. "You don't have any choice. Any more than I do. Unless we can do something about it."

Jake said a dirty word.

"Honey, you've tried to leave, you've seen for yourself how well that works—just trying to walk away. Am I right?"

Again, Jake didn't answer.

At bottom he knew that she was right. It was crazy, but she was right. But his feelings were mixed up. Despite himself he found the idea of working and living here kind of intriguing, in a kind of crazy way. Sharing Camilla's bed every night would be part of it, and that would be great. But being free to leave was essential.

He said: "You tell me old Edgar sleeps every day, all day."

"That's right."

"What about the days when you go out drawing and painting, like when we first met? You mean he was back here sleeping then? In that—that little hole?"

Camilla hesitated briefly. "Right."

"So you had a chance to get out then, didn't you? But you just sat there on a rock, drawing your pictures, talking to me when I came along. Why didn't you just walk out, if you're so anxious to leave? The way was open that day, right?"

Camilla's answer was quite calm, and came with depressing readiness. "No, the way wasn't open, Jake. Not for me to go out. Only for you to come in."

"I don't get that."

She made a helpless gesture. "It's the way Edgar had things arranged. He can open the doors and close them. He opened a door for you."

"He *knew* I was coming? You knew?"

"How could either of us have known that? Did you

know yourself where you were going when you started out that day on a hike? But he left a door open—so someone could come in."

Jake had to admit that on the day he first met Camilla it was only chance that had brought him hiking down the south bank of the big river, to Deep Canyon. "But yesterday you *did* know I was coming."

"Sure, you told me you'd come back on Sunday."

"Did Edgar know?"

"I—I had to tell him that I'd met you, Jake."

"Was he angry?"

"No. He wanted someone to work for him. Anyway, he doesn't care if I—have a friend. As long as I do what he wants me to do."

"And you're saying he actually wants us both for something more than work."

She nodded silently. Then she burst out: "But I had to bring you anyway. Don't you see, Jake? I needed you, never mind what Edgar wants."

Jake pressed on. "But the first two times I met you, it was in the same place, and I wasn't trapped like this. *I* could still go back to the camp. I did go back."

"Those first two times you didn't follow me up here to the house. Coming this far up Deep Canyon was what got you in too deep to turn around."

"So. You sucked me into this deliberately. I'm just wanting to make sure."

She nodded slowly. "But I couldn't help myself."

And Camilla cried again. She looked so pitiful that Jake couldn't make himself be rough with her.

Under the circumstances he couldn't bring himself to be tender, either. Not right away. Leaving Camilla weeping on the sofa in the big room of the little house, Jake spent the last hours of daylight roaming up and down the little canyon, never getting more than a hundred yards or so from the house and cave, looking for something. He didn't really know what he was looking for. Anything, anything that might connect this place with the world he knew, the universe in which he'd spent the first twenty-two years of his life.

As sunset drew near, moments of panic came over Jake. He kept feeling caught in a cage whose walls he couldn't even locate with any precision. He'd already looked, reasonably, upstream and down for a reasonable way out. Now he circled the steep amphitheater made by the widening of the side canyon, seeking intently for any way up the walls. Except for the place he'd already climbed, near the waterfall, they looked impossible. He'd have to be desperate to try them, and even if he succeeded, he'd only find himself up on the impossible version of the South Rim again.

He wasn't yet completely desperate. But there were moments when he was getting close.

The sun had disappeared behind the western cliffs, though daylight still held the sky. Jake paused in his restless, almost pointless prowling, still hoping for a sudden insight that might solve his problems. At best he was going to be more than a full day AWOL from camp—but that was rapidly getting to be the least of his worries.

Coming back to stand between the house and the cave, he once more surveyed Tyrrell's workplace. The more Jake stared at the entrance to the grotto-cave, and the futuristic electric lights within, the more intrigued he was with what he saw, though almost against his will.

Returning to the house, he found the shotgun still standing in its corner in the main room. Jake picked up the weapon and broke the action open. The chambers were loaded, all right, with what looked like regular shells.

Camilla, her face looking swollen from weeping but

eager to please, had come to stand close beside him, watching.

Jake made his voice gentle when he spoke to her. "Camilla? If Edgar thinks he's keeping me a prisoner, how come he's so accommodating as to leave this for me?"

She went back into the kitchen, where, as Jake now noticed, she had started the process of baking bread. " 'Cause it won't do you any good."

"What if I pointed it at him? Told him he was gonna do what I want, from now on?"

"You could point it all you want. You could even shoot it at him, and it wouldn't help. I've seen that done." Camilla, pausing with bread-dough on her fingers, nodded.

"Somebody took a shot at Edgar? With this?"
Another nod.
"Who?"
"Somebody who was here before you were."

Then he wasn't the first one she'd enticed in here. Well, that hardly mattered now. There were moments when Jake thought all three of them must be crazy—Camilla, the hard-to-find old man, and not least himself.

"Shot at him but didn't hit him?"

"Hit him all right. Shot went right through him, tore the clothes he had on all to pieces. Didn't hurt *him* any, though." Jake got the impression that in relating this lunacy Camilla was describing something she'd seen herself, or was convinced that she had seen.

Jake decided to let the question of this impossible shooting drop, for the time being anyway. And he let the loaded shotgun stay where it was—for the time being.

"You're baking bread. That must mean you're staying for a while."

Camilla didn't say anything to that. The movements of her working hands were brisk and forceful.

"Why'd you come here in the first place?"

"Didn't have anywhere else to go. Met Edgar in a tavern in Flagstaff, and he was nice-looking—he looked years younger then—and a real smooth talker. He told me how his wife had left him, just walked out. Didn't ask me to marry him. Asked me if I'd come and model for him. I said all right, though I figured he'd expect more than modeling. I was right." Abruptly Camilla stopped talking.

"How come his wife could walk out, but we can't?"

"How do I know? After she was gone, he must have fixed it somehow so no one else could go."

"He sounds like a magician."

"Don't laugh. You haven't seen much of him yet."

"I'm tryin', I'm tryin'. So once you came here and took your clothes off, he wanted something else besides just looking at you."

"At first he did." Camilla shrugged. "For the past year all he's done is use me as a model."

"You've really been here more than a *year?*"

She glared at Jake, for once seeming to be angry with him. "What've I been telling you? How'm I supposed to get away?"

In response to further questions, Camilla admitted that she still did sessions of modelling for old Edgar, though not as often. "Been almost a month now."

Once she'd put her bread dough aside to rise, Jake got her to walk with him back to the cave. This time he found the switch for the futuristic lights and turned them on himself.

And this time he noticed that there was one more room in the cave, an unlighted chamber far in the back. It was accessible, if you could call it that, only by a crevice as narrow as the one leading to the place across the canyon where Tyrrell supposedly slept.

"What's back here?"

"That's where Edgar does a lot of work. I don't know

what he works on, but he spends a lot of time back there."

"Got a flashlight?"

"I think there's one on the workbench." Camilla sounded reluctant.

Jake found the flashlight and used it, trying to peer into the recess. He caught one glimpse of something that made him jump, a moving object that he didn't know what to make of and didn't like. The impression Jake received was of a figure, a ghostly-looking thing as big as a man, a featureless, faceless glowing form that stood for an instant in the light and then moved away, into a part of the half-hidden chamber that he couldn't see. Or had it been not a figure at all, but only an odd reflection of his own light on the strange rocks?

Jake gritted his teeth and tried to find the thing again. No dice. It must have been only a strange reflection of the flashlight's beam, he thought. There was nothing else to be seen now in the blockaded chamber, just another area of the cave, empty except for some marks of cutting with hand tools on the walls and floor. It looked like someone had been working hard in that back room. Maybe there was another way in and out of it, some passage that Jake couldn't see from where he was.

When Jake and Camilla were back inside the cottage, he confronted her again. "So, up until six months ago you slept with him. And now he doesn't care about that kind of thing?"

"Even at the start, when I first came here, I only— went to bed with him a few times. In a way. But what he really brought me here for was to model."

"What do you mean, you went to bed with him in a way? He didn't like to do it the normal way?"

"Nope."

"How, then?"

"Does it matter?" Camilla wasn't eager to talk about

that part of her story. "You don't need to be jealous of
Edgar, lover. What you've got to be is careful of him."

"You think old Edgar is jealous of me? He's keeping
me here so's he can have someone to be jealous of?"

"No. Not that way. But you better believe he's dangerous."

"Well, I'm not that worried. I won't need a shotgun,
either, if he tries to give me a hard time."

"What'll you do, hit him with your fist?" Camilla
looked scornfully at Jake. "That won't do you any more
good than the shotgun. But I s'pose you've got to find out
some things for yourself."

Jake could only gaze at her in hopeless puzzlement.
"Where's he really sleep?" he demanded at last. "I have
to talk to him."

"I showed you where he sleeps."

"Bullshit."

Camilla only sounded worried. "Honey? Edgar's a
very unusual man."

He nodded grimly. "That's what you keep telling me.
I'm ready to take your word for that."

"He's a very nasty man too. I wish to God I—you and
I—could get away."

"Well, honey, we will, just as soon as I get some
things figured out. You keep telling me Edgar's the one
who's somehow keeping us here. How can that be?"

"He has some way of controlling time. Making door-
ways in it. Opening and closing them."

"Huh?"

"Jake, I told you, time isn't just time down here.
Everywhere else hours and days just go by normally. Not
here, not in the Deep Canyon. Down here it's what I call
deep time. Edgar's tried to explain to me how it works,
some of it anyway, but I don't get it. Maybe you can get
him to explain it to you."

"Maybe I can. I bet I can."

Jake spoke those words softly, but his tone must have alarmed Camilla. She said: "Don't think because he looks old you can just twist his arm or beat him up. He's stronger'n any man I ever met."

"Yeah?"

"Take my word for it, honey." She paused, looking at Jake. "You're not gonna just take my word, are you?"

Jake made a large, solid fist, and looked at it. There was no fat on him, and every muscle in his body was hard, from four months of building trails. "Doesn't seem like I'm gettin' anywhere without fighting him. And you tell me that whatever's happened, it's up to Edgar to straighten it out if he wants to."

"Don't just jump in and fight with him, honey." Camilla leaned very close to Jake. "Honey? You hear me? And that shotgun, leave it alone. I tell you, that doesn't mean anything to Edgar. Just make him mad, if he thinks you're ready to kill him."

"What do you mean, a shotgun doesn't mean anything?"

She leaned back and spoke confidently. "All right then, go ahead, try using it on Edgar and see. Don't blame me if it makes him mad."

Jake didn't say anything. He could imagine himself using a shotgun on someone, but only as a last resort, if his life depended on it.

Camilla moved toward him smiling, and they kissed. But even this woman's lips, even her body, could now distract Jake only briefly.

"You haven't seen anyone besides Edgar in all that time?"

She hesitated. "I've seen a couple of people."

"Who?"

No answer.

"Like the person who shot at him with the shotgun."

A nod.

"A man."

"Yes."

"You mean these other people were here and then got out? Where'd they go?"

"Nobody got out." Then Camilla added: "The man who shot at him is dead."

Try as he might, Jake couldn't get any more details out of her about the supposed shooting.

"All right, all right. So, Edgar sleeps in there, does he? That means at sunset he's gonna come out of that cave where you say he sleeps? Come out through that little crack?"

Camilla nodded.

At sunset Jake was across the creek, over on the other side of the amphitheater, watching the little cave from no more than twenty feet away. It happened after the sun was completely down. One moment there was no one else in sight, and the next, Jake couldn't see how it was done, Tyrrell was standing there in front of him.

"Camilla's been talking about me, I see," said the old man, looking at Jake with no particular surprise or anger.

Jake was too stupefied to answer right away.

The old man nodded slowly. "All right, maybe it's just as well. Let her talk. Now maybe you'll believe her. I hope you're ready to learn your job?"

Jake ignored that. "I want out of here."

"I have no interest in what you want. I asked you a question about your work."

"To hell with your work. I'm telling you what—"

The open-handed slap came at the side of Jake's head so fast that he had no chance to block it or dodge it. It hit him so hard that both of his ears rang, and he staggered away, almost falling.

In a moment he had got his legs under him again and was coming back. He launched a hard swing with his right fist, aiming for the old man's jaw.

—and in the next instant Jake's arm was caught. Camilla was yelling, screaming something in the background. Jake tried to jerk free, but there was no chance. His right arm felt like some heavyweight wrestler had his wrist in both hands, twisting, but he could see plainly enough that it was only little old Tyrrell, gripping him casually with one.

"I'm not really going to hurt you," the old man told Jake patiently, when Jake had given up struggling. "Because I want you to work, and I still have hopes that you'll be bright enough to learn what you need to learn, with only a little pain."

One-handed, Tyrrell twisted the arm a little farther, not very far, and Jake cried out helplessly and went down on his knees.

"Enough?"

"Enough!"

"Are you working for me? Taking orders?"

"I'll take orders!"

Tyrrell let him go. Then the old man turned half away and started walking, then paused, turned, and motioned for Jake to follow him. "Come along, I'll show you what I expect you to do. By this time tomorrow you'd better have something accomplished."

Jake struggled back to his feet, nursing a wrenched but not disabled arm. The old man's strength just wasn't human.

Tyrrell was waiting to see what Jake was going to do next. Jake wasn't going to do anything.

Tyrrell said: "If you want to live here, you're going to

have to work. You've had a day to get used to the idea. Now come along."

Jake was aware of Camilla, watching fearfully from a little distance. But he didn't even look at her. He followed the old man.

~ 9 ~

Startled by the sound Bill had made, the girl who sat by the fire turned her head. Slowly she got to her feet, staring warily at Bill. Just beyond the other side of her compact encampment there yawned a chasm; if she were frightened of him, she had no place to run.

Actually she seemed more surprised than afraid. She said to Bill: "Who are my friends? Who sent you after me?"

Doing his best to appear non-threatening, he spoke in soothing tones. "Your father sent me. And your great-aunt Sarah. They both wanted me—us—to try to find you."

"Us?"

"I work for a firm of private investigators."

"My father," said Cathy Brainard. The two words came burdened with an unhappy commentary that Bill could not begin to decipher.

He said mildly: "Well, maybe you don't get along with him, but I can assure you he's been worried."

Cathy took a few seconds to think that statement over. "How do I know you're telling me the truth?" she asked finally.

Bill stood back a step, continuing to try to look

relaxed, but ready to make a grab if the reluctant object of his search, so serendipitously located, should make an effort to run past him. He said: "True, you don't know me. I'm just a hired hand, but I'm your friend. My name's Bill Burdon. I can show you some ID if you like."

Cathy considered that, and gave a nervous little laugh. "I'm not sure that a piece of paper or plastic would tell me a whole lot."

"Okay, I thought I'd offer. Tell me, are you about to cook something on that fire?"

She considered again, and laughed again, this time with some real amusement. "I don't know if I am or not. Are you hungry?"

"Yes ma'am, rather. I've been out all night, with one candy bar to eat."

"Out looking for me in the dark?"

"I know it sounds foolish. It didn't start out that way." Bill looked around at the spectacular scenery.

In a moment he realized that Cathy was almost smiling at him. She said, with something like amusement: "Don't tell me you're lost."

"All right, I won't admit it. That would be bad for the image. But I'm really *damned* if I can see how the whole South Rim and everything on it can disappear like this." He gestured at the surrounding spires and buttes.

To his surprise, Cathy didn't smile. Nor did she answer directly. "I'm getting hungry myself. All right, I can cook up some freeze-dried glop," she said. "There's a spring handy, just over here."

Walking with her when she went to get the water in a little aluminum pot with a folding handle, Bill looked around at her camping arrangements with approval. It was obvious to him, though he said nothing on the point, that she hadn't been here a month, or anywhere near that long. "Nice camp. I can see you know how to do this."

"Thank you."

"How long were you planning to stay?"

"I haven't decided that as yet. You can tell that to anyone who's interested."

"Your father's very worried about you. So's your aunt Sarah."

"Really?" The tone was sarcastic. Then she asked, as if the question really puzzled her: "How did you manage to get in here and find me?"

"Well, there was some kind of—disturbance—at the Tyrrell House last night. I ran downhill in the dark, chasing someone I thought might have been involved."

That had Cathy's interest, all right. "Who?"

"Never got close enough to him to form a good idea about that."

She relaxed slightly. "Probably lucky for you."

Back at the camp with water, Cathy arranged the pot where the little wood fire would heat it nicely, and dug into her pack after the freeze-dried food. "Probably just as well for you," she repeated.

"Why do you say that?"

She shrugged.

For the next half hour they talked mainly about the mechanics of camping, even as they dealt with such matters in a practical way. The food was as good as could be expected.

When the meal was over, Bill said casually: "Thanks. Shall we get started back?"

Cathy fed another bit of deadwood to her fire, and shook her head. "I'm in no hurry to go anywhere. I've still got some heavy thinking to do."

"They're really worried, you know. It's been a month now, after all."

"Oh my God." Her hand went to her mouth, and her eyes searched his. "It's been that long? But of course—I suppose it might have been."

Her surprise sounded so genuine that Bill stared at

her in puzzlement. "How long did you think it had been?"

Cathy, scrubbing out her cooking pot with water and sand, only shook her head.

Bill pursued: "It would be nice if you came home with me—came back to your folks, I mean. Of course maybe you don't want to call that home any longer. As a favor to me, just to show them that I've earned my money. Then you can resume your camping trip, for all I care."

"My folks," she said. And suddenly she was angry. She looked around as if she might be trying to find something suitable to throw.

"Or at least tell me why you don't want to come home. Let me say it again, your father misses you a lot."

She blinked at him. "Really?" Now she sounded totally unconvinced, and genuinely angry. "What do you know about my father? You think that—that—" Whatever was upsetting her this time had left her speechless.

"I met him briefly. All I can report is how he impressed me. And your aunt Sarah's really upset."

He thought that Cathy softened slightly at mention of Aunt Sarah. But she gave no indication of changing her mind.

"Well, I'm certainly not going to try to drag you back against your will."

"I should hope not."

"Well, I'll be going, then, and tell them that you're safe. Or that you were safe when I saw you."

"Yes, you do that, Bill. Think you can find your way back?" A faintly wicked gleam that had begun to glow in Cathy's blue-gray eyes faded again. "I'll come part of the way with you. Maybe I can point you in the right direction."

"Good. Thanks." Bill smiled, thinking that this would at least give him a little more time to try to talk her into coming home. "Oh, by the way. Would you mind if I took a snapshot or two? Just to prove to everyone that I really did find you?"

She considered this. "No, I don't mind."

He got out his camera. "One last question, also?"

"Let's hear it."

"Who do you think those people were, who came to the Tyrrell House last night and got me chasing them?"

"I wouldn't want to guess."

Bill left it at that. He took a couple of Polaroids, and announced that he was leaving.

Cathy, coming with him to show him the way as promised, evidently felt secure in leaving her camp; the terrain and weather conditions seemed to make it safe to leave the small fire unattended.

They hiked for half an hour or so, up and down across country in a direction that seemed doubtful to Bill; but he was ready to admit that he was the one who was lost. Then Cathy stopped and pointed out the way he had to go.

When he took leave of her at last, Cathy stood looking after him, her arms folded.

After fifty paces or so Bill turned back to wave, but his would-be rescuee, already hiking briskly back in the direction of her camp, did not see, much less return, the gesture.

Bill pushed on in the direction she had indicated. He couldn't really believe Cathy's story the way she'd told it. For one thing, she wouldn't have been able to pack in a month's provisions on her back . . . would she? That freeze-dried stuff was very light.

Before Bill had made any headway in his thinking, or traveled fifty paces more, he was distracted by the sudden impression that something had gone strange about the air, or the light; as if the sun might have dimmed in a partial eclipse, though the sky was cloudless.

After a few moments of looking about him, he had to admit to himself that he could pin down nothing really wrong with sky or sun. But both were disturbingly different.

Still following the directions given him by Cathy, and pondering what seemed strange alterations in weather and time of day, in half an hour Bill Burdon came in sight of El Tovar. So suddenly and unexpectedly did this discovery occur that he endured a moment of serious disorientation. On topping what he had thought was only a minor ridge, he found himself actually standing on the South Rim after all. At the same time the unmistakable landmark of the great log hotel popped into view, less than half a mile to the east.

With a sense of relief, mingled with shame at having got lost like a rank tenderfoot, Bill strode toward Canyon Village.

. . . and yet today the central building looked somehow different, strangely smaller, than the hotel he'd seen at close range only last night.

Thoughtfully he scratched his chin—and then stopped in his tracks. He could distinctly remember shaving, just yesterday morning, before setting out from Phoenix. And yet now he had, he swore he had, what felt like a three days' growth of beard.

Shaken, Bill walked on. Then again he paused, squinting even though his eyesight was ordinarily excellent for distance. Now he could make out a handful of antique cars, of thirties vintage, in the shrunken and unpaved parking lot beside El Tovar. No other vehicles were to be seen.

Bill rubbed his eyes. Maybe he was just tired. Maybe it was just the heat-shimmer of the atmosphere making the automobiles look strange. But—heat-shimmer in December? Come to think of it, the air did seem unseasonably warm . . .

* * *

He hiked on, entering a portion of the rim-trail that took him briefly back in among the pine and cedar, out of sight of El Tovar and its attendant marvels. During this interval he managed to convince himself, despite the continuing warmness of the air, that he had really managed to find his way back to the mundane world he had left last night, in late December of 1991.

But in a few moments the trail brought him out of the woods again. There, unarguably there, was El Tovar—but, disturbingly, it really was a smaller version of the hotel he thought he could remember from last night.

All Bill could do was push ahead.

He passed, and recognized, the Bright Angel trailhead, though the fences here looked different than the fences he'd passed last evening, and there were fewer guest cottages overlooking the Canyon than he seemed to remember.

Moments later, Bill arrived at the Tyrrell House.

It was a warm day, yes, all right, a summer afternoon—with the sun threatening to set much too far to the north for December—but Bill didn't want to think about that just now—and he had first unzipped his jacket and then taken it off.

Some tourists, their numbers much diminished from those of yesterday—as Bill recalled yesterday—were moving toward Bill along the rim trail, which now ran at a somewhat greater distance from the house than he remembered. Today's sightseers, Bill had to admit, were dressed for summer. If he looked at them carefully, and allowed himself to think about what he saw, he would have to admit something much more disturbing. They were very strangely dressed indeed. You would have to say they were costumed like people out of his grandfather's photo album from the thirties. . . . Some of them, who glanced at Bill, also appeared to be impressed by what they saw.

Bill turned his back on the costumed sightseers. His feet dragged to a stop in front of a building that had to be the Tyrrell House. No doubt about it, this was the same location, and the same house. He could recognize the familiar outlines of the structure, practically unchanged from yesterday evening.

But . . .

Today the front door of old Edgar Tyrrell's dwelling stood ajar. From just inside, Bill could hear children's voices, toddlers it sounded like. At least a pair of them.

And the area just in front of the house was no longer paved with a Park Service sidewalk, as he was sure that it had been last night. Now there was only a little un-paved footpath worn in the hard earth, leading to the front door.

Even as Bill stood gazing at that door, it opened wider. Out came a young woman and a little girl of four years old or so, in toddler's overalls. The young woman was garbed in a thirties dress, and a wide-brimmed gardening hat.

The little girl, thought Bill, had remarkable eyes. Their soft blue-gray reminded him much, very much, of the eyes of the girl named Cathy whom he had just left.

Both of them looked at the strange man who had stopped near their front door.

"How do," said Bill to the young woman, in his best mild country manner, and bobbed his head.

"How do," the young woman answered softly, as if perhaps she thought straight imitation was the safest course. Then she did a mild double-take as something in Bill's appearance appeared to register with her. "Can I help you?" she asked slowly.

"I didn't know," he said after a pause, "that anyone lived here. Beautiful place to live." That was certainly inadequate. "Oh, my name's Bill Burdon, by the way."

The young woman studied him for another ten or fifteen seconds. Then she introduced herself: "I'm Sarah Tyrrell." Pause. "If you're looking for my husband, he won't be back until after dark."

~ *10* ~

O n the morning after Bill Burdon's disappearance, Joe Keogh was awakened in his hotel room by a discreet tapping on the door. Cursing, Joe reached for his watch and learned that the time was eight A.M. He rolled off the bed, only to find himself barely able to stand. His twisted ankle had swollen and stiffened since last night, notwithstanding the fact that he had eventually applied ice packs. He was worse off now than when he'd taken off his shoes and thrown himself down on the bed barely four hours ago.

The tapping was repeated, and Joe muffled his curses and somehow hobbled to the door. Last night at the Tyrrell House he'd taken the next-to-last shift of waiting for Bill to call in again. Eventually, some time after midnight, he had abandoned that vigil and, at his client's urging, allowed John to help him back to his own room.

He reached the door, and called, "Who is it?"

"Maria." The answer was barely audible, but Joe recognized the voice. He relaxed and let her in.

The young woman, who had been up practically all night, naturally enough looked tired, but she said that in a couple of hours she'd be ready to go again. There wasn't much to report, she added, since nothing had happened at the Tyrrell House after Joe's departure. While delivering these remarks Maria was taking off her boots and unrolling her sleeping bag on the sofa.

"Mrs. Tyrrell didn't offer to let you sack out over there?"

"Nope. In fact, a little while ago she started hinting pretty strongly that I ought to go to my own hotel room, if I had one, and get some rest. Of course I said I had one."

Joe grunted, and stumped over to the window. Last night's clouds and fog were gone, and the sun, now about half an hour high, was having things its own way. At least, he thought, we ought to get a look at the scenery today.

Two seconds was all he could spare for scenery just now. Joe ran fingers through his hair. "I'm going to have to talk to John."

Maria, on the point of disappearing into her sleeping bag, hesitated. "Want me to get him on radio?"

"I'll do it. You'd better get some rest. We're going to need you later."

But Maria delayed again. "Boss? When do we go looking for Bill?"

"Soon. I promise, you won't miss out on that."

"And how come that person, or those people, whoever it was, was able to get past us last night?"

"I have some ideas on that. Ideas I want to talk over with you and Bill—as soon as he gets back."

"Sure." Maria, sounding really tired, had put her head down again and was already drifting off.

Trying to let her sleep, Joe moved into the next room, where he soon reached John on the radio.

In five minutes John Southerland entered the suite. He had nothing further to report regarding Bill. "Brainard was unhappy to see me leave. But I figure we're working for Aunt Sarah, and she seemed all in favor. Say, where'd Mr. Strangeways get to?"

"England, he said."

"What?"

"You heard. I have no real explanation. Why don't you get some sack time while there's a chance?" Maria's faint snores came drifting from the other room.

"At the moment I'm more hungry than tired."

"Okay, order up some room service. For three, I guess. I like pancakes."

Moments later, Joe was shutting himself in the bathroom. There he swallowed a couple of aspirins, and enjoyed—if that was the right word—a shower, conducted largely while balanced on one leg.

Emerging in fresh clothing, he found both Maria and John sleeping, she in her sleeping bag and John, boots off, stretched out on the floor, where he had wasted no time in creating a kind of padded nest with jackets and chair cushions. Joe, keeping as quiet as possible, established himself in a chair, where he silently cursed his injured ankle.

Staring at the phone on the little table at his elbow, he contemplated getting in touch with his home base in Chicago. John's wife Angie ought to be minding the office, and there might possibly be a thing or two that she could do to help.

Before Joe could make up his mind about the call, room service arrived, inevitably awakening his colleagues. Maria roused herself and stretched, catlike. "Strange dreams . . ." she murmured, her expression one of remote dissatisfaction.

The two younger people were glad to join Joe in an experience of white linen and what looked like silver, with food and coffee suggesting anything but proximity to the wilderness. Joe, with one foot propped up on cushions, consumed a delicious though unavoidably gloomy breakfast, then ordered an extra pot of coffee.

From time to time he glanced at Bill Burdon's unused

sleeping bag, which lay accusingly in a corner of the room, still rolled up.

Over breakfast the three discussed the situation. They'd had only the brief and somewhat garbled radio messages from Bill, assuring them that he was all right, though having trouble finding his way back.

Maria said: "That just doesn't sound right to me. From the way Bill described his background, his experience, I'd expect him to be able to find his way home from the North Pole."

Joe looked at his watch. "I think it's still too early to call in the Park rangers. He said he might have to wait for sunrise to start back, so let's give him a little longer. You two finish eating and get some rest. If we don't hear from him by ten o'clock or so, we'd better start looking."

Observing the difficulty with which Joe hobbled about the hotel room, Maria suggested that maybe he ought to see the local doctor. But he shook his head, reluctant to do that. He didn't think any bones were broken, and there was probably little any doctor would be able to do for him, except tell him that he ought to rest. He sat down with his foot propped up on the bed. At least the swelling wasn't any worse. John and Maria offered contradictory advice as to whether heat or cold would be best to apply at this stage.

As soon as they had finished eating, both John and Maria proclaimed themselves ready to get back into action. Joe, silently praising the resilience of youth, grunted approval. In a few minutes the two younger people had left the hotel and were descending in clouded winter daylight to search the slope immediately below the Tyrrell House. They were going to look for some clue to Bill's fate, or, failing that, anything that might help explain last night's strange events.

Maria and John had hardly left the hotel when another tap sounded at Joe's door. He opened it to discover

Brainard, gazing anxiously back over his shoulder in the direction of the lobby, then almost pushing over his aunt's chief investigator in his eagerness to get into the room.

"Somebody after you?" Joe inquired.

Brainard affected not to hear that. Staring as Keogh hobbled back to his chair after closing the door, he commented disapprovingly: "That looks fairly serious."

"I'll manage." Joe eased himself back into his chair. "I've got some young people to handle whatever legwork needs to be done. Who are they and what do they want?"

"Who?"

"The people who are after you. I'm assuming there's more than one. I'm assuming also that you're the one who shot off a gun last night."

G. C. Brainard sat down and closed his eyes. "A federal offense here in the Park, I know."

"That's right."

"But there are other things that worry me more." Digging into a jacket pocket, Brainard produced a heavy-caliber, stubby-barreled revolver. "I want your advice on what to do with this."

"Do the other things that worry you more have any connection with your missing daughter?"

Brainard blinked at him. He seemed saddened and even injured by the suggestion. "No, nothing directly to do with her. Why?"

"Because the job your aunt Sarah originally wanted me to do was to get her back. Now everyone, my client, and you, the girl's father, are trying to edge me away from that. Tell me, Mr. Brainard, how did you come to adopt Cathy?"

"I'm concerned about my daughter. I want her to be all right," said Brainard, in an injured tone. His eyes looked hurt.

"So tell me about the adoption."

"All right, if you think it'll help. My late wife and I adopted Cathy in 1978, when she was—four. We were childless, so . . ."

Joe probed for more details. As far as he could learn, the Brainards had adopted Cathy largely at Aunt Sarah's urging. Sarah had apparently encountered the girl through some kind of charitable work with which she was then involved, and had been drawn to her. But at that time the old lady had been already in her sixties, too old to be approved as an adoptive parent.

Brainard suddenly blurted, "I can't believe I'm actually carrying a gun."

"Can I take a look at your weapon?" Joe asked.

When Brainard gingerly handed over the gun, Joe broke it open and inspected the loading.

"What're you looking for?"

"I was wondering," said Joe, "if your bullets might be made of wood."

"What?" No comprehension showed in Brainard's face.

"Never mind."

The stocky man shook his head. "It was dumb of me to carry that thing; I hardly know one end from the other. I'm liable to kill someone I'm not aiming at. If you're willing to help me out, maybe you can get rid of it for me?"

Joe put the pistol down carefully on the arm of his chair. Later, he thought, he would unload and disassemble it, and pack the pieces away separately in his own luggage.

Then he faced Brainard. "If you expect me to help you," he said to him, "you'd better tell me why you're carrying a gun. Who are you afraid of, and why?"

The other closed his eyes and leaned back in his chair. A pulse beat visibly in the side of his throat, just below his unshaven jaw. "I owe some people a lot of money. Jesus, how did I ever get myself into such a mess."

"What kind of people?" Though to Joe it seemed fairly obvious from the way Brainard was behaving.

Brainard's eyes came open, and he lifted his head slowly. "Mainly a man named Tuller. Ever hear of him? But why should you, I suppose there are a thousand like him. I think he's in with some branch of the New York mafia. Loans out money at a nice clean fifty per cent per month. I thought I had a chance to make a killing, clean up a lot of old debts . . ."

"How much?"

"I borrowed eighty thousand. He wanted a hundred and twenty back by the middle of December, about two weeks ago. I couldn't pay, I couldn't come close to paying, and so here I am. Aunt Sarah won't hand out that kind of money, and I don't blame her."

"Maybe you're here hoping to get something from her, or from Tyrrell, that you can sell."

"Hoping to stay alive until I can do something like that." Brainard tried to smile. "But no such luck. Now I'm on the edge of dead." He did smile. "Get me out of here, somehow, Keogh. Get me away from this bottleneck and give me a running start somewhere. There won't be any conflict with what you're doing for my aunt. You'll be well paid, I've got enough cash stashed away for that."

"No thought of going to the police?"

The other made a sound somewhere between a moan and a laugh. His soft hand bounced on the chair-arm as if he were testing the hardness of the wood. "That would really put the seal on it. They'd really kill me, then. So far, I don't think they're actually quite ready to do that. It's just that I have this prejudice against having my balls smashed, or my kneecaps broken."

Joe nodded thoughtfully. "If you help me out a little first, then I'll see what I can do for you."

"Help you how?"

"To begin with, tell me all you can about Tyrrell."

"There's not a hell of a lot I can tell you." Brainard shivered slightly. "We do business, we don't have long, chatty visits. He never talks about himself. And he's definitely not looking for publicity."

"I don't suppose this Tuller knows about Tyrrell? That the old man is still alive and doing business?"

"No way. He's never heard about it from me . . . and Tyrrell is not a man I'd want to appeal to for help."

"I see." Joe thought for a minute. "Does your aunt know about this Tuller and his people being after you?"

"She knows I'm in some trouble of that kind. I don't think she realizes how bad it is. I've told her that people are actually here looking for me, but I don't know if Sarah believes that."

"All right. Stay here in my room for the time being. Make sure who's at the door before you open it."

Joe's next move was to dispatch a hotel bellhop to bring him a cane, or failing that, a crutch. Both items, the youth assured him, were available in the general store near the park's Visitor Center, and he would deliver a cane shortly.

Joe thought the next knock on his door, a few minutes later, might be the bellhop, having established some kind of a land speed record; but a cautious opening of the door revealed Sarah Tyrrell.

A few moments later, old Sarah, her nervous nephew, and Joe were all seated at the small conference table.

Sarah wasted little time in preliminaries. "Mr. Keogh, the disturbance at the house last night was caused, at least in part, by my husband. I did see him."

"Why didn't you tell me then? And why do you tell me now?"

"Others were present then. Besides, I wanted to think the matter over. I am convinced now that Cathy is in no danger from my husband. I wish that I could say I believe her to be in no danger."

Brainard was staring at his aunt. "I hope to God you're right, about Edgar. But look, what I saw—what I shot at last night—that wasn't Edgar Tyrrell."

"There was another visitor to the house last night," Sarah confirmed. "Another presence. Something—came with Edgar."

Joe looked from one of his visitors to the other. "I wasn't in a position to see what was happening. Is that all either of you can tell me? 'Something' came to the house?"

"At first," said Brainard, "I thought it was one of the people trying to collect from me, somehow outside the window. But all I could really see was a—pattern of lights. My nerves were ready to crack, and I took a shot at it." He shuddered faintly.

"Mr. Keogh." Sarah was doing her best to be businesslike. "In the light of what happened last night, of everything that we know now, I would like you to tell me, with complete honesty, whether you think you really have any chance of finding Cathy and helping her."

Brainard nodded and looked hopefully at Joe.

Again Joe looked from one of them to the other. "I don't know that what happened last night really changes anything, except that now one of my people is missing. I hope to be able to tell you in a few days, what I think our chances are of helping Cathy. Meanwhile you don't have to keep us on the payroll."

Brainard continued to look the part of the anxious father. "What will you know in a few days that you don't know now?"

Joe was trying to frame an answer, when his little two-way radio buzzed. The device was lying where he'd left it, on a small table across the room. "Excuse me."

He got to his feet and hobbled over to the unit. A

moment later, Maria's voice was speaking from the instrument in his hand: "Boss? We've just heard from Bill."

Joe's two visitors were listening as attentively as he was. "Where is he?" Joe demanded.

Maria sounded enormously relieved. "Don't know exactly, but we were talking to him, and he sounded good. He says he's now definitely on the right track home. He'll be coming up Bright Angel within an hour."

It was almost noon when Bill Burdon, looking somewhat dazed, finally emerged from the depths. John and Maria went about a hundred yards down Bright Angel to meet him, as he appeared against the solemn background of a Canyon almost fully visible, a panorama grand enough to distract any newcomer at least briefly from any task.

"What the hell happened to you?" demanded John, getting angry now that it seemed the missing man was safe.

"You won't believe it." Bill stared at him, then at Maria, shook his head and started past them up the trail. They fell in beside him. When he was a little below the Tyrrell House he stopped again, to gaze up at the odd structure as if expecting some kind of a revelation.

Maria hardly noticed Bill's behavior. She was looking downhill, past an antlike mule-train of tourists on a switchback far below. She was frowning, as if considering something in the distance.

Neither of the men were paying her any attention. John, regarding Bill intently, abruptly remarked: "You didn't have a beard last night." That got Maria's attention back.

Bill only shook his head again. Then he reached out and took each of his discoverers briefly by the arm, as if to assure himself that they were real. He smiled at their solidity.

"Where's the Boss?" he demanded. "I've got a report to make."

An hour or so later, Bill was seated with Joe at a table on the balcony overlooking the lobby of El Tovar, and its massive genuine Christmas tree. Holiday music was playing somewhere, tourists by the hundreds were enjoying themselves, or trying to, and Bill was halfway through the second version of his report. Joe had bought him a drink, and was getting him to start the report over, because the first version had been notably lacking in coherence. Joe's newly purchased cane stood leaning against the table at his side.

Bill's beard was drawing curious glances, because it was now mostly on one side of his face. He had started to shave it off, then decided he had better let it be for the time being, as providing some kind of corroboration of the story he had to tell.

"—and she was just there, camping out to be alone, was the impression I got. Trying to get her head together, like we used to say."

Briefly Bill balanced a couple of Polaroid photos in his strong right hand. Then, with the air of a gambler playing cards which he did not really expect to win, he tossed them faceup on the table in front of Joe.

Joe picked up the photos and examined them. "That does look like the girl who was described to us."

Bill gestured at the pictures. "Oh, that's Cathy Brainard, all right. I don't have the least bit of doubt. She seemed unhappy with her family, and she didn't want to come back to them. At least she didn't want to come back with me. She was very firm on that point, and there was no way I could drag her."

"No, I can see that. So what did you do then?"

"She pointed me in what turned out—I guess—to be the right direction, and I—walked out." Bill paused for a long time. He swallowed half his drink, and grimaced. "Now comes the part you're not going to believe."

Joe sipped from his own glass. "You might be surprised. Try me."

"All right. I found my way—or I thought I found my way—back to the Tyrrell House. Except it wasn't this Tyrrell House. Not the one that's sitting over there on the rim right now."

"Go on," said Joe encouragingly.

Bill said defiantly: "It was the Tyrrell House in the thirties, before it became a museum. And Tyrrell himself was still living there, with his family."

"Wait a minute. You talked to Tyrrell?"

"No."

"What, then?"

"His family. Including—including Mrs. Tyrrell."

Joe was silent for a moment. "You mean the same Mrs. Tyrrell we're working for?"

Bill nodded slowly. "I think it's the same woman, boss. Only the Mrs. Tyrrell who hired us is about sixty years older. And then . . ."

"Then what?"

"There was a little girl, too, with young Mrs. Tyrrell. Her daughter, I assume. Maybe four years old."

"And?"

"And this little girl had what I'd call a strong family resemblance with Cathy."

Joe smiled faintly at Bill's anxious gaze. "Let's go talk to the old lady," he said.

Leaving the hotel, going west once more along the rim walk, Bill paced slowly beside Joe, who hobbled with his cane. They found old Sarah warming her hands before a fire in the main room of her house.

"Mrs. Tyrrell? I was wondering—can you remember

ever meeting Bill, here, before you were introduced last night?"

The old woman looked from one man to the other. "I feared there might be complications," she said at last. "Is there trouble with time now, gentlemen?"

"I don't know," said Joe. Bill, his mouth slightly open, stood looking from one of them to the other.

"Young man," said Sarah, looking at Bill. "I thought last night that we might possibly have met before. But a great many strange things happened to me in the comparatively brief time that I lived with Edgar Tyrrell."

Haltingly, at Joe's urging, Bill told the story of his recent wanderings.

Sarah heard him out. "I suppose that what you say is not impossible, young man. The house as you describe it sounds correct. Perhaps a young man, who seemed out of place, did once drop in when I lived there. Perhaps I was able to advise him as to which way to walk, to get home— before the sun went down."

"And the little girl?" Joe asked.

"I have told you that I had a daughter."

"Where is she now?"

"I don't know. Tell me of my grandniece. That's what I'm paying you for."

Old Sarah's reaction to what the young man had to say of Cathy was definitely positive. Her eyes greedily devoured Bill's pair of Polaroids.

"Oh yes, yes, that's her," she murmured. "And living freely, by herself? Then there may be hope."

A few minutes later Joe and Bill returned to Joe's rooms in the hotel, where they had left John acting as bodyguard for Brainard.

John opened the door for them. "We had a transatlantic call while you were out. From Mr. Strangeways."

Joe paused in the act of pulling off his coat. "What'd he want?"

"He suggested we call our home office, and start Angie looking into other vanishings that have taken place in this area. He thought, and I agree, that over the years there have probably been a fair number."

"Okay." Joe grunted with relief as he settled himself in a chair. "Then ring her up."

In a minute Joe himself was talking to Angie, John's young wife. He asked her to find out how many people disappearing in or near the Canyon had any known connection with the Tyrrell House and its inhabitants.

He added, "Of course even those with no known connection might possibly be Tyrrell's responsibility."

When Joe hung up the phone, Brainard, who had been peering cautiously out the window, turned and called in a low voice: "Keogh?"

"Yeah?"

"That's one of them out there now. One of the men who are after me. Just standing there on the walk, as if he wants to make sure I see him."

Joe picked up his cane and got on his feet. He looked out cautiously, past the curtain that Brainard was holding back a little. "The big guy with the fur collar."

"Yeah."

"Sure?"

"Of course I'm sure. After what these people have said to me I'm not likely to forget what they look like."

"Got a name for this one?"

"This one introduced himself as Preston. Mr. Smith and Mr. Preston is what they told me. Of course I have no idea if those names are really . . ." Brainard, with a fatalistic shrug, let his words trail off.

"All right. I'll just go say hello," said Joe, and reached once more for his jacket. At the same time he sized up Bill and John, then let his gaze settle on the former. "Bill, you look bigger and uglier. Come out with me and back me up. Don't say anything and don't do anything unless it looks like I really need help. John, mind the store."

Preston, who had heavy, dark eyebrows and a mustache to match, hadn't moved. A second man, sharp-featured, built on a smaller scale but also strong and solid-looking, came from somewhere to join him, as Joe, with Bill staying a step behind, came hobbling out from the hotel. All four of their hands in jacket pockets, Smith and Preston watched their approach without expression.

Joe halted a couple of steps away. "You're looking at my window. Anything I can help you with?"

"I don't think so," said Smith, evidently giving the question serious consideration. His sharp features split in a smile. "If I decide I need a shoeshine, I'll let you know."

The big man in the fur collar took a more direct approach. "You a cop?" he demanded.

Joe shook his head. "Not any more," he answered mildly. "But they're not far away. Smith and Preston, huh?"

Smith turned his head to Preston. "D'ja hear that? I think the gimp is threatening us with cops. Maybe our lawyer ought to talk to him."

Preston gave what was probably a well-practiced impression of a man whose inner rage was mounting swiftly. He spat in the general direction of Joe's shoes. Out of the corner of his eye Joe saw Bill start to step forward and then hold back.

A couple of Park rangers in their tan uniforms and Smokey the Bear hats were coming along the walk, among the usual gaggle of tourists. The rangers were talking geology, not paying any attention yet to four unhappy-looking men who stood in a loose group. Balancing on his cane, Joe reached out with quick, deft fingers, and snatched the cigarette from between Preston's fingers. He crushed out the glowing end on the furry lapel of the man's expensive jacket, so a fine thin wisp of smoke went up into the air of the winter afternoon. The gesture was quick and unobtrusive, as if he were only brushing away a little dust.

Preston twitched and started, as if the fur had been his skin. He said three foul words in a low, distinct voice. He started to sway forward.

Smith, aware of the Rangers nearby, put out an arm to hold him back. It was more of a gesture than a tug, but it succeeded.

To Joe, Smith said, in a new, dangerous voice: "Tell Brainard he better pay his debts. Paying debts is a law of nature, see, gimp? Sooner or later we all have to do it. Sooner or later."

"I'll tell him," Joe said flatly.

Old Sarah was sitting with her eyes closed, trying to remember. Was it only her imagination, or did a ghost of memory really come teasing back, a strangely-dressed young man who had dropped in at the house on the Rim one warm afternoon in the early thirties?

So many peculiar things had happened to her in the thirties. When you lived with a vampire, when you lived with Edgar Tyrrell, what difference more or less one strange young man?

Had the young man stayed until Edgar appeared, shortly after sunset? Or had Sarah, as she hoped she was remembering, managed quietly to save his life?

But the thirties were gone now, out of reach for her if perhaps not for Edgar. The most important thing, of course, was the modern evidence provided by Bill and his photographs, evidence that Cathy at least was still alive, and not being held somewhere against her will.

Nothing really helpful about Edgar, though. What

helpful news could there ever be about him? The only helpful news would be, perhaps, that he was dead; sooner or later the true death came for all, even the *nosferatu*. But in Edgar's case, in the case of a man who so often did tricks with time—or perhaps, one with whom time so often played its own tricks—not even a confirmed report of death would guarantee that he could henceforward be considered harmless.

Sarah shuddered.

She had never really understood the work to which her husband had devoted his life. The research, the art— whatever the right name for it was—which had fascinated her husband and evidently still obsessed him, beyond all the attractions to which normal humans could be subject.

Sarah had never understood his work. But she had learned to fear it terribly.

Joe, re-entering his hotel room, said to the waiting Brainard: "They're gone for now."

"Thanks."

"Por nada. I don't think they've gone very far."

"I know it."

"But I've at least given them something to think about. I can get in touch with some people I know, try and see if these guys are wanted for anything."

"A temporary expedient. I appreciate it, but . . ."

"You're right."

Maria Torres, roused from a reverie by someone's voice calling her name, found herself leaning over a balcony at the Tyrrell House, contemplating the depths. Something very alluring was down there . . .

Daydreaming. She was daydreaming on the job. Maybe this was just the kind of thing the Canyon did to people.

~ 11 ~

Half an hour after sunset, on the day after Jake's abortive attempt to start a fight with Edgar, the two of them were in the workshop-cave together, talking calmly and unhurriedly about the job. Jake's right arm still ached when he moved it in certain ways, but other than that it was almost as if yesterday's scuffle had been forgotten.

Edgar was inspecting the day's work Jake had just accomplished. Basically the boss's comments were favorable, though now and then he pointed out some detail with which he was not completely satisfied.

Jake had spent the day mining the deep Vishnu schist in the bottom of the cave for small white nodules. Edgar kept a sizable collection of these on his long workbench and in bins just below it. He used some of the nodules for his carvings. Jake had seen him carry others back toward the secret rear chamber of the cave, putting them down on the floor of the cave just in front of the crevice, as if sooner or later that would be their destination.

The mining itself, working hard rock with nothing but hand tools, had gone very slowly today. To Jake's relief, Edgar didn't seem to care that the process was a slow one, only that the search for nodules should be thorough and that Jake should occupy himself with it during most of the daylight hours. Every time he discovered one of the lumps of peculiar white stone, he had to excavate it carefully, undercutting to free it at the bottom. Then he carried it to the workbench, where he sorted all nodules by shape and size.

The bench was a long, crudely built but well-lighted wooden table, running along one wall of the cave beside the entrance. Here a dozen or two of the white nodules of modest size were scattered, a couple of them fixed to the bench in jigs and clamps, obviously in the process of being carved into the likenesses of living things. The white stuff was stone—at least Jake wouldn't have known how else to classify it—but in its feel and texture unlike any other material that he had ever handled.

Edgar told Jake that he, Edgar, had gathered some of the nodules already on the workbench, from the local rapids in the Colorado. Edgar also cautioned him—quite unnecessarily—that such methods of collection were not something that either Jake or Camilla could undertake and expect to survive.

There seemed to be plenty of white nodules here now, as Jake could see for himself. He wondered momentarily whether Edgar really needed or wanted more of them, or if he just wanted to keep Jake busy and out of mischief. Camilla's warning that Edgar really wanted something else from both of them came back to Jake now.

Most of the day Jake had worked with his shirt off, sweating like a pig. The cave was a little cooler than the sunbaked canyon outside, but not much. He took frequent breaks, and at intervals during the hot hours Camilla brought him cold lemonade. He had had the electric lights turned on for part of his workday; he needed them if he really wanted to get a good look at what he was doing, unless the sun was coming in the entrance at just the proper angle. They were still on now, of course. Jake noted that Edgar's vision seemed to be extremely good. The old man could see small details from a distance, and he wore no glasses.

On the job Jake used hammers and pry bars and chisels. Edgar had explosives on hand—Jake had seen the little locked-up shed, just outside the mine—but said he rarely employed them.

Edgar was saying to him now: "I've tried dynamite, but this is a ticklish place to try to blast; much better to dig out what's wanted carefully, with hand tools. That's where you come in."

Jake nodded. The old man today was taking such a reasonable, businesslike attitude that Jake couldn't help getting the feeling, in spite of everything, that there was some chance this would turn out after all to be a decent, acceptable job. It was a crazy attitude, he realized whenever he stopped to think about it; but somehow when Tyrrell was talking so reasonably it seemed only natural.

"What's back there?" Jake inquired, nodding toward the almost completely blocked chamber at the rear of the cave. Things were going so reasonably at the moment he thought he might receive an answer.

Edgar looked at him. Then: "My work," said the old man shortly, putting a slight emphasis on the first word.

"Hey," said Jake, half an hour after arriving back in the little house, about an hour after sunset. It was almost the first syllable he'd uttered since Edgar had told him he could go home for the night.

At the moment he was standing in front of the electric refrigerator, holding the door open and looking in. A strange fact had just caught his attention, and he was wondering how he could have been so slow to notice it.

"What?" Camilla, moving around behind Jake, was in the prosaic process of getting dinner ready.

"Somebody went to the store, looks like."

Only last night Jake had become aware, without really giving the matter any intelligent thought, that the stocks of supplies in the refrigerator were starting to run short. The cabinet shelves had still been deep in canned goods; there was no prospect of actual starvation, and so he hadn't really thought about where the eggs and ham and cheese were coming from. But this morning there had been fresh food, as there was now.

Overnight, somehow, the refrigerator had been newly stocked. "Where'd all this stuff come from? There's eggs, there's beer, there's apples—"

"Edgar brings it. He brought stuff last night. Every week or so he goes on what he calls a shopping trip up to the Rim. The real Rim, the one where there are people. Some of the stuff he steals from El Tovar, some he gets in other places."

Thoughtfully Jake hefted a little wooden box of Kraft cheese. The familiar brand name on the box was heartening. It proved that the real world wasn't entirely out of reach. "Somehow I thought he stayed down here all the time."

"He says he'd like to stay here all the time and work; he grumbles about having to go out. But he needs tools and other stuff. So while he's up there he gets some breathers' food."

"Huh?"

"That's what we are. You and me. We're breathers. Edgar isn't. You didn't notice yet? Edgar doesn't breathe."

Jake stared. But now he was beginning to know that here in the Deep Canyon, the stranger a thing sounded, the more likely it was to be true.

Camilla was nodding. "That's right. Watch him close, next chance you get. No breathing, unless he needs

the air to talk." She lowered her voice to a whisper.
"Jake, that's what vampires are like."

"Vampires. You mean like in the movies."

"No. Not like that." Looking at the restocked
shelves, Camilla giggled strangely. "The way he stocked
up this time, it looks like he really wants to keep both of
us going."

After a time Jake said: "He must need food for himself."

"He doesn't eat like you and me. Not like breathing
people."

"Huh?"

"Warm blood is all that Edgar really needs. Could be
my blood, or yours, or a dog's. He sometimes catches him
a wild animal, big or small, and drinks its blood."

Jake couldn't answer.

Too many things, impossible things, had forced themselves into his life, made themselves part of his vision of
reality, over the last couple of days. By his own subjective
reckoning, he had only been gone from the CCC camp
three days now. He wondered if that was, if that could be,
right. He could believe Camilla now, that time, like the
big river itself, ran different here in the Deep Canyon.

He said now: "I wonder what they're doing back at
camp."

"Ha. They might have forgotten you already. On
their calendar, you might have been gone a month."

Yesterday Camilla had talked casually about taking
the shotgun, loading it with something lighter than what
the bears required, and bringing in some rabbits. And
there didn't appear to be much trouble catching fish. Behind the house she had also started a small kitchen garden, where Jake could identify carrots and tomatoes,
among some tough western weeds that were threatening
to take over. A branch line from the waterpipe that came

in to the house from the creek was arranged to water the garden at the turn of a spigot.

But the old man's foraging expeditions were much more interesting. "So, Edgar brings in all this store-bought stuff, eggs and canned goods and beer?"

"Right. He wants us well-fed." Again she giggled. "He'll bring you some new clothes if you want. He brings me some. I ask him for cigarettes, but he says they're bad."

"How does he get out of here, when he goes on these trips to the rim? I mean what path does he follow?"

She shrugged. "He just goes. Vampires can do it. Maybe not all of them, but he can."

"Come on." Softly Jake was trying to coax her out of being crazy. "How d'ya know he's a vampire?"

"I know." Camilla raised one hand to rub her throat.

"Come on."

Camilla shook her head, as if she could read Jake's thoughts. "You'll know I'm crazy, lover, if I tell you all about what Edgar can do. You just watch for yourself. You're gonna see a lot of him from now on. And you better do the job he gave you in the cave, lover. You really better."

Remembering the strength that had caught and wrenched his arm, made him helpless as a baby, Jake had to agree with that, at least.

When Jake went back to work in the morning, he discovered that sometime during the preceding night Edgar had harvested a massive chunk of deep Vishnu schist from somewhere in the bed of the river—the rock was still wet, and there were tiny shellfish still clinging to one side. Then he had somehow brought the slab, which must have weighed five or six hundred pounds, up the side canyon to the workshop.

All by himself? Jake could believe that now.

On the workbench was a small note, in neat, precise handwriting, changing Jake's orders for the day, and signed 'Tyrrell.'

Jake started to work accordingly, concentrating on the slab, breaking it up and mining it for nodules.

Tyrrell reappeared promptly at dusk, just when Jake was getting ready to knock off work for the day. He examined Jake's crop of white nodules carefully, and declared himself reasonably satisfied.

A few minutes later, alone in the house with Camilla, Jake said: "Jeez, the way he handles tools, the strength he has, he could have done in half an hour what took me all day. Maybe he could have done it even faster. What's he need me for? Why's he need either of us?"

"I told you once what I really thought."

"I remember. About him wanting our lives. But I just don't understand."

"I don't understand it either, lover. It's just a feeling."

An hour or two before dawn, Jake snapped awake. Some alien force or presence had shaken the bed that he was lying in. He came fully awake to realize that Edgar was in the bedroom with him and Camilla.

There was only the faint light of the night sky, coming in through the curtains on the shadeless windows, to illuminate the room. But this was light enough for Jake to see Edgar, dressed as usual, standing at bedside, one arm around Camilla's naked body. She was already half out of bed, with Edgar's help getting an unsteady balance on her feet.

Jake, with his right arm still aching from yesterday's combat, put one foot on the floor and started an unthinking, angry lunge at Edgar.

Edgar effortlessly shoved him back, so that he went staggering across the little bedroom, striking his head against the far wall, sliding down to a sitting position on the floor.

Slowly Jake rose and regained his balance. Camilla, her arms at her sides, was now standing beside the bed. He saw with a chill feeling of horror that she appeared to be still asleep, her body swaying lightly. And Jake saw, with a minor shock, that her eyes were still closed, her face serenely untroubled.

Edgar stood nearby, the fingertips of his right hand barely touching Camilla's upper arm. With gestures and a single whispered word, he conveyed to Camilla what he wanted her to do. After a moment's hesitation she obeyed the command, whatever it had been. Walking to the door, naked as she was, she went on out. Edgar followed her.

"Cam! Wake up!" Jake shouted as she disappeared. But neither she nor Edgar paid him the least attention.

Jake pulled on his trousers and rushed after the receding figures. He detoured sufficiently to grab up a bread knife from the kitchen table, and still caught the deliberately moving Edgar and Camilla at the front door of the house. He aimed the knife at Edgar. Edgar effortlessly caught Jake's arm and once more, with an almost absentminded motion, hurled him aside like a small child.

Jake scrambled for the shotgun that stood leaning in a corner of the room. He swung the weapon around and aimed it, squarely at the old man in the doorway. Jake pulled the trigger, and the hammer fell with a dry snap.

Jake screamed at Camilla to wake up.

At last the old man seemed to notice him. "She'll awaken when I want her to," said Edgar quietly. He smiled, as if finding mild enjoyment in Jake's tantrum, went out calmly with the sleepwalking woman, and closed the door of the house behind them.

Jake stood staring at the blank panels for a few moments. Then he broke the shotgun, saw that its load had been removed, and cast the useless weapon down. Opening the door, he followed Camilla and the vampire out of the house.

With Camilla walking a step in advance of her escort, who seemed almost deferential, they were going in the direction of the workshop-cave.

Jake continued to follow the pair, at a distance of ten yards or so. If either Edgar or Camilla was aware of Jake's continued presence, they had chosen to ignore him.

The figures disappeared inside the cave, which remained dark. Jake, following cautiously, standing first just outside the entrance, and then just inside, peered into the darkness. A faint white glow that somehow impressed him as unhealthy was coming from the inner chamber.

Dimly he saw that the huge stone blocking the inner chamber had by some means been swung or tilted back; there was room, just room, for Camilla to squeeze her naked body through the aperture. Edgar went after her, his body somehow gliding easily through the gap.

Fascinated, frightened but unable to help himself, Jake crept closer, step by step.

Until he was close enough to see how the two bodies, Edgar's and Camilla's, came together. Camilla moaned as the old man pressed her back into the corner of the chamber. Jake could see only heads and shoulders, but from the angle between them, they couldn't very well be in contact below the waist. But Jake saw now what Camilla had meant by the vampire's love-making. The old man's teeth, suddenly turned as sharp as a rat's fangs, were on her throat . . .

Jake, sickened, watched for no more than a few seconds; then he retreated to the cave entrance, where he sat on the threshold of stone, staring into the cave at nothing, trying not to hear the occasional moans—perhaps they were of pleasure—that came from the inner room.

An hour passed—or it might have been several hours. The eastern sky was growing steadily brighter when Camilla came stumbling out of the inner chamber. Jake raised his head to see her slow emergence, her form ghostly and somehow pitiful in the dim light. At the same time Jake could hear the huge rock grating, and knew that Edgar must be moving it back into place, so it would block the aperture as before.

When Camilla reached Jake's side, he stood up and put a supportive arm around her.

"Cam? Cam, are you all right?"

She moaned again, and mumbled something. At that moment Edgar appeared briefly, standing before them in the entrance to the cave, apparently paying no attention to either Jake or Camilla. A few seconds later, the figure of the old man disappeared.

Jake looked around, dazed, in the slowly increasing light. There was only Camilla, sobbing, with him now.

Jake could see the little blood-beads on the whiteness of her throat.

Leaning on each other for support, the two of them made their way slowly back to the house. Into the bedroom, where their clothes were still scattered about. Where their master, as Jake now fully realized, could enter any time he chose.

There was no hope, no thought, of getting back to sleep, no effort at it. Half an hour after coming back to the house, sitting at the table in the main room, pretending to drink coffee, Camilla suddenly said to Jake: "I think he wants you to get me pregnant."

Jake goggled at her. "What? Why'd he want that?"

"I don't know, I don't know." Then she gripped Jake by the arm. "When he had me back inside that little room . . ."

"Yeah?"

"The two of us weren't alone. There was someone else in there too."

"What?"

"Someone—or something."

Jake remembered the vague form he had seen with his flashlight, in the course of his earlier exploration of the cave. He could feel his scalp creep. "What's that mean?".

"I don't know. I don't want to know. Jake, *get me out of here! GET ME OUT!*"

Jake had no answer ready for that demand.

In an hour or two, leaving Camilla, fully clothed again, lying sleepless on their bed, he shuffled back to the cave, where he got to work, once again following orders to mine nodules of the nameless white rock. There was nothing else that he could do, and the labor at least gave him some way to occupy his time.

And for Jake the really crazy part, the part that made him think that maybe he'd gone around the bend himself, was yet to come.

It came that evening, an hour after sunset, when he found himself once more standing with the vampire-sculptor at the workbench. It came for Jake as he stood there with old Edgar, and heard himself talking calmly about tools and rocks, weights and shapes, almost as if the horrors, sexual and otherwise, of the night before had never happened.

Jake, watching the old man handle the rocks, seeing him shatter Vishnu schist with hard blows of his metal tools, could only marvel again at the master's strength and skill. Despite his fear and hatred, he could almost feel himself starting to develop enthusiasm for this project.

* * *

For the second night in a row Jake's and Camilla's bedroom was invaded without warning; this time Jake slept through the intrusion as if he had been drugged. He was not aware of what was happening until Camilla was already gone. Then, hurriedly throwing on his clothes, he followed her and her abductor to the cave, which was once more dark and silent.

The scene of the night before was re-enacted, with minor variations in detail. Once more the old man forced the young woman back into a corner of the inner chamber, where Jake could see only a small part of what was happening. Once more, more strongly than before, Jake got the impression that Camilla was at least on the way to becoming a completely willing partner in this act— whatever it might be exactly.

And this time, peering into the inner chamber of the cave, Jake got a better look at the third presence there, as insubstantial but as real as light.

He could see the whitish, translucent shape, whatever it was, move in such as way as to suggest that it was enveloping Camilla's body and, like the old man, nursing at her veins. While this was happening, the old man withdrew himself as far as the small size of the inner room permitted.

Then he stepped forward again. . . .

Jake carried away with him the very distinct impression of having seen three forms locked in an orgiastic embrace.

Headed back to the house again with Jake, minutes after sunrise, Camilla said: "Jake, lover, if he keeps on doing that to me . . ." She let the sentence trail away.

Jake could imagine half a dozen outcomes if it went on. None of the ghastly pictures evoked in his mind were coherent, but each seemed more horrible than all the others.

"We can't let him keep on," he said. Then he added, as if in afterthought: "We've got to kill him."

Those last five words just hung in the air. He had pronounced them quite easily and naturally, as he might have said that they needed more firewood.

Almost casually, Camilla was nodding her agreement. "And even so, I don't know that he's the worst thing we've got to be afraid of."

For a long time after they returned to the house that morning, Jake and Camilla sat in two chairs at the table, saying little, doing nothing.

For a while, perversely and frighteningly, she was in a mood to giggle and tease Jake—as if getting free from Tyrrell's control was, after all, the last thing she had in mind.

"Oooh, are you jealous, Jakey?" She pouted, mock-pleading in the tones of baby talk. "Don't ooo be jealous? Old Edgar's not a bit jealous of ooo!"

At last he jumped up without answering her and ran out of the house, going to his work. When she brought him his lunch, sometime past midday, she was sober and serious again.

~ *12* ~

The time at the Greenwich meridian, only ten minutes of longitude east of London, was two minutes past midnight. The penultimate day of the old year just beginning. The man who in Arizona had called himself Strangeways was now standing alone in the darkened parlor of a large Kentish country house, perhaps a quarter of a mile from the center of the village of Down.

For many years no one had lived in this house. But for some forty years of the nineteenth century it had been the home of Charles Darwin, and on most days of the late twentieth century it was open as a museum. Tourists came with some regularity, a comparatively small number of them who were interested enough to make the effort to find the place. At midnight, naturally, there were no other tourists and even the caretakers had long since retired to their own homes and beds.

For almost an hour the moderately tall figure of the sole nocturnal occupant had been standing, virtually motionless, in the great scientist's study. Shortly after the stroke of midnight he moved at last, lightly touched with his fingertips some of the shelved books, drew a deliberate breath to smell the furniture polish of the museum-like preservation in which the house lay bound. Standing close to the tall, dark case of Darwin's great old clock, he listened carefully to the heavy soft voice of the mechanism within. The silent visitor's investigatory methods, honed through centuries, were older than those of modern science, and in certain matters even more successful.

At almost three minutes after midnight the tall man turned his head sharply—his ears had caught a sound just outside the house. Someone was trying to get in. Smiling, he murmured a soft invitation, confident that ears as keen as his own, out there in the winter night, would hear.

Presently there came a gentle shimmering in the dark air of the study, followed by the quiet appearance of a soft but solid feminine form, brown-haired and youthful in appearance, dressed in the English fashion of a century ago.

Offering the newcomer a courtly bow in the style of a bygone age, the foreign visitor exchanged with her a few words of private tenderness.

Then he said: "I am sure you are aware, dear Mina, that this year marks the centennial of my first visit to England—and, of course, of our first meeting?"

The youthful-looking lady smiled. "Perfectly aware, dear Vlad. I was wondering if the entire year would pass before you commented on the fact." Her voice was as undeniably English as her dress.

"I have been busy," her companion said abstractedly. For a moment he stood with hands folded in front of him, looking almost like a vicar.

"Of course you have. And with important matters. I did not mean to chide." Graceful and poised, Mina patted the visitor to Britain on the arm.

"So." He drew a deep breath—an occasional habit of his which still persisted—and looked about him. "So, this is Darwin's house."

"No doubt about that, there's a sign outside." Mina was practical as always. "He lived and worked in this building for most of his life—I take it this is not your first visit?"

"A natural assumption on your part, my dear, because I entered the building without any recent invitation—but the truth is that I have never entered this house before. Once, however, almost a century ago, I *was* invited in. That was on my second—or was it perhaps my third?—visit to England. After a hundred years many such details escape me."

Mina laughed softly, an almost breathless sound. "To be sure. No doubt your invitation came from some maiden, the revelation of whose name you would still deem inadmissibly ungentlemanly . . . Vlad Drakulya, do you still suppose me jealous of the breathing kisses you received so long ago? For that matter, of those that, I am sure, you continue to receive?"

Her companion acknowledged the comment with a blink and a faint smile. "Kisses? Yes, indeed, kisses there were, to be sure . . . by the way, my dear, I have spoken with several of your countrymen since my arrival in Britain yesterday. I have even consulted at some length with one man in particular, who somehow—I confess I do not know how—knew that I was coming."

Even practical Mina appeared to be impressed. "An elder counselor, perhaps?"

"You may say so. One whom I have, for the past few years, been privileged to call friend. He was almost a thousand years of age when I was born. I will not speak his name . . ."

"I understand." The power of some names was not to be taken lightly. "And from this ancient and venerable Briton you have learned something that will be of help to you in your current difficulties across the sea?"

"I have learned several things." Drakulya spread out his arms. "To begin with, a man named Edgar Tyrrell once stood in this very room . . ."

The visitor spent the next minute or two telling his beloved Mina about Tyrrell.

Frowning, she asked: "And was your mysterious Tyrrell one of us, *nosferatu,* before he left England?"

"I cannot be sure, but it seems likely. Darwin died in 1882, nine years before I first visited Britain. And Tyrrell, so interested in Darwin's work, did not appear in Arizona until almost fifty years later. That would argue a long life for a mere breather."

Presently, having absorbed as many useful impressions as he thought he might on this his first visit to Darwin's house—having at least temporarily sated his curiosity as to what might be discoverable in the dim study—the investigating vampire, with his vampire lady friend beside him, approached a tall window giving on the garden, and passed outside into the dank wintry English night. Both gentleman and lady traversed the locked window without disturbing either glass or wood, having no more difficulty than they had experienced with their entrance.

Pacing the frosted garden, with crisp grass crunching under his boots, Vlad Drakulya took note in passing of a helpful little sign intended to explain details of the grounds to tourists. Moments later he and his companion, following an arrow on the sign, had entered on Darwin's looping rustic footpath, used by the great breathing scientist for both exercise and meditation.

The footpath led them across a winter-quiet field, and through a little wood. Along this way the vampires stalked thoughtfully, speaking seldom, communing in silence with each other and with their surroundings. The man in particular was trying to sense the vibrations of the past and hear its deep inhuman voices. Not Darwin's past, no, he had already finished with that. Let Darwin rest in peace. His life, his house, his work, had served the investigator beautifully as the entrance way. But now entry had been accomplished. The real goal lay vastly deeper in the past. Almost immeasurably deeper. Darwin and Merlin were indistinguishably contemporaneous, seen from the perspective of the depth of centuries, of innumerable millenia, of incalculable ages that now required to be probed. . . .

Recalled from reverie by the banal stirrings of physical hunger, the male vampire paused to tempt a fascinated rabbit closer among the trees of the small wood. Then a pounce—mercifully quick—and with a good appetite he and his companion fastidiously shared between them the small creature's blood.

Overhead, the dark skeletal fingers of Darwin's trees probed and questioned the chill sky.

Mina, her red lips again as clean as those of any breathing maiden—indeed, cleaner than most—indicated the bent limbs with a subtle gesture. "As if they might be sifting the starlight for messages; don't you think so, Vlad?"

"Very poetic; as to what I think, I think I have now, at last, begun to understand, my dear."

"To understand—?"

"I think I am ready to return to the Grand Canyon."

"A very fascinating place, I'm sure. Some day you must show it to me. And someday—but not now, for I can see that you are in a hurry—you must explain to me what it is that you have just come to understand."

"Some day I shall."

The pair kissed chastely. Moments later, the man changed form and spread his wings. Tonight the wings of his own altered body would carry him no farther than Gatwick; for transatlantic movement his fastest travel option was the same as that of the most mundane breather. He was about to board prosaic British Airways.

* * *

A few hours after leaving Darwin's house, snugly ensconced in driven, roaring metal at some forty thousand feet over the Atlantic, speeding westward toward Chicago, the vampire found time to think, and a great deal to think about.

To begin with, had Tyrrell as a mere breathing boy really known Darwin, who had died in his house at Down in April of 1882? About fifty years had passed between that possible meeting, and the time when Tyrrell—himself by then an old man on the breathers' scale—had met and married Sarah in Arizona.

Old Sarah would certainly know whether her husband had been a vampire when they were married. He, Drakulya, was going to have to talk to her as soon as possible after he reached the Canyon.

Or was it possible that Tyrrell had never known Darwin, though he, Drakulya, had now convinced himself that the former had at least once—whether breathing at the time or not—stood in the great scientist's house?

Whatever the exact relationship between Darwin and Tyrrell, the artist—and this was the important fact— had certainly absorbed some of the ideas of the scientist.

Not many hours after his departure from England, the returning passenger was standing in one of a row of phone booths in the great terminal at Chicago's O'Hare Field, trying his best to reach Joe Keogh in Arizona. But the effort was fruitless. Evidently no one was occupying Keogh's hotel room at the moment.

Drakulya thoughtfully replaced the receiver, ruminated for another moment, then tried a Chicago number, one he did not need to look up. In a matter of seconds he was speaking to Angie Southerland, young John's slightly younger wife.

When a woman's voice said, "Hello?" the caller intoned: "This is your Uncle Matthew, my dear." Of several of his names that Angie would probably have recognized, that was the one the caller thought most likely to put her at her ease.

"Oh," said Angie. The caller had been recognized. He was not surprised to hear how the young woman's voice dipped for just a moment into chill uncertainty, before it genuinely warmed.

When the initial exchange of civilities had been concluded, he said: "Your stalwart husband and I are currently engaged upon the same project, in Arizona. We have come to it by different paths, but . . ."

"I know." Angie sounded practical, as usual. "John told me he thought they would have a job at the Grand Canyon. He didn't tell me much about it, because he didn't know much himself."

"It would be helpful if you could do some research for us. For me, specifically."

The caller, in making this request, knew that Angie had at her fingertips electronic connections with such esoteric things as data bases and so-called bulletin boards. By such means Joe Keogh's agency in Chicago had access to vast realms of information across the country and around the world.

"Joe's already called and asked me to look up some things having to do with the case. I can tell you what I've found out so far."

"Ah. I would appreciate that."

Angie said: "To begin with, Edgar Tyrrell was declared legally dead in 1940, at the request of his widow. He had disappeared seven years earlier, around the middle of 1933, on one of his frequent hikes into the Canyon. He's described as 'elderly' at the time of his disappearance, when he'd been living on the South Rim for around thirty years."

"Would you be good enough to read me the entire account, my dear?"

Angie would, and did. The newspapers of 1933 reported concisely that the eccentric sculptor and near-recluse had left a young wife and a small child, both of whom were reported as living in the old house on the rim. By 1940 Sarah Tyrrell was living on the East Coast, and there was no further mention of a child.

At least one small item in another old newspaper suggested that eventually Sarah Tyrrell had begun to get a name for being as eccentric as her aged husband had been.

"And the little girl," asked Drakulya. "What happened to her?"

There was a silence on the phone, except for the noise Angie's busy fingers were making on her keyboard, evoking knowledge from some electromagnetic cache perhaps again halfway across the continent.

What, thought the man on the other end of the phone line, would Merlin think of this means of divination?

At last Angie said: "1933 is the last mention of any Tyrrell child I've come across. As far as I've been able to tell from looking at old newspapers, she dropped out of sight permanently at that point."

"And the child's name?"

"Do you know, I can't find one for her."

"And the subsequent activities of Mrs. Tyrrell? After 1940?"

"Have been only very scantily reported in the news. Starting in the sixties, there are a few items—a small mention here and there, as inheritor of her husband's estate. Oh, and there's this. From the sixties on, this Mr. Gerald Brainard, her nephew, evidently began to be involved in his aunt's business affairs."

"Confirming what we had heard. Thank you."

Presently the phone conversation was over. Ignoring the noise and bustle of the world's busiest airport swirling around his phone booth, the returning traveler tried once more to reach Joe Keogh in Arizona. This time the effort was successful.

The man in Chicago communicated his thoughts to the man in Arizona. Then the caller was moved to philosophize.

There was no reason, Drakulya commented, no good reason why a vampire could not be a scientist, or an artist. "As we know, the two abilities are similar."

"I suppose you're right."

"Of course I am right. Quite a few of the *nosferatu* breed, myself included, collect *objets d'art,* but almost none of us create such works. This fact has for some time puzzled and worried me, Joseph—but I am keeping you from important work."

A minute later, Joe Keogh in his suite in El Tovar was hanging up his phone and reaching for his jacket and his cane. He wanted to question Sarah Tyrrell about her daughter, and since there was no phone in the Tyrrell House, he was going to have to make the trip on foot yet again.

People in the lobby of El Tovar were talking about snow in the forecast, and once Joe was outside, the look of the wintry morning sky and the smell of the cold wind confirmed that a real snowstorm was almost certainly on the way.

~ *13* ~

F ollowing a second change of planes in Phoenix, an ordeal accompanied by additional infuriating delays, the last leg of the returning traveler's long flight westward deposited him at the small Flagstaff airport after midnight. He sniffed keenly, testing the local weather. From that point on, eschewing snowy roads, he returned to the Canyon in beast-form, at a four-legged cross-country run.

Only upon his arrival in the immediate vicinity of El Tovar, shortly before dawn, did the traveler resume manform. On the morning of New Year's Eve the rising sun—fortunately for him obscured behind thick clouds—found him on the South Rim, contemplating the view along with a scattering of like-minded early-rising tourists.

As soon as Mr. Strangeways could comfortably make private contact with his breathing colleagues in Canyon Village, he told Joe Keogh and John Southerland something about his sojourn in England, with emphasis on his stop in Darwin's house. There and from other sources he had been able to gain key information about Tyrrell and his doings down through the decades.

Even as he relayed this information, Mr. Strangeways was administering a massage to Joe's injured ankle, accompanying the physical treatment with certain suggestions delivered mostly by non-verbal means.

Joe, stretched out on the sofa in his suite, and feeling curiously relaxed, enjoyed the relief of pain in his sore leg, and made sure that Strangeways was brought up to date on what had happened at the Canyon in his absence, particularly regarding Bill Burdon's disappearance and return.

Joe was somewhat apologetic on the subject. "I know you warned me against going after Tyrrell. I didn't think I'd have to warn Bill; he was supposed to watch the house, not chase people."

Drakulya's strong, pale fingers paused in their healing work. "And did the young man sustain no injury?"

"Not that I can see."

The massage resumed. "Well, it is impossible to ward against all the impulsiveness of the young—where is Maria, by the way?"

"Keeping Mrs. Tyrrell company, as usual. Hey, that's starting to feel a lot better."

Presently Joe was bidden to get to his feet, and test his leg. For a moment he thought his ankle might be as good as new—but only for a moment. He had not been miraculously cured, but he had been definitely helped.

Brainard, on being introduced to Mr. Strangeways, had stared at him, as if there were something about the bearded man he recognized, or felt himself on the verge of recognizing. Then he had retired to the other room of Joe's suite.

He might have saved his trouble, for Drakulya had little interest in him. Instead he now wanted to talk to Sarah Tyrrell.

This muted, clouded winter daylight was not sharp enough to give a toughened, experienced vampire any trouble. Not really, once he had put on a broad-brimmed hat. Thus prepared, he approached the Tyrrell House, where no one answered his tap at the front door. Nor could his keen ears discover the presence of any breathing lungs inside. Quietly setting out to locate Sarah, he expected no great difficulty—a breathing woman of her age could not have gone far—and experienced none.

He came upon her near mid-morning, when brief periods of sunshine were alternating with snow showers, the former tolerable to Strangeways under tree-shade, the latter providing a good tracking snow. Only the most elementary craft was needed to follow the rather wandering trail of the old woman's boots from the point where she had left the traveled rim-trail and set off through the thin growth of hardy trees.

On coming at last in view of his quarry, Strangeways stopped momentarily that he might observe while himself remaining for the moment unobserved.

Sarah Tyrrell was standing, looking at the ground, in what might have been one of the prettiest spots of all the pretty spots on the South Rim. The size and position of the live trees and visible stumps suggested that this scene had been a clearing fifty years ago. Now it was wooded with a second growth of piñon and oak.

Sarah had not visited this spot for decades, and now, having reached it after some uncertain searching, she stood looking about her sadly. The truth was that the exact location of the grave of her younger child was no longer easy for her to pinpoint with any confidence. A distinctively twisted pine, growing on the very rim, had served her for decades as a secret landmark, but it was gone now, not even a stump remaining. Perhaps even a few feet of the rim itself at the tree's location were missing now. Even the Canyon changed with time.

Still, enough local landmarks in the way of massive

rocks endured to let Sarah feel confident that she was at least within a few yards of the right place.

Her uncertainty was made worse by the fact that she had visited this place no more than half a dozen times in all the years since she'd left Edgar. Whenever her preceding visits had been in spring or summer she had unobtrusively brought flowers. There had been no way to do that unobtrusively now, on this dull winter afternoon. She supposed that if she tried she would be able to buy them at the gift shop or the general store, or order them delivered from somewhere outside the Park. That last, she thought, would draw too much attention. Sarah still had her reasons for wanting secrecy, and she clung to them—though sometimes she doubted they were valid.

This time she had considered trying to order a small holly plant, or perhaps a potted poinsettia—she supposed there must be a florist available in the Village. But so far she had not made the effort.

In every year of the more than fifty that had passed since the child's death, Christmas season had been an especially hard time for Sarah. She prayed at every visit to this unmarked grave, and felt that her prayers were heard; yet it bothered her still, that almost furtive unchristian burial in this unconsecrated ground.

She had certainly baptized the baby before it died, creek water from the Deep Canyon poured from a cupped hand on the small pale forehead, in the time-hallowed private ritual of worried mothers. As indeed Sarah had seen to the more formal baptism of the older girl in church. That had been in California, before she had ever known Edgar Tyrrell . . .

Lost in her thoughts, Sarah was not aware at first that she was no longer alone. When the fact was borne in upon her, without her quite understanding how, she turned around quickly.

Standing a few paces away, watching her from between two oaks, was a brown-bearded man who at first glance appeared to be about thirty years of age. When he saw that she had noticed him, the watcher, in an obvious gesture of respect, touched the broad brim of his hat.

"Who're you?" Sarah demanded.

There was no immediate answer, and without giving the man much time she repeated her question, sharply.

Patiently he responded, "One who would like to be your friend, Sarah. I do not believe that you have ever shared willingly in any of your husband's crimes."

She drew in her breath sharply. "Sir, my husband has been dead for many years."

The stranger only shook his head slightly, and showed her the ghost of a smile. "We both know better than that."

"What do you want? And how do you know my name?" At this point Sarah paused, belatedly becoming aware of some subtle things about her visitor that put her in mind of Edgar. In a different voice she added: "I see that you are . . ."

"Yes. I assume you mean that I have certain things in common with your Edgar; indeed I do. My name for the last few days has been Strangeways, but I have had others. Perhaps you have heard of me under another name."

Sarah nodded slowly. "It is possible that I have." Now she appeared to be frightened.

"Let me assure you again that I mean you no harm." Her visitor smiled reassuringly, and with a few unhurried steps diminished by half the distance between them. He looked around him, carefully, at their immediate surroundings, the spot that had once been a clearing.

He said: "I have visited the cemetery near the visitors' center. All who lie there sleep in peace. I had not known till now that another burial ground was here."

After a pause he added: "But I believe that only one is buried here."

"Yes. As far as I know, only one. My own child, who died in infancy. But I—I have forgotten exactly where . . . ?" Tears came to Sarah's old eyes.

"Perhaps I can help."

"I would be—I would be grateful."

Sarah was silent then, while her companion moved about, pausing every step or two to gaze intently at the snowy ground. Once or twice he tilted his head, as if he were listening intently.

At last he pointed silently.

The mother came to the spot and looked at it, then raised her head and looked around again. "Yes," she said then. "Yes. Right here."

After a brief silence, her companion remarked softly: "I too know what it is to lose a child."

"Do you?"

The man nodded abstractedly. He looked about him at the clouded sky. He squinted and momentarily lowered his gaze under the brim of his soft hat, as the sun threatened and then failed to break through. Wind murmured in the pines, and a jay screamed, sounding like a spirit tormented by some primal hunger.

At last he said: "When I, in God's wisdom, am someday granted the privilege of a permanent grave, I could pray for it to be in some such spot as this."

Sarah stared at him again. This time she perhaps saw something that, for the moment at least, offered reassurance. Presently she said: "I think that *he* expected you to come seeking him one day—or someone like you."

"Indeed? Why?"

"I never knew. Perhaps it was that he had broken some law of your kind, and his . . ."

"From what I have been able to discover about your husband, I should say that he had good cause to fear our law. Our law does not allow killing without just cause, or the keeping of slaves. Or unprovoked theft, a crime I consider particularly reprehensible."

Sarah stared out over the Canyon. "I make no apologies for Edgar," she said at last. "He had chosen his own life, as we all do. And he will have to accept the consequences. But I wish . . ."

Almost half a minute passed before Drakulya asked softly: "What is it that you wish, Sarah?"

Sarah looked down at the earth again. "That I had some flowers," she said, "to decorate my child's grave."

Her companion bowed lightly. "Let me see what I can do."

He had no need to go far, no trouble in locating several specimens of mistletoe, growing low enough to be easily reachable, on one of the nearby oaks. Mistletoe, the parasite ripening in winter, with one pale berry already on the sprig. No trouble to find, to pull a sample from the tree, to bring it back to the still-grieving mother.

Going down on one knee, with some difficulty, Sarah placed the simple offering on the otherwise completely unmarked grave.

She accepted the help of a strong arm in getting back to her feet.

"Now," said Mr. Strangeways. "Will you tell me how the infant died?"

That was a terrible thing for Sarah to talk about, but eventually she managed.

"Then you are not sure that the death was your husband's fault?"

"Not sure, no. I never could be sure. But the doubt—I couldn't stay. I had to get my surviving child away."

"I see. I understand."

By silent agreement they had left the unmarked

grave behind them now, and were walking slowly back in the direction of paved walks and people.

Sarah asked: "Are you—working with Mr. Keogh?"

"I am his colleague, yes."

"Now I can begin to understand how he expected to be able to help me."

A few minutes later, Sarah and the old vampire were talking freely, back in the Tyrrell House. There, once a smoldering fire was stirred to life, Sarah could be physically warm and comfortable. For the time being they had the place to themselves.

Though she felt she could speak more freely now, still her mind was far from easy. "He was a good man once, and I loved him. I came to fear him too—I came to fear him terribly, and sometimes I still do—but for all that I love him still."

"Have you spoken to him, Sarah, since Cathy disappeared?"

"Only very briefly, at the house the other night. Nothing you could call a real communication. About all we did was exchange looks, and curses." The old woman's voice was hesitant, but Drakulya thought that she was telling the truth. He could not be absolutely sure. Even after five hundred years he was sometimes wrong.

Sarah pleaded with Mr. Strangeways to do all he could to help Cathy. "I appeal to you as a man of honor. She is still missing, and I am greatly worried, in spite of what the young man told me."

"If you appeal to me in such a way, then I must do what I can." He smiled, and patted Sarah's arm. "Is there anything else?"

"There is another matter, Mr. Strangeways, since you are gentleman enough to ask. I would like, if I could, to protect my nephew from the consequences of his own folly. He is a great fool in many ways, but he is not a vicious man. And he is the only father that Cathy has ever really known."

Mr. Strangeways frowned.

"At least—if it is possible—can you protect him from serious harm as long as he remains here in the park?"

"I do not promise anything."

"Please."

"Very well, I will do what I can."

"Thank you. You are a gentleman."

~ *14* ~

J ake was taking the morning off from work, without permission.

Dragging with him a numb and resigned Camilla who wore her hat and sunglasses, he had sought a place well away from the house and cave, where he felt they had a chance of being able to talk safely, at least in broad daylight. They had gone down the little canyon, Jake leading the way and looking about him earnestly, until Camilla had asked him what he was looking for.

"The place where you used to sit drawing. Where we first met."

She shook her head slowly. "I don't know if we can get there, lover. If we can, it won't do us any good. Why d'you want that place?"

"I just did." He sighed. "I want a place where we can talk."

Camilla repeated what she had already told Jake several times: that during the hours of daylight they could talk freely anywhere, that Edgar was sure to be in his daytime refuge at this hour. But Jake still had a hard time freeing himself from the idea that the old man was likely to be in hiding, listening to them, anytime and anyplace.

At last, reaching an area that looked familiar,

Camilla and Jake sat down side by side on a rock, right on the edge of the creek, whose voices today were only noise for Jake.

As soon as they were seated, he said: "I can't take it, Cam, watching him do that to you."

"How do you think I feel?"

"I don't know." He turned his head to gaze at her steadily. "When I was watching the two of you last night, it looked to me like maybe you were enjoying yourself."

"That's a rotten thing to say."

He was silent.

"There's only one way we can get out of this, Jake."

"I know. That's what I came out here to talk about."

"I guess I know what that one way is. I guess you've already told me. And you're right, but I'm still afraid."

Jake didn't want to speak. He couldn't shake the feeling that the old man was just waiting behind a rock somewhere, listening to them, ready to pounce.

"You know as well as I do, Jake. The only way to get ourselves out of here is—

"Is."

"—is to kill him."

The words had been said again. Nobody pounced.

"Kill him. Then we'll have time to think, to look around, to find our way."

Camilla unpacked her sketch pad and some pencils. It was as if she had to do something with her hands. Now, at the same spot where Jake had first met Camilla, he once more watched her draw. They had a lot of planning to do, but neither of them said anything for a time.

She was wearing her hat and sunglasses, but still, after a little while, she had to move closer to the cliffs, seeking the shade. It seemed to Jake that she was growing ever more sensitive to the sun.

"Cam."

"What is it?"

She had turned her head toward him, and he stared at her mouth, her slightly parted lips. "Nothing, I guess. Just now I thought there was something funny about your teeth."

Slowly, somehow, the real planning started between them.

In all her months of living with Tyrrell, listening to him talk and observing him, Camilla had come, or believed that she had come, to understand not only the horror of the man but something of his weaknesses.

Jake with a conscious effort was building up his nerve. "All right, I'm ready to kill the son of a bitch. Truth to tell, I've been ready for some time. Now tell me how. How're we going to kill him?"

Camilla needed only a few seconds to think—as if she had already asked herself this question. "There's only one time—maybe two times—I've ever seen him hurt."

"Tell me."

"First time was only a little while after I moved in, when he got a wooden splinter in his hand, from the handle of one of his tools."

"That hurt him, huh?"

"More than a shotgun charge could do. He started to suck the blood out himself, after he pulled the splinter out—then he saw me watching him—then he got me to—"

Jake could all too readily visualize her, sucking blood. He made an effort to blot the picture out.

Camilla shivered. From the look on her face now, Jake guessed that she'd found the act exciting also. She smiled sheepishly at Jake.

"What was the other time?" he asked.

"What . . . ?"

"You said that twice you've seen him hurt."

"Oh. Well, he wasn't really hurt the other time . . .

but he looked mighty uncomfortable. He was up late one morning, when the day dawned really cloudy. Then a hole opened up in the clouds suddenly, and the sun came through . . . Edgar looked sick for a moment, he looked really scared."

"Huh."

"And the next second he was gone. Not to the place where he always sleeps, but back into the cave. He spent that day in the cave with the lights out, making it as dark as he could. After sunset he came out, looking—tired. He'll never take a chance of getting himself caught out in bright sunlight."

For a moment they stared at each other.

Jake said at last: "No way we can make him do that."

"Doesn't seem like it, does it?"

Jake squinted at her. Presently he asked: "What about fire?"

Camilla had to think longer on this point; perhaps it was a new idea to her. At last she reported that Tyrrell was at least not indifferent to fire. "I can't remember seeing him stick his hand in flames, anything like that."

"Then let's figure fire is something we might try."

Another hour of discussion brought no great enlightenment. There seemed to the two young breathers to be three possible means by which they might accomplish their oppressor's destruction: wooden weapons, fire, or sunlight.

"There's another thing I'm worried about, Jake."

"What's that?"

"What if I got—pregnant?"

"Jesus. Are you?"

"I don't think so, but—*he* asked if I was. That last time we were—we were in the back of the cave."

Jake was silent, pondering. Maybe this didn't actually make his own situation any worse, but he didn't like it.

"And he was listening to me," Camilla said.

"Listening? What?"

"Listening. Putting his ear against my belly."

"Can he tell that way?"

"Said he couldn't be sure. If I was, it was too early to be sure."

"Anyway, what does the old man care if you're pregnant or not?"

"I don't know! I—don't—know!"

Jake took her in his arms. What began with the giving of mutual comfort and reassurance soon turned into passion.

When Camilla opened her mouth to cry out in pleasure, Jake recoiled with horror, rolling away from her.

"Jake, what happened? What is it?"

"It's—your teeth. They were—they looked like—"

She sat up, her eyes wild with fear, her hands to her mouth.

In the afternoon, Jake returned to work in the cave, digging and sweating and breaking rock, gathering the precious nodules. Somewhat to his own surprise, he found that he still wanted to work. That he was doing a good job, even taking pride in the fact.

That evening, back in the cottage, Camilla found Jake standing in the child's bedroom, contemplating the stuffed animal, and the forlorn lunch box.

"What're you doing, lover?"

"Thinking. Trying to think. But not getting anywhere." He pulled open the door to the bedroom closet. There on a shelf was the small clock that no one ever wound, that no longer ran. A metal box, inconspicuous, sat on the same shelf. Jake took it down and opened it.

Old papers and old photographs, looking like the kind of stuff that any family might save, but here somehow out of place.

Camilla was alarmed. "Better put that back, Jake. Tyrrell doesn't like either of us in this room, let alone going through his things."

Jake riffled through the stuff in the box, saw nothing that caught his interest, closed it, and put it back up on the shelf. "How come this house has a kid's room in it, anyway?"

Camilla took him by the arm, tugging him out of the room. She said: "Looks to me like his wife must have had a little girl."

Jake let himself be tugged. He tried to picture Tyrrell as a father. Oddly, it seemed possible.

Back in the main room of the house, Jake sat looking at the calendar on the kitchen wall, which still maintained that this was June of 1932.

Camilla saw him staring at the calendar. "What year was it, Jake? When you came in here?"

Jake turned his staring gaze on her. "Whaddya mean what year was it? This is nineteen thirty-five. I came in here only—a few days ago." The frightening thought returned that maybe it really had been a month. Maybe even longer. Raising a hand, he rubbed his chin; it was quite definitely bearded now.

He demanded: "What year did Tyrrell bring you in? Last year? Nineteen thirty-four?"

"Jake, you're wrong by thirty years. Thirty-one. I met him in Flagstaff in nineteen sixty-five."

Tyrrell, as far as his two breathing victims could determine, was practically indifferent to time—or if he kept time, it was only by some method of his own.

Jake noticed, however, that the old man was usually

willing to talk about time. In fact it was one subject on which he tended to speak compulsively. Time, he once told Jake, hardly mattered to him, as long as he felt confident of being able to access the mundane world in at least the approximate era that he wanted.

Jake and Camilla continued sharing the house and the single adult bed. But only in the hours of daylight, shortly after dawn or before sunset, did they any longer make love, with a passion that had grown fierce and somehow hopeless.

Few nights passed during which the master did not summon Camilla to accompany him into the cave.

Once when Jake, driven by anguish, dared to demand a reason, the old man said with a wicked laugh that he wanted her to model for him.

Jake, knowing what he would see if he followed the pair, now usually remained in the house when Camilla was summoned. For hours he paced restlessly from one room to another, on the verge of doing something desperate—and more than likely suicidal.

Eventually, after an hour or so, Camilla would return to him. And now she refused to talk at all about what had happened between her and Tyrrell.

Several times she came back from these midnight excursions dreamy-eyed and looking openly happy, and Jake knew a sudden anguished impulse to murder her.

It troubled him also that she had now begun to sleep most of the day, in a troubled and exhausted fashion, and to be restless and wakeful during the night, as if waiting for the vampire's summons.

The next time that Jake tried to talk to Camilla about killing Tyrrell, she put him off, saying she was too tired.

* * *

How much time had really passed since he had been confined in this strange world, Jake could no longer even attempt to guess. But there came a day when he again was walking out of doors, beside the creek, with Camilla, feeling relatively safe in morning sunlight.

When he returned to full awareness of where he was and what he was doing—returned from a waking dream of something horrible—he heard himself pronouncing the words: "Then we'll get him with wood."

Camilla, for the moment looking no different than on the day he had first met her, strolled beside him, shaded as usual by her sunglasses and hat. She said: "Can't, not while he's awake. You've seen how strong he is, how fast he can move."

"If we could only get into that place where he sleeps," said Jake. Then he stopped suddenly, staring at the canyon wall a hundred yards away with red unseeing eyes. "Dynamite," he whispered, to himself.

The planning went on, intermittently.

"There's fire. You say that fire hurt him too."

Camilla nodded slowly.

Fire made Jake think of gasoline or diesel fuel, or kerosene. None of the first two were here in the Deep Canyon, but there was certainly kerosene, stored for the household lamps in a fifty-gallon drum that lay on its side in a homemade rack under a cottonwood some thirty yards or so behind the house. Presumably Tyrrell brought in more, somehow, from time to time.

As for the dynamite, Jake knew that Tyrrell had some stored for use in his quarrying. And Jake had learned something of the uses of fuses and blasting caps in his CCC work building trails. Edgar kept the dynamite locked up, but Jake, looking at the little shed, didn't see any reason why it couldn't be broken open.

"Maybe if we did it that way, we could still burn him

up back there in his den. Even if the dynamite doesn't get him, or it doesn't open up the rock as neatly as we'd want it to."

No matter how they tried, any other ways of killing this monster were harder to imagine. Camilla swore repeatedly that the shooting she had witnessed had had no effect, and Jake, after what he'd now seen of Tyrrell with his own eyes, was ready to believe her.

Jake could think of no way to trap the evil one out in the bright sunlight. Could he possibly reflect sunlight in on him somehow when he was in his den? They'd need two or three big mirrors, which they didn't have, and then just hope it worked. That idea was too impractical even to mention to Camilla.

Jake demanded crazily: "Are you going to tell him, the next time he bites you in the neck? Tell him that we want him dead?"

Camilla shuddered and said she was revolted at the thought of doing that. She pleaded with Jake to take it easy on her.

"Tomorrow morning, then," said Jake at last. "As soon as the sun is up."

"Tomorrow morning," Camilla agreed, in a whisper.

Jake walked alone, thinking to himself. He still trusted Camilla because he had to, even though she was no longer always the same person. He trusted her—but not entirely—because he had no choice.

Jake sat hollow-eyed beside the canyon's stream, listening to its voices. Telling himself he was trying to listen, but he thought that really he was maybe trying not to hear. There were exhortations to murder in the voices, and even stranger commands, that he had trouble understanding, and dared not wholly acknowledge even to himself.

Tyrrell, working that evening in the cave with Jake, informed his prisoner that, according to mundane science, only very simple fossils were known to occur naturally in the deepest life-bearing rock down here, a layer of schist whose formation lay beyond an unimaginable gulf of time. Below those simple relics, the layers of lifeless Precambrian rock stretched back an enormously greater distance toward eternity.

"Are you capable of imagining even a million years, Rezner?" asked Tyrrell, as the two men paused in the midst of their labors on the deep rock.

"Why not? Anyway, I don't have to imagine. I've already seen stranger things, since I met you."

~ 15 ~

On leaving Sarah Tyrrell, Drakulya walked back to El Tovar, intending to consult once more with Joe Keogh, and also to ask some questions of the adoptive father of the missing girl.

Brainard, still lying low in Joe Keogh's suite, was made uneasy by the way Mr. Strangeways looked at him. Brainard in fact impressed his caller as a man who would dearly love to become invisible.

Under steady scrutiny, Brainard looked from Joe to Strangeways and back again. Then he ventured:

"You're maybe—a friend of Mr. Tyrrell's?"

Strangeways shook his head. "I have not yet had the pleasure of meeting him. We do share a certain background, however."

Brainard nodded slowly. "I thought so. So maybe you'll be able to find my daughter?"

"As I have told your aunt, I will do what I can to help her. First, I would like you to tell me all you can about Tyrrell."

Brainard fumbled through several pockets before he found his cigarettes. "That won't be much. He's alive, down there somewhere, as far as I know. I haven't seen him for a long time. And I've been doing business with him over the years. Honest business. There's nothing wrong with that, is there?"

Another question elicited the information that Brainard himself had never been down into the Canyon, not even the most mundane modern version of the place, and he seemed to have no clear idea that a Canyon of any other time or shape might be accessible. He had never even set foot on the main trails that descended from near the Village and whose upper portions at least were trampled daily by a thousand tourists. He was not expert or even interested in the out-of-doors. In fact, Brainard seemed to think it believable that a man had been hiding out for sixty years, in some sanctuary accessible without magic or its equivalent in science, within a mile or two of the swarming tourist activity on the South Rim.

Drakulya said to him: "Tell me more about the business that you do with Tyrrell, and—since you ask—I will venture an opinion on its honesty."

"Well sir, there's nothing wrong with the kind of business I do with Mr. Tyrrell. I'm a dealer in art. Specifically in his creations. There's nothing very complicated about our arrangement—except that most people think he's dead. But I'm not defrauding anyone; the pieces I deliver are genuine. Mr. Tyrrell carves statues, and I sell them for him. Unlike paintings, carved stone is very difficult to date, so the buyers just assume these items were done in the thirties, or even earlier. The man has a right to sell his own creations, doesn't he? And a right to employ me as an agent?"

At this point Joe interjected: "His wife also has a legal right to his estate. But as I read the situation, she's not getting most of the money from these deals that you conclude."

"Is Sarah complaining?" Brainard demanded.

Mr. Strangeways made a slight gesture in Joe's direction, as if to silence him. Looking steadily at Brainard, he said: "Tell us, please, just how this arrangement began, between the two of you."

"Sure." Brainard looked at the ceiling, considering. "It was back in the early sixties, and I was here looking over some things for my aunt—she usually does her best to avoid spending any time here. But she never has wanted to turn the place over to the Park Service completely.

"Well, I'd come here one day to take a look at some of the furnishings in the Tyrrell House, to see what they might be worth. I was staying in the place overnight, when—*he* showed up, in the middle of the night. Surprised the hell out of me."

"Showed up—under what circumstances?"

"I was sitting there in a chair, thinking—actually I supposed I dozed off in front of a fire. Then something woke me up—a dream, I thought at first. Then I heard someone in another room. I went to look, and he was just standing there. At first I thought he might be a burglar—but he soon convinced me he wasn't."

"Then he made no strenuous effort to avoid discovery."

"I—suppose not. Maybe he was curious about me."

"And how did you recognize him?"

"Oh, I'd seen several of the old photographs. And, being in the house, I'd also been thinking about him . . . but above all I think it was the way he just told me who he was, when I asked him. Very calm, low-key, and self-assured. Still, that he was really Edgar Tyrrell was a little more than I could believe at first—also, I may add, that meeting was one of the spookiest experiences of my entire life. Here's this man who was supposed to have been dead for thirty years . . . but, to make a long story short, I believed him. Had to. We got to talking about art, and he excused himself—disappeared, almost as if he were a ghost—and in twenty minutes he was back, carrying something that convinced me."

"What was that?"

"A pretty little piece, a coyote as I recall, not one of those really strange animals—he told me he'd come up to the rim to compare one of his new pieces with an old one he remembered being in the house. Of course the one he remembered wasn't there. All that was left in the house, even then, were reproductions.

"We talked some more. When he found out I was his wife's nephew—well, his own nephew too, of course, though I could never imagine myself calling him 'uncle'— he started asking me questions about Sarah. Apparently they'd had no contact since she left him.

"He was really curious about her, and seemed concerned. But he also made it a condition of our doing business that she was not to know I'd met him and talked to him. In fact, no one at all was to know that he was still alive."

Brainard considered. He lit a cigarette, with hands afflicted with a noticeable tremor. "To make a long story short, after we'd talked for a considerable time, he left me his new piece to sell for him. In return he didn't want money—he had a list of tools, construction materials, things like that. 'I could obtain the material by other means,' he said. 'But this will save me time.' "

"Always," said Mr. Strangeways, "always a question of time. In one way or another. Does it not seem so, Joseph?"

"Yeah," said Joe abstractedly, and turned back to Brainard. "Go on."

Brainard crushed out his cigarette in an ashtray, and went on. "After he'd gone, I began to think, and the more I thought, the less I could credit what I'd just seen. I mean, this guy would have to be ninety years old, and still active, the way he was."

"And that was almost thirty years ago. By now he'd have to be well over a hundred. Maybe a hundred and twenty? But you're still doing business with him."

"All right, it's crazy. I don't know. You tell me. Maybe it's his son who meets me now, or his grandson. Maybe it's his younger brother. Maybe it's Tyrrell's ghost—I don't know, though I have my own ideas. All I do know is that he keeps bringing up carvings and I've never had any trouble selling them as authentic. I know what the collectors think, that my aunt and I have this secret hoard of Tyrrells that we're putting on the market gradually, one a year or so, just to keep the price up.

"The one time an expert did question authenticity, I took his objections back to Tyrrell. And the next item Tyrrell gave me, and all the ones after that, were done in such a way that those objections wouldn't hold. I guess some people are still doubtful from time to time, but I've always been able to find a number who believe."

"And what did you do for Tyrrell, in exchange for being made wealthy?"

"Brought him stuff. He never wanted money, said he had no use for it. He's got some kind of cave, a hideout down there in the Canyon, that no one's ever managed to find."

"He told you that?"

"In a way. Little things he said from time to time. That sounds crazy too, that nobody could find his hideaway. Until you stand on the Rim here for a while and take a real look at the place." There was no doubt that Brainard believed in the plausibility of what he was saying.

"What sort of things, exactly, did you bring him?" Joe asked.

"I'd get him catalogs, and he'd pick out what he wanted from them, and tell me what specific tools to buy. A few times he wanted chemicals, and I'd go to a scientific supply house. Explosives, once in a while. That took a bit of doing, because you usually need a license, but I know some people. Usually it was things like rope, and generator parts, and some men's work clothing, in specific sizes. Tyrrell's sizes. Drafting materials, once . . ."

"And all of this has been going on for thirty years?"

"Almost that long, yes. He told me he'd tried other ways of getting supplies, before he met me. He said he kept running into problems with the other ways—but he didn't go into any details on that."

"And finally you did break your agreement. You did tell Sarah that you had met him."

Brainard nodded. "I had to, after our arrangement had been going on for a year or two. I kept coming up with more statues, and I couldn't keep that a secret, not from her. The sales were common knowledge in the field. She knew too much about her husband's work and his affairs, that there hadn't been any such backlog. So I had to explain where the statues were really coming from."

"And what was her reaction?"

"About like yours." Brainard sighed. "She wasn't surprised—not nearly as much as I'd expected her to be. She asked a great many questions about Tyrrell—indirectly, the way he'd asked about her."

"She didn't want to meet him, though?"

"No. Never suggested anything of the kind. She really didn't want to come anywhere near this place. Though she's been here a few times over the years; just in and out, never staying in the house overnight. Until now, when Cathy turned up missing."

"And did Tyrrell ever find out that you'd broken your agreement with him?"

Brainard shrugged wearily. "If he did, he didn't say anything. He might have guessed I'd told his wife at least. He probably realized all these posthumous sales couldn't be kept secret from her. But he must have decided just to let things go on."

Joe's radio was buzzing, and something in the quality of the sound suggested—to him at least—that it was urgent. Answering, he heard Maria's voice.

"Boss? Cathy Brainard is alive and well, back up on the South Rim."

"You've seen her?"

"I'm standing here looking at her now, right near the mule corral. She's come back up Bright Angel, just the way Bill did."

The three men, each surprised in his different way, looked at one another for a long, silent moment.

Joe grabbed up his cane while Maria on the radio was still giving details. In a moment he was hobbling at his best pace—notably improved since the massage by Mr. Strangeways—after the other two men who had been with him. Now Joe could almost keep up with the overweight and puffing Brainard.

In a minute he caught up with the others near the mule corral, which was deserted at this time of day, the morning's convoy of tourist riders having descended into the Canyon hours ago, and the afternoon's contingent of returning adventurers not yet arrived.

Maria was standing there, with a young woman who could only be Cathy Brainard. As the men arrived, Maria hurried away, with a quick word to Joe that she wanted to inform Mrs. Tyrrell.

Joe saw Drakulya look after Maria, frowning slightly.

Cathy was just standing still, looking weary. A large backpack that must be hers was lying at her feet.

Brainard, his fears for himself forgotten for the moment, was standing just in front of his daughter, staring at her with obvious relief. "Thank God, you're back."

"Hi," the girl said to him, a certain reserve in her voice. She submitted tiredly to a somewhat awkward hug.

Holding her at arm's length, the stocky man said to his adopted daughter: "I was afraid—I never wanted you to get caught up in any of my own troubles. I never wanted that."

"Your troubles?" It sounded to Joe as if the young woman didn't know what her father was talking about, and wasn't trying very hard to find out. As if she had to make a considerable effort to bring her mind back from her own concerns.

Nor did it escape Joe's notice that she avoided calling this man "father."

"Kid," said Brainard. "Cathy. I'm not going to ask you any questions. I'm just glad you're back." He awkwardly stroked her hair.

"I'm going to ask you some questions, though," Cathy flared back. "And I have some for Aunt Sarah." She looked at the strangers present. "But I guess they can wait." Brainard, looking bewildered, let her go.

Then Cathy turned her gaze toward Strangeways. The look she gave him, casual at first, became something of a stare. "Who're you?" she demanded, with the bluntness of one determined to concentrate on matters of importance.

Strangeways bowed slightly. His face under the broad hat brim was shadowed. "A friend of your mother's, Cathy."

Joe put in: "He's working with me, Miss Brainard." Then it became necessary for Joe to explain his own identity, and the reasons for his presence.

When Cathy had heard him out she looked at the investigators with some bitterness as well as weariness. "Well, I'm back now. You can call off the hunt."

"Cathy! It was old Sarah's voice; she was approaching, as swiftly as her years would allow, from the direction of the Tyrrell House. Cathy ran toward her with open arms, and the others witnessed a more emotional reunion.

A few minutes later, Joe, in the company of John and Mr. Strangeways, was hobbling back toward his hotel. Sarah, Cathy, and Brainard had preceded them. Silence obtained during the first part of the walk.

"I guess we can start packing?" John suggested, when they were halfway to their destination.

"Not I," said Mr. Strangeways.

"How's that, sir?" John inquired.

"I am thinking, gentlemen," said their elder companion, "of the *Origin of Species*."

Joe Keogh thought for a moment. "You're talking about the book written by Charles Darwin?"

Dark eyes turned toward him. "Not so much the book as its subject—the laws governing the development of life on earth. Tyrrell's real interest seems to be in those basic natural laws, which Darwin began to discover more than a century ago. My people as well as yours are subject to those basic laws. We are all human, all children of the earth."

"All right. Well, Cathy's back, apparently unharmed. My client is probably going to thank me for my trouble, pay me off, and send me on my way."

"Yes, your mission seems to have been accomplished, Joseph. But I am not yet satisfied that I am free, in good conscience, to depart. Not yet."

Joe did not hesitate. "What can I do to help?"

"Yeah," seconded John.

"I cannot say just yet, gentlemen. But the offer is gratefully accepted."

In Joe's suite Sarah Tyrrell put down the borrowed phone, having just finished reporting to the law that her grandniece Cathy Brainard had returned safely, under her own power.

The old lady commented: "They didn't sound very excited or surprised."

Joe said: "A lot of runaways come back under their own power. Where's Cathy now?"

"Getting some sleep." Sarah paused. "Where's Maria?"

Joe didn't know. He looked at Bill, who was standing by. "And where's Brainard, by the way?"

"Said he was going to the lobby to get some cigarettes. Didn't seem to want an escort."

The day's snow showers were picking up in intensity as Gerald Brainard, wearing a winter coat, small suitcase in hand, turned from a pedestrian path into one of the small sightseers' parking lots scattered around the Village area. Looking left and right through the gloomy day, he pulled a set of car keys from his pocket as he approached a small snow-covered Pontiac.

He had not looked in all the necessary directions, evidently. He barely had the car door open when a large form, wearing a fur-collared coat, loomed over him.

"Think you're going somewhere?"

A few minutes later, the Pontiac was parked again, this time in a snowy byway of the winter Park, a long, comparatively narrow expanse of paving, half drive, half parking lot, surrounded by pine woods, much used by summer crowds. Now the place was all but deserted; only one other car stood there, besides the Pontiac.

Three men were sitting in this second vehicle; Smith was behind the wheel, Brainard beside him on the right, and Preston in the rear seat.

"We're just gonna sit here for a while," Smith was saying. "No hurry, is there? We got all day, right?" He turned his head slightly. "Pres, was there anything else you wanted to do this afternoon?"

"Nope." Preston was lighting a cigarette. He made no move to offer a smoke to anyone else. "I got all day. Nothing I want to do but sit here this afternoon and talk about money. How the man we work for is going to recoup a certain investment."

Brainard had nothing to say. Pale and shivering, he was staring straight ahead of him, at the band of snowy woods some distance beyond the windshield.

"I want some suggestions, Brainard. Deadbeat."

"I don't have the money to pay you now. I—"

The speech ended in a yelp. Preston had reached forward to burn the back of Brainard's neck with his cigarette.

"Just sit still, sweetie. That's not what I call a suggestion. You're gonna come up with some better ones than that."

"Nobody here in this part of the park," Smith remarked conversationally. "You couldn't plan to find a deserted place like this around here at the holiday season, could you? But it's our lucky day. I'm waiting, deadbeat. How are you going to come up with a hundred and twenty grand?"

"I'll pay it," said Brainard. He started to pull his coat collar up, covering the back of his neck. Preston behind him pulled it down again.

A moderate snow was falling. "They say," said Smith, "that sometimes the whole park gets snowed in for days."

"No tourists in sight anywhere," said Preston from the rear. "No rangers. Nobody here but us. We're waiting, deadbeat."

He burned Brainard again.

* * *

And then, suddenly, they were not alone. The figure of a bearded man, wearing a broadbrimmed hat, was standing at the edge of the woods. And then purposefully approaching the occupied vehicle, passing the empty Pontiac.

Brainard made a little sound, almost too faint to be called a groan, deep in his throat.

"What the hell now?" remarked Smith.

Drakulya stopped some twelve or fifteen feet in front of the car. He stood there motionless, hands in pockets. His lips moved and he was saying something.

Smith ran a window partway down, and the voice of the man standing outside could be heard plainly. "Mr. Brainard, patience. You will shortly be free to leave."

At those words Brainard made a convulsive effort to open his door. The man behind him grabbed him by the collar and pulled him forcibly back into his seat. Then Preston opened his rear door and got out of the car, which resettled itself on its springs with the removal of his considerable weight.

"Get lost, punk," fur-collared Preston told Mr. Strangeways. "Go chase the squirrels somewhere. This is a private conversation."

Brainard gave a desperate cry for help, a cry he choked off when the man in the driver's seat beside him jabbed him with an elbow.

Drakulya looked from Brainard's captor behind the windshield to the other who stood in open air. "Mr. Smith, I presume? And Mr. Preston? I see it is too late to urge you to allow this man to leave the Park unharmed. Well, I suppose I must make allowances. I hesitate to interfere in the collection of a just debt. So may I ask—"

"I already told you once," interrupted Preston. "I told you nice, go chase a squirrel. You wouldn't listen. Okay." He strode forward purposefully, heading straight for Mr. Strangeways.

At the last moment, just before he reached his goal, a frown as of puzzlement appeared on Preston's face.

Then he reached out for the waiting Strangeways. But the grip he wished to obtain had been pre-empted. Mr. Strangeways already had him with both hands by the front of his furred jacket, and a fraction of a second after that Mr. Preston squawked aloud, in sheer surprise that his body had so rapidly become airborne. He made a shrill noise for such a large man. And for a mere breather he was quite well-coordinated, able to execute a kind of dance step in middair, a doomed attempt to regain balance that had, alas, already been lost forever.

His body, carefully aimed, smote with considerable force the front end of the occupied but motionless vehicle. In the first phase of the impact, the flying man's legs struck the hood. A fraction of a second later his bulky torso crashed into the sloping windshield. Strong glass caved in, but did not shatter. The hurtling body glanced from the deeply slanting surface, mounting almost straight up into the air for a distance of several car-heights before coming down on pavement covered with, so far, only a very inadequate padding of new snow.

Even before Preston's body had undergone this secondary impact, Drakulya was standing beside the driver's door, pulling it open. Incautiously Mr. Smith had neglected to fasten his seat belt, a fact which did not escape his caller's notice.

Taking the back of his second subject's neck firmly in one hand, and with the other seizing the steering column just below the wheel, Mr. Strangeways brought the two together with an effort that approached the maximum force he could exert.

A fraction of a second later he was recoiling in startlement, and hissing his annoyance as he realized that this part of the exercise would have to be done over again. His effort with the steering column had only succeeded in popping an airbag, leaving Mr. Smith hardly worse than disconcerted, rather as if a shotgun loaded with cream puffs had been fired in his face. Smith tried to wave his arms, and let out a rabbit-like squeak that some listeners might have found comical.

But Mr. Strangeways still had him by the back of the neck.

Intent on concluding this distasteful business, the bearded man recovered his aplomb with commendable speed for one of his advanced years. The airbag had already deflated itself, and a second try with neck and steering column produced the desired result.

Brainard, though physically almost intact, required help to leave of the battered vehicle.

"Thanks. My God, how can I thank you?"

"You have just done so. That is sufficient."

"I didn't see either of 'em watching the hotel. I thought I'd take a chance . . . now Cathy's back, I didn't want her getting messed up in my troubles."

After advising his client to try some snow on his burned neck, Strangeways methodically but quickly went through the pockets of Brainard's tormentors. Preston, sprawled in the snow, still breathed, but painfully, and the examiner judged that that condition would not persist for long. In Smith it had already passed. Strangeways also rifled the more obvious places of storage in their car, looking for anything that might connect them with Brainard.

He found nothing in that line, but did collect almost five thousand dollars in cash. Considering this the spoils of war, Strangeways handed it, in the form of an untidy bundle, to Brainard before sending him on his way.

"Some of that's my own money. They took it away from me just now."

"You may have the rest," the rescuer said.

"Can I pay you something, for your help?"

"Decent of you to offer. But no, thank you. The weather is turning bad. I advise you to drive carefully."

"Thanks." Brainard gingerly scooped more snow onto the back of his neck. "God, maybe my luck is turning at last."

When Strangeways arrived back at the hotel suite, Joe Keogh asked him if he had seen Brainard.

The bearded man nodded. "Yes, as a matter of fact. When last I saw him he was driving peacefully toward the main exit from the Park. I have little doubt that he will be well on his way before the worst of the storm arrives."

"What about the people who were after him?"

Strangeways looked at his well-kept nails. "Also on their way."

After a pause Joe asked: "Still after Brainard?"

"No. They had taken a different direction . . . careless, improvident men. I doubt that they have managed to get far. The roads are becoming treacherous." He made a sighing noise, faintly reptilian. "For the careless, accidents are almost inevitable in such conditions."

"Oh," said Joe, with finality. He had known the other for many years. After a moment he said: "Oh," again.

"Joseph?" the other asked him mildly.

"Yes?"

"Are a great many automobiles now equipped with airbags?"

"Most of the new ones, I guess."

Drakulya nodded thoughtfully. "Now I must rest. All this activity by day is wearing, even in weather so beautifully gray—I can see why my compatriot Tyrrell was so drawn to this country, dangerous as it is for us."

"Why?"

"The sun, Joseph. We, our kind, are much concerned with its presence, absence, and intensity."

"With avoiding it, I'd think."

"Yes, of course. Only with the full bulk of a planet between our bodies and the sun are vampires entirely shielded from all of the potentially harmful emissions and effects. Though it is still my contention that we may depend on some emission from the sun, as yet unknown to science, for much of our true nourishment . . .

"But also we have no trouble in grasping the idea that something really odd might be expected to happen when the sun strikes directly, for the first time in a billion years, upon the freshly shattered surface of some deep rock.

"Who can say, Joseph, what would happen then? Perhaps most likely nothing. On the other hand, I can visualize strange possibilities . . ."

"And Tyrrell was thinking along those lines when he came here."

"I am sure it was not idly, merely by chance, that he came to settle here in sun country, as it is called; on the contrary, anyone coming here as a vampire would require a strong reason."

"Connected with Darwin, maybe?"

"With life, Joseph. Connected with nothing less than life itself.

~ 16 ~

Lying side by side in bed, almost silent and almost motionless, Jake and Camilla had clasped hands, his left holding her right. Both were listening intently to the normal noises of late night in the Deep Canyon. Something that sounded almost like a coyote was howling in the distance. Through the open window of their bedroom there drifted, reassuringly, the worksounds made by the old man, demonstrating that he was on the job as usual.

Neither Camilla nor Jake was anywhere near sleep, though hours had passed since either of them had whispered a word. The night had been hell, any kind of sleep all but impossible. Sleep had become nearly impossible anyway in recent nights, with neither of them able to guess when their demonic master might appear suddenly in their darkened bedroom, demanding the blood, the life, of one or both of them.

Both Camilla and Jake were nearing the last stages of physical and mental exhaustion.

Jake could only thank God that Tyrrell had not intruded on them during the night just past. There was no working timepiece in the cottage. Until the sun actually rose, the breathers had no choice but dumb endurance of the fear that the vampire had somehow discovered their plan. No relief from their suspicion that the satanic Tyrrel was only toying with them, that he would appear to confront them in the last hour, or perhaps even the last few minutes, before dawn. Jake kept going over and over in his mind everything that Tyrrell had said to him yesterday, every change of expression on the vampire's face—had Tyrrell guessed?

One of the windows of the bedroom was on the east side of the house. Jake lay staring at the edge of the curtains, wondering for a long time whether the sky was really, at last, starting to lighten in that direction, or whether he was deluding himself with hope. When he was sure that the night was really fading, he reached out a hand silently and squeezed Camilla's wrist. Thank God, thank God, at last!

Moments later, the sounds of Tyrrell's labors ceased. That was a sure sign that dawn was coming.

Unless, this morning, he was quitting early to deceive them.

"Listen!" Camilla had been lying as tautly awake as Jake.

"Shh!"

No more noise came from Tyrrell. Undoubtedly there was daylight in the east.

Moments after reaching that decision, Jake was up and pulling on his clothes.

The sun had still not cleared the canyon's eastern rim when Jake and Camilla began trying to break into the little shed in which the old man kept his explosives jealously, if not very effectively, locked up. Camilla said that she was certain, or almost certain, that Tyrrell usually wore the key to the explosives store on a chain around his neck. But the long crowbar in Jake's hands proved quite adequate for wrenching away the padlock and its hardware.

Jake pulled open the door of the shed and took out the box of dynamite, stubby sticks wrapped in heavy, waxy paper which bore red warning labels. For a moment his heart sank as he thought the necessary blasting caps must have been hidden elsewhere; but no, there they were, another box, printed with warnings, way back on the top shelf. And there on the same shelf as the caps was the wire, several big spools of it; and down in the bottom of the cabinet the electric blasting machine, a little square box with a big handle sticking up on top, newer-looking than the one the CCC used.

Why hadn't the old man locked this stuff up more securely? He supposed it was because Tyrrell didn't think his current slaves would have the wit and the nerve to do what they were doing.

Now Jake could hear Camilla's hurrying footsteps. She had already drawn kerosene from the drum behind the house, and she was carrying two containers full of the smelly liquid when she met Jake on the way to the little cave across the creek where Tyrrell was supposed to sleep. One container was the two-gallon can normally used to bring kerosene to the house and fill the lamps, the other their biggest cooking pot.

The plan, worked out over a period of days, was to drench the sleeping vampire with kerosene, running the liquid in on him with hoses or a length of metal pipe. Then they would use dynamite in an attempt to blast Edgar out of his snug sunless hiding place—the blast, Jake calculated, might itself set fire to the drenching liquid. If not, they would have to ignite the kerosene by tossing burning rags or torches into the recess.

Jake started carrying the blasting materials to the slab of rock that shielded the vampire. Meanwhile Camilla was busy filling all the glass jars she could find in the house with kerosene.

As soon as she brought them across the creek, Jake

took one, screwed the lid on tight, then hurled the container carefully into the vampire's shady recess. The glass shattered quite satisfactorily, and the liquid splashed and dribbled inside the shaded recess. Cam and Jake looked at each other. As far as they could tell, the stuff had gone right where they wanted it.

No reaction had been provoked inside the miniature cave. The smell of kerosene, oily and pungent, quickly filled the air.

"He's got to be covered with it now. He's got to be."

"If he's there. If he's there."

"He's there. He's got to be."

Neither of them could be one hundred per cent sure of that. Yet there was nothing to be done but forge ahead. As Camilla tightened the lid on a second jar of kerosene, Jake wished aloud, not for the first time, that they had gasoline available.

"Why?"

"Burns hotter."

"This won't work?"

"Of course it'll work. Kerosene burns hot enough. I wouldn't be trying it otherwise. Give me that." Jake hurled another missile, scoring another direct hit.

Gasoline just wasn't available, nor was diesel fuel. Tyrrell had no motor vehicles in the Deep Canyon, no need for the stuff, and so none was kept on hand. The generator ran on water power, and Jake had made sure that there was no auxiliary engine for it.

He capped and hurled a third jar, and winced as this missile shattered on the stone atop the cave, wasting most if not all of the precious deadly stuff.

Handing him the last filled jar, Camilla suddenly shouted a question. "Jake, goddam it, Jake, what if this doesn't work?"

"Too late now to worry about that."

"But what if—?"

"You said you'd seen him hurt by burning."

Camilla shuddered. "No, what I said was I never saw him stick his hand in the fire."

"He'll burn, he's got to burn, goddam it. We're going to kill him, one way or another, now we've started. We've got to." He hurled the last jar into the cave.

Their pitifully small collection of jars was used up already. Now it seemed to Jake that the jars hadn't held nearly enough kerosene—it seemed to him crazy that he had ever thought they might. But no time to worry about that now. On to part two of the plan. A piece of garden hose taken from the little irrigation system was pressed into service to convey the flammable liquid to where they wanted it.

As Jake had foreseen, using the hose was very awkward. First one end of it had to be pushed over the barrier slab of rock, well back into the cave where Tyrrell supposedly was sleeping.

(Would the eyes of the vampire open? Jake wondered. Would he see what was coming at him? You'd think he'd have to smell it, anyway, unless he was completely dead.)

Then the other end of the hose had to be elevated, held high by straining human hands, while kerosene was poured into it by other hands, through the funnel which was normally used to fill the two-gallon can from the drum. Jake had to run to the house to get a chair for Camilla to stand on while she poured.

Between episodes of these lifting and pouring efforts for which all four of their hands were needed, Camilla went running back, again and again, eventually draining all of the kerosene from the storage drum into their pot and can. Jake was cutting the wire that he'd found, and closely inspecting the slab of limestone that guarded Tyrrell's refuge, picking out the places where he wanted to put the dynamite. He thought two sticks should do it.

As soon as they had done all that they could do with kerosene, Jake started hand-drilling the holes for the explosive. In his left hand he gripped the drill, a simple hand tool shaped like a long chisel with a steel shank and a star-shaped cutting end. With his right arm he swung one of the middle-sized hammers from the workshop. Dust and fine chips spouted from under the biting end of the drill with every blow, and after each blow Jake rotated the cutter slightly.

The drill, driven by no more than human muscle, sank into the rock with painful slowness, a small fraction of an inch with every blow. The workshop boasted a few electric tools, but there was no way to get power to any of them back here.

Camilla stood by him, watching for the most part in silence, and stinking, as he did, of kerosene. Their clothes were wet with the stuff. All either of them needed was for someone to strike a match.

"What can I do to help?" she pleaded.

"Nothing, right now."

The smell of kerosene saturated the air. Jake could imagine the puddle of it that must lie back in among the rocks all evaporating, dissipating into the atmosphere before they were ready to put a flame to it. He told himself such thoughts were foolishness, and labored on.

At last, the first of his hand-drilled holes was deep enough. Thank God it was only limestone that he was trying to drill, and not granite, nor the strange black Vishnu schist.

Camilla asked again: "What can I do?"

"Okay. Here, you hold the drill."

Now, starting the second hole, he could use a bigger hammer, and grip it with both fists. The work went faster. Once he hit the drill only a glancing blow, and it leaped free of Camilla's grip to clang with what seemed awful loudness on the rocks. She screamed at Jake to be careful what he was doing, not to hit her arms.

At last they had drilled the holes. Putting the dynamite and blasting caps in place was not all that difficult, but the job had its tricky aspects. Really, Jake knew very little about this, only what he had picked up before he came to the Deep Canyon, watching the experts employed by the CCC.

He was tamping a blasting cap and its attached wire in on top of the first charge, when Camilla said suddenly: "I have to see him dead, Jake, it won't be enough to just think he's probably burned up back in there. If I don't see him with my own eyes today, I'll die waiting for it to get dark tonight—not knowing if he's really dead, or if he's coming out after us."

Jake grunted and went on working.

Finally the dynamite was set, tamped into both of the drilled holes with wire and blasting caps in place.

Jake was ready to set it off. There was no reason to delay.

He had set up the blasting machine in what he thought would be a sheltered place, behind a huge rock a hundred feet from Tyrrell's sanctuary. He attached the wires to the machine and had raised the handle to deliver a jolt of electricity when Camilla clutched at his arm.

"What was that?" she demanded in a whisper.

As soon as she called his attention to the sound he could hear it, sure enough. It was an inhuman or half-human sound, and Jake was sure that it came from the direction of Tyrrell's little cave. It reminded Jake of the time when as a child he'd come across a cat dying with its foot caught in a rat trap.

There was no use waiting.

"Here goes nothing," Jake muttered to himself. Camilla, seeing what he was about to do, crouched down.

Jake said: "Put your head down."

He leaned his weight on the handle, heard the armature whirr, an instant generator inside the machine. He'd put everything together right, because a hundred feet away the blast went off, two charges ripping the atmosphere in the same heartbeat. In the open air, dynamite always made less noise than Jake expected.

He was on his feet at once, jumping out from behind his sheltering boulder and running toward Tyrrell's sanctuary through the small rock fragments falling back to earth. A dozen strides and Jake skidded to a halt, seeing with fierce despair that the explosion had not shattered the barrier rock. Only perhaps a tenth of the obstruction had been removed; the deep recess was every bit as inaccessible as before.

Camilla joined him, saying nothing. The sight of failure wasn't the most immediately sickening thing for Jake. Worse than that was the noise now coming from the little cave. There was no longer any doubt that Tyrrell was really there, just where Camilla had kept saying that he had to be.

There was fire back there, behind the rock, what must be a miniature lake of kerosene going up quickly in black stinking smoke. Kerosene was burning, but not only kerosene. There was something else.

It had taken the screaming, a horrible inhuman sound, a little while to get started. But there was no doubt about it now.

"Jake! Jake, what do we do now?"

He stared at the remaining barrier rock, trying to visualize where its weak points must lie. He had been wrong before, but there was nothing to do now but keep trying. "Get more dynamite. We'll have to blast again. Hurry!"

Camilla ran off at once. Jake stayed behind, planning where to drill the next set of blasting holes. If there would be time to drill them before the sun went down. The first pair seemed to have taken forever.

The screaming coming from the deep sanctuary went on and on. On and on, unceasingly.

~ 17 ~

Cathy Brainard was once more trudging her way down Bright Angel Trail, headed for the Deep Canyon. This time she had left all of her camping equipment behind, except for a canteen.

And this time Maria Torres was walking stride for stride down the trail with Cathy. Maria had not even bothered bringing a canteen.

The two young women had met, without conscious prearrangment, up on the broad pedestrian rim walk, near the Bright Angel trailhead. They had scarcely seen each other before this meeting, yet on encountering each other on the walk they had agreed within moments, with a minimum of discussion, on what they were going to do.

"It'll be a big help if you can show me the way down," Maria had said, almost by way of greeting, staring into the gloom below. Mountain-sized buttes made purple shadow-shapes down there, beyond a miles-deep band of sunken clouds and snow-showers. "Down to where I have to go. That will save me valuable time."

"So," Cathy had said. "They've given you the job of keeping an eye on me."

Maria had frowned, as if she were troubled by some distant memory. "No," she had said slowly. "Maybe I'm supposed to be doing that, and maybe Joe thinks I am, but

I'm not. No, my reason for going down is personal. This is extremely important to me."

"All right," Cathy had said, disbelieving. "Whatever you say, however you want to come along, for the private detectives or just for fun. How you get there is supposed to be this damned big secret, you know. A secret I wasn't supposed to remember, but I did anyway. To hell with them and their secrets. My parents, I mean. Whatever they did to me when I was a kid. I don't quite know yet what it was, but I'm going to find out."

Maria had said nothing. She had been staring into the depths, apparently at something far, far beyond the afternoon's returning convoy of mule-mounted tourists, who were just coming into view in the middle distance, ghostly centaurs climbing out of snow and time.

Cathy had started down the trail.

"This time," Cathy said now, "I left a note for Aunt Sarah. She's a good lady. No use worrying her unnecessarily."

"Maybe you shouldn't have done that," Maria said.

"Left a note? Why not?"

Maria didn't know why not; she couldn't say, and only gestured vaguely. But somehow the thought of Cathy's note made her uneasy.

"You see," said Cathy, "going down the first time, I mean at Thanksgiving, that was a lot different. I didn't really know where I was headed, then. I only had a kind of memory." She paused. "Do you ever have—dreams—about your early childhood?"

"Not any more," Maria said.

"Memories, I should say. More like memories than dreams. Going down that time was like a dream. I saw things, real things, that I had convinced myself were only figments of my imagination. Like a certain little house. Seeing that house scared me, so I just—went camping for a while. Now I've got to go back and make sure about things, like that house, and my parents. I . . ." Cathy did not seem to be able to find words to complete the thought. "You work with Mr. Strangeways?" she asked finally.

"No," said Maria, in her new vague, indifferent voice. "Not really. I've barely met him. Why?"

"There's something spooky about him."

"I think you're probably right about that."

The two young women trudged on down the trail.

They had gone no more than fifty yards when Cathy noticed that Maria was carrying nothing—not even a canteen—in the way of camping supplies or equipment.

"Aren't you going to need anything?"

"No. I'm not really—going that far." Maria was staring straight ahead of her, as if she were thinking very intently indeed. Cathy almost hesitated to interrupt such concentration.

"You're following me, right? Checking up on me? So how do you know how far I'm going?"

Maria shrugged.

"Well, you're all right." Cathy shook her head, tossing her hair. "You're not going to need a canteen, because it isn't very far."

"How do we get there?"

"You have to know a secret. But that's all right, I remember the secret. Or else I'm crazy, and I've only been imagining things all along."

"What kind of secret?"

"It's a trick my father—the man who must have been my real father—taught me when I was very small. For a long time I forgot it; but once you learn something important like that, it's never quite forgotten. You know what I mean? Like riding a bicycle."

Maria didn't answer. She was still gazing straight ahead of her as she walked, as if her thoughts were really elsewhere.

Snow blew in the faces of the two young women, and flurries obscured the trail, above them and below. The mule train, mounting methodically, led by a mounted ranger, came into view once more, this time immediately ahead. Cathy and Maria moved as far as possible to the inside edge of the trail, letting the big, sure-footed animals walk past, each carrying a half-frozen tourist. The mounted men and women, at this stage of their adventure intent on getting back to warmth and civilization, scarcely glanced at the waiting hikers.

The trick that Cathy had mentioned, of course, was a technique required of any traveler bound in or out of the place her parents had called the Deep Canyon. The proper technique was essential, not only to pass the barrier of time, but to arrive on the other side of that barrier somewhere near your chosen destination. It was of course necessary that the destination had been rightly chosen—and for Cathy, as she herself now thought, this journey of exploration, of rediscovery, was not only right, but inevitable.

She tried, without much success, to discuss all these things with Maria, as the two young women continued walking down Bright Angel Trail together.

Maria at last paid enough attention to say: "It's all new to me down here. You'll have to show me."

"Oh, I can show you easily enough. When I was a little girl, I came down this way more times than I can remember—than I *could* remember. But now I'm here again, it's all coming back."

Now the two were alone, cut off on all sides by the falling snow that had driven other visitors to cover. Cathy as she descended the trail pondered yet again the questions of her own origins: Who had her real mother been? Somehow she was almost entirely certain that her real mother, whatever her identity, had been dead for a long time. And who, really, was the man that she remembered as the father of her childhood?

Gradually, in the course of growing up as Brainard's adopted daughter, Cathy had come to realize that her adoption had made her a relative of old Edgar Tyrrell, an important but vastly eccentric artist who in the dim past of the thirties had built the Tyrrell House, among his other achievements. But until very recently Tyrrell and his ancient affairs had never loomed large in Cathy Brainard's thoughts. She had never had any cause to connect the half-famous artist, whose name appeared on statues, in books, and in museums, with the vague memory she nursed of her 'real' father. The dates were just hopelessly wrong, to begin with.

Nor, until Cathy arrived by chance at the Canyon this year, at the age of seventeen, had she ever had any reason, or any desire, to visit the house on the South Rim.

Cathy was vaguely aware that her adoptive father sometimes visited the Canyon on business trips—though Brainard seldom discussed business in front of her. But people at home almost never talked about the Tyrrell House in her presence, and she had had no idea that she had ever been there before.

Until she saw the place. Then, at first glance, she was certain that it had once been her home.

Cathy, absorbed in thought, almost passed up the turning when they reached it, almost missed the proper place to work the trick. But she did recognize the place in time, despite the snow. The two young women turned off Bright Angel, following what looked like a deer trail, leading nowhere. But Cathy made the turnoff without hesitation.

In Cathy's awareness there had been floating the memory of certain old photographs of Edgar Tyrrell, pictures she had come across from time to time, in magazines or books. She was certain of having seen at least one such photo, framed, in the Rim House, and it seemed to her there had been another in one of the Canyon guidebooks she and her girlfriends had seen in the early stage of her Thanksgiving visit, in their room at one of the lodges.

And at Aunt Sarah's home on Long Island, Cathy knew, the old lady still kept one or two such photos, black and white, taken with a boxy old thirties camera. On rainy childhood afternoons young Cathy, browsing through a past in which she had never thought to find herself a native, had come across those pictures more than once. Somehow those pictures had become confused—or so she had long thought—with her real memories, of a real man she once had called her father.

The snow inside the Canyon stopped falling, and the air warmed. The sky remained cloudy, but the quality of light changed, suggesting dusk in the Deep Canyon, but no longer suggesting winter. Visibility increased.

"Yes, this is the place," said Cathy quietly. They were in some kind of a side canyon now, vastly smaller than the big one. A creek, narrow enough to step across, came gurgling down the middle. The narrow trail, or path, generally following the creek, took the young women in single file around some dwarfish cottonwoods. They had arrived in sight of the cottage, which stood only fifty yards or so ahead. Its windows were lightless, and the whole place looked uninhabited and uninviting.

Cathy stopped in her tracks, gazing at the little structure. Maria halted uncertainly beside her.

"I lived in that house once," Cathy said. "Not for very long, I think. But I did live there."

She glanced at Maria, who, silent and dreamy-eyed, was obviously thinking her own thoughts, not paying much attention to her companion or to the cottage.

A strange way for a detective to act, Cathy thought. But Cathy was concentrating on her own thoughts too. She added aloud: "I bet my father still lives here, maybe not in the house but somewhere nearby. I have that feeling."

That caught Maria's interest at least faintly. "Your father? Gerald Brainard?"

"Not him." Now Cathy sounded contemptuous. "My real father. The one I remember from when I was a little girl."

Slowly the two young women approached the silent cottage. A faint steady roar in the background, half-smothered by the noise of the stream, suggested some kind of machinery at work.

"How long since you've seen him?" Maria asked. She appeared to be trying to pull herself out of her apathy, struggling against the half-awake feeling and behavior that had claimed her all the way down.

"It must be about twelve years," said Cathy. She frowned, having made an unsatisfactory mental calculation. "And my great-aunt Sarah might have lived here too—but that would have been more like fifty years ago. No, maybe even sixty."

Lately Cathy had found it almost impossible to make anything satisfactory regarding time. Two days of her Thanksgiving trip had turned somehow into a month; at least, everyone else agreed that she had been gone a month, though on her personal time scale the camping trip could have lasted no more than a couple of days.

Nearing the cottage, Cathy and Maria were accosted by a large calico cat, looking no more than half domesticated. The creature sat in the narrow path before them, mewing as if demanding something; then it darted away into the sparse shrubbery as they approached.

"It's Beagle," breathed Cathy in an awed voice.

"Beagle?"

"That's his name. He was my own pet kitten once. Or a cat that I remember as looking just like that one. My father got it for me. I remember wanting a kitten, and wanting one so much, and I think I remember telling my father . . . a cat can live twelve years, can't it?"

"Sure. I think so."

When the visitors reached the door of the cottage, Cathy tried the latch and found it open. There was no other lock. She started to go in.

Maria took a step back. "Are you sure this is all right?"

"Of course it is. I live here."

"But you don't any more." Maria raised her hands, rubbed her eyes, shook her head, and looked about her. "What am I doing here? Where are we, anyway?"

But Cathy had already disappeared into the darkness inside the little house.

There were electric lights, in the main room at least, and Cathy knew where to find the switch.

"Just like I remember it," she murmured, looking around the large room. "Except that everything's so small. I seem to remember even the furniture. This chair—" She dragged a hand across the rough-carved wooden back.

Maria was looking out one of the windows into gathering dusk. She said: "Someone's coming."

Cathy turned. The man, dressed in dusty workman's clothes and looking calmly angry, was already standing in the door. His was the righteous look of a homeowner confronting unexpected intruders.

"Father?" The word burst from Cathy at once, impulsively. "Then you are still alive!"

The man's face was changed, scarred and darkened,

from the face that she remembered. But in her mind there could be no doubt.

The man in the doorway froze into position for a long moment. Then he glanced briefly at Maria, before fastening a penetrating gaze on Cathy. His face now betrayed little or nothing of what he might be feeling.

He asked, in a rasping voice: "Who are you?"

It was as if Cathy did not even hear the question. She stood where she was, her hands on the back of one of the wooden chairs, gazing back at him. "Daddy?"

"My God—is it possible?" Still staring at her, the man stepped forward, groping for the nearest chair. When he had it in hand he pulled it to him and sat down. His sitting was a sudden movement, as if his knees were no longer to be trusted.

He said, slowly: "What do you call me?"

"You are my father, aren't you? You must be. I can remember you—and I remember this house." She looked around her. She looked back at him. "I lived here, once."

"What's your name, girl?" It was an old, old voice.

"I'm Cathy. Don't you know me? I can remember you as if it were yesterday. You haven't changed—not much."

"Cathy. For a moment I thought that you were young Sarah, somehow finding her way back to me. It's a wonder—a marvel—how much you resemble your mother."

At once, as if the question could be held back no longer, the girl demanded: "Why did you desert me and my mother?"

"Desert you? I?"

"She left me in an orphanage, when I was four or five years old. That much I know. She wouldn't have had to do that, if you hadn't deserted her. Am I mistaken?" Cathy seemed anxious to be told that she was.

Edgar Tyrrell drew himself up straight in his chair. "I deserted her? And abandoned you? Who told you that?"

"It seems obvious. Am I mistaken? I can remember the two of you quarreling. Up on the rim, the day—someone—was being buried."

The man in the chair looked old. After a moment he said: "Your sister was buried up there. I'm surprised you can remember that." He shook his head slowly. "After that, your mother walked out on me. She blamed me, somehow. She took you with her and walked out on me one bright day, without warning. And she never came back."

After a pause Cathy asked: "What was she like? My mother?"

"In her youth, you mean? You speak of her—in the past tense."

Cathy stared at him. "She's dead!"

Old Tyrrell stared back. Then he looked about the room, remembered something, and in an instant was on his feet, in a fluid movement that belied his look of age.

"Where is your companion?" he demanded sharply.

Cathy needed a moment to understand. "Maria? I don't know. She was right here a moment ago."

Tyrrell stood listening, in concentration. "It doesn't matter," he said at last. "She will not have got far. She doesn't matter." His gaze fixed on Cathy again. "You matter, though."

"Father?" Cathy, letting go of her chair, came toward him, at first tentatively, then in a little rush that ended in an awkward embrace. Tyrrell's arms, at first raised as if to ward her off, closed about her slowly, gently.

"You are my father," she said against his shoulder.

Gently and slowly he disengaged to hold her at arm's length.

"I am—I was—your stepfather, child. When I first saw you, you were perhaps two years old. Your sister was a babe in arms. Your mother was—or is—the only woman—perhaps the only person—I have ever truly loved. You—and your sister—were the only children I could ever have. Therefore you matter to me. And you always will."

He added gently, "You told me just now that your mother was dead?"

"My real mother? She's been dead since I was six." Cathy paused, suspicion being born. "Hasn't she?"

Tyrrell ignored the question for the moment. "When did you leave the Rim, in what year? And how did you get here, into the Deep Canyon? The way should not be open."

"The way was open for me," Cathy said simply. "Because I lived here once, I remembered how to find the turning. I came looking for you."

"What year? Tell me, what year?"

"I don't know what you mean. *This* year? This year is nineteen ninety-one."

"Ah," the man said.

Moving past him to the open door, looking out into the gathering night, the young woman sampled the air, the strangeness of the place, with a deep breath. Smells strange and familiar at the same time, unknown since childhood, keyed into her memory.

She said: "I could always remember this place—very much like this. Except now the house and everything seems so much smaller. But when I remembered these things I thought my memory was playing tricks on me. There were other things, too, that didn't seem to fit. Cars, and radios, that I gradually realized looked like they were from the thirties. Old-fashioned clothes and toys. When things like that puzzled me, I always thought my memory was playing tricks."

She looked at her companion closely. "And there were even stranger things. Things that I saw *you* do, or seem to do, that would have been impossible for anyone."

"My dear . . ."

Cathy indicated with a gesture that she had not finished. "Not only my memory," she added. "People have been lying to me all my life. I didn't know if this place was real. When I tried to talk about it, no one would pay attention. My mother abandoned me in an orphanage, and you, my father, never tried to find me—did you?"

"No," the man said, after a silence, "because I came to realize that your mother was right to take you away from here."

"Why was she right?"

"It was a dangerous place for you. I realize that now."

"Now you live here all alone?"

Tyrrell looked faintly surprised. "Alone? No, far from alone."

The girl asked: "What year did she leave you?"

"Who?"

She stared at him. "My mother!"

"Nineteen thirty-four."

"Nineteen thirty-four?" A moment of mental calculation. "That isn't possible!"

"Ah, but it is."

"No. It's the time, you see—Father. You're saying that Mother left you in nineteen thirty-four. But I'm only seventeen. How could I possibly be . . .?"

"My whole life is a question of time, Cathy. Time does not run smoothly for me. Nor does it for anyone who lives in the Deep Canyon—as you did. It's as if there were rapids in the flow. Like those in the river, you see—do you remember my showing you the river?"

"I remember—the river. Yes!"

"And I must have shown you the white rocks? The rocks as old as the earth, that make big rapids in the flow of time? I have spent my life at work upon those rocks—the spirit of the earth is in them."

Cathy cared little about rocks. "Father—it was Aunt Sarah, my grandaunt, who left you in nineteen thirty-four."

"It was Sarah, your mother, who left me—ah, I begin to understand."

"But—how could—"

Tyrrell walked to the bedroom door. "Come here, girl. Let me show you something."

A minute later the two of them were in the room that had been briefly hers in her young childhood. Entering, the man touched a switch beside the door. A lamp came on.

"I don't remember there being an electric light."

"I put that in a few years after you were gone. There was some—trouble with the kerosene lamps."

Reaching into the closet, Tyrrell took down the stuffed animal and showed it to Cathy.

"Do you remember this, daughter?"

"Yes, yes!"

"And this?" He set the childish lunch box in front of her. "I brought this down from the Rim, for you, at your special request. It was something you remembered from the world outside, before you came here. And you wanted one, I don't know why." He paused. "Perhaps you still had hopes of going to school one day. Well, I suppose you've managed to do that."

"Yes, I've gone to school. I don't know either—Father—why I wanted the lunch box. But it seems to me I remember that I did."

"And this." Now he was opening a very different metal box, also taken from the closet. "I believe your birth certificate is still in here somewhere."

In a moment he had brought out an old paper. The folds in the document were stiff with age.

"Dated May eighteenth, you see, nineteen thirty.

Your mother had it with her, for some reason, when she came here."

Cathy looked at the paper. " 'Catherine Ann Young,' " she read aloud, wonderingly.

"That's you. Sarah's maiden name was Young. She was never married, you see, to your biological father. She must have loved him, of course, to have two children by him. Perhaps he was a married man. I never asked her much about her past. I was content to have her as she was." He paused. "More than content."

"But I can't believe this." Cathy was shaking her head. "This would mean that there were years—decades, out of the middle of this century—when I didn't exist at all."

"You might also reflect that you were also absent from existence during the entire nineteenth century— and for a good many centuries, millenia, geological ages, before that."

"Of course, but—it's so strange."

"I doubt, my dear, that your life is any stranger than my own." Tyrrell took thought, and hesitated. "Well, perhaps it is, in some details. But I also doubt that either yours or mine is the strangest human life that anyone has ever lived." He smiled. "Of course, neither of us have quite run our full course yet, have we?"

The birth certificate was marked by two tiny baby footprints in black ink, showing a left foot and a right.

"Those prints would match yours," said Tyrrell gently. "My dear, you were born more than sixty years ago. Evidently in California, as it says. Your mother can tell you the details, I'm sure."

"My mother. Then Sarah is my mother."

"Indeed she is. I'll see that you get back to her safely."

Cathy's eyes closed as she stood over the little table, and for a moment she looked faint.

Then she reached out, groped for her father and gave him a tighter hug than before.

Again he responded awkwardly.

Releasing him, she looked around. "I wonder where Maria's got to?"

"I must go to the cave," Tyrrell said suddenly, as if the question about Maria had reminded him of something. "It will be safer for you if you come with me, rather than waiting here."

"Safer?"

"The Deep Canyon is a dangerous place to visit, girl. You have been lucky, so far. And when you were a child, you were well protected. Your baby sister—was not so fortunate. And for that your mother blamed me." His voice had dropped to a kind of whisper. "Come with me. If your companion is important to you—perhaps we can still help her as well."

"Help her? What's the matter?"

"Come with me. Now."

On reaching the entrance to the work-cave, Cathy paused just inside. "I remember this place," she whispered. "It's where you worked. My mother would tell me: 'Daddy's working.' And I would come to the doorway and look in here—at the darkness."

"I still work here, daughter." Tyrrell stood with his head turned slightly, listening carefully. "Your companion is not here now." He turned on the lights.

"What do you work on, Father?"

"On the lifeblood of our planet, my dear. On life and death. On the ways that the two can come together. You see, neither can exist without the other."

"Father? What's happened to you?" Here in the cave's harsh electric lights, she could see how the old man's face showed scars. What must once have been hideous burn marks had healed and softened with time, leaving little more than a suggestion of what must once have been disaster.

"What are those scars?" Cathy repeated. "I don't remember them."

"Someone attempted to kill me." Her father turned from his workbench to answer tersely. "Actually, they wanted to burn me to death."

His look softened when he saw his daughter's reaction.

"It doesn't matter now," he assured her. "They failed. And that was a long time ago. Here, here are the rocks I work on. Not the silly things I carve from ordinary stone, for Brainard to sell. I gave up most of that sort of work a long time ago."

Tyrrell broke off, listening. He looked at Cathy, and his face grew worried. Moments passed before she could hear what he heard, approaching voices, sounding like those of two women and a man.

~ *18* ~

In the bright sunlight of midafternoon Jake stood, momentarily immobilized by the screams that poured out from behind the chipped and blasted but still solid barrier of rock. The man Jake was trying to kill obviously still survived.

Camilla, standing beside her breathing lover, had covered her ears with her hands, but now she added scream after scream of her own to Edgar's.

Anger brought Jake out of his momentary paralysis. He slapped Camilla viciously, trying to knock her out of her hysteria.

A moment later she was clinging to him, sobbing, and he was trying to comfort her. Then he grabbed her by the arms and shook her. Almost shouting to make himself heard above Edgar's cries of agony, he commanded: "We've got to try the dynamite again. We've got to finish him off."

Camilla shuddered. "I know, I know—I'm all right now."

Already Jake had picked up his hammer and drill again; the only practical hope was another attempt at blasting. He still had dynamite, and wire, and blasting caps.

Camilla had an inspiration. "We forgot about the kerosene in the lamps in the house. I can get that."

"Good idea. Throw the lamps back there. Keep that fire burning."

She ran off.

Hastily Jake ran his hands over the barrier rock, selecting the spots where he wanted to drill the next set of holes. In a few moments he had begun hammering again. The failure of his first attempt had made him more keenly aware than ever that he didn't really know what he was doing when it came to blasting rock.

In a couple of minutes Camilla was back, walking now, carefully carrying three kerosene lamps. She hurled these accurately, one at a time, the glass bowls shattering inside the cave. The fresh shower of flammable liquid made the black smoke pour forth with increased volume.

Then she came to help Jake. "It'll go faster if I hold the drill."

"Yeah."

She gripped the steel tool, rotating it after each blow as she had seen Jake do. Jake switched to a bigger hammer, as he had before. A slowly growing frenzy of fear and horror fueled him with energy. The work went faster.

When Jake and Camilla prepared to start the second new hole, he happened to look back into the little cave. What had been a deeply shadowed recess was now well lit by flames. To Jake's horror, he was able to see a portion of Tyrrell's head, scorched gray hair and blackened skin, at about knee level. The old man in his torment must somehow have managed to pull himself up on hands and knees.

Black smoke obscured at least half of what the orange flames were trying to reveal, but still Jake could see that Tyrrell's clothing was largely burned away, at least around his neck and shoulders, and the vampire was looking out at his assailants. His eyes, set in the scorched ruin of his face, were glassy and staring. His blackened lips writhed, uttering strange sounds.

On Jake's next swing his hammer missed the drill completely, fortunately missing Camilla's hands as well. She yelled at him in fright and dropped the tool.

Jake bellowed back at her, and she picked up the drill again.

Then suddenly it was all too much for her. Screaming, she dropped the tool clanging on rock and started to run, heading down the side canyon in the direction of the river.

Jake's shout of desperation—"Cam, get back here! I can't do this alone!"—stopped her in her tracks.

Quivering, she came back. But then she slumped weakly to the ground, unable or unwilling to do any more.

Again he gripped the drill in his own left hand, though both his arms were trembling with fatigue. Again he swung the smaller hammer with his right.

The drilling progressed, slowly. Time passed. Tyrrell's screams slowly subsided into hideous moans, as the fire in the recess burned itself out, the black smoke diminishing to a greasy trickle in the air. Jake could not believe that the moans were ever going to stop.

Slowly, slowly, the last hole that Jake would have time to drill deepened in the limestone. Somehow the sun had passed the zenith and was going down. Despite oddness of the way time was passing, and the urgency of passing time, he had to pause frequently to rest his arms.

He didn't look into the cave again, but with the wind blowing the last traces of smoke away he knew that now the fire was out. Whatever damage the burning kerosene was capable of doing had been done, and their enemy had somehow survived it.

"Jake, I'm sorry, lover. I'll help you now, I'll help."

Camilla had pulled herself together and come to stand beside him.

Jake nodded and smiled, saving his breath for work. He put down his hammer for a moment, leaning against the barrier rock to rest, wiping sweat from his forehead, and from his face, long days unshaven, with the sleeve of his work shirt.

Camilla came to give him an embrace.

Without warning, Tyrrell's scorched hand came groping out of the recess. The thin limb struck like a black snake wearing the ashen remnants of a sleeve, the arm extending itself unbelievably far. The grab missed Jake's arm by a fraction of an inch, and caught Camilla by the collar of her shirt.

Jake let out an incoherent sound of horror, dropped his hammer and jumped back. But the vampire's groping hand had now fastened on Camilla—she was being dragged helplessly into the small aperture between two unyielding surfaces of rock. The sound she made now was less a scream than a prolonged sob.

Jake stepped forward again. He picked up the metal drill, half as long as a baseball bat, and heavier, and swung it directly against Tyrrell's almost skeletal wrist— to no effect. The sensation of impact that traveled back up the drill and into Jake's own hands was as if he had struck the massive rock itself. The blackened hand did not release its grip.

Camilla's body was braced, all her muscles straining as she struggled to keep herself from being forced, crushed, into the narrow aperture. Her sobbing made coherent words: "No, Jake, use wood! Use wood!"

Jake dropped the drill. He grabbed up the longest hammer, and tried pounding with the handle at Tyrrell's arm. When that had no effect he changed his tactics, using the handle like a lever, jamming it into the narrow crevice between rocks, making a fulcrum of one angle of the big rock slab. With all his strength he forced Tyrrell's burned wrist against another rock.

Once more, the man in the cave screamed horribly.

His blackened, bony fingers still refused to release Camilla's collar, but now the fabric of the shirt was ripping.

Part of the garment, collar and shoulder and sleeve, tore completely away. With a final cry, as if she might be dying, the young woman fell to the ground, out of the vampire's reach.

Jake grabbed her under the arms, pulled her even farther from the blackened arm that still groped in search of breathing flesh.

"Come on, Cam, we're not done yet. Come on, you've still got to help me. We still have to drill another hole." It would have to be done, obviously, in a place where Tyrrell could not possibly reach them as they worked.

"All right." Camilla dragged herself back to her feet.

They worked, in a nightmare of heat and exhaustion, in a persistent numbing stench of kerosene, while the treacherous sun slid swiftly down the sky. Sometimes, from the corners of their eyes, they saw one of Tyrrell's ruined arms come groping desperately out again.

There came a time when Jake had to rest. Camilla, now almost wholly recovered as far as he could tell, brought him food while he rested.

At last Jake, measuring with the drill, decided that the final hole was deep enough to hold a charge.

Once more, with shaking fingers, he crimped high explosives and blasting caps together, along with one end of a length of wire.

"Hurry, hurry." Camilla, in a shaking whisper, had begun to chant a litany.

It seemed to Jake that time was going crazy. How could a full day of sunlight have slipped away so quickly?

Shadows were lengthening, the hours of daylight almost gone.

Inside the cave, darkness was firmly re-established, and the man in there had ceased to struggle visibly. He had fallen completely silent.

Eventually, with the two breathers huddled in the same shelter as before, Jake managed to set off a second blast.

Running out from his shelter as before, amid a shower of splintered rock, he needed only a single glance at the barrier to know that he had failed again. Once again a thick slice of the obstacle had been blasted away, but the main bulk still stood. Maybe one more shot would do it. Maybe.

Fatalistically Jake surveyed his tools and blasting materials. Even if he had the stuff for a third blast, which was doubtful, he lacked anything like the time to prepare one.

Dragging Camilla to her feet, he started moving with her, an exhausted shuffle down-canyon in the direction of the river. "Come on," he urged.

"Where, Jake? Where?"

He kept his mouth shut. He didn't want to say anything, for fear that the half-dead thing in the little cave might hear him.

Dragging, half-carrying Camilla with him, Jake made the best time he could, down the trail to the river.

All along he had had in the back of his mind this final try at escape, something to do when all else failed. If they could get to the river there was a chance they might survive the rapids. And now there was a chance that Tyrrell, injured as he was, would not be able to pursue them past that barrier, or could not catch them if he did. If the rapids killed them, well, any quick death would be better than what was coming for them here at sundown.

Leaping freely beside Jake as he stumbled along, too weak to run, the foaming water of the little creek babbled warnings and strange curses.

Camilla at his side seemed to be delirious, or almost, mumbling warnings. The last rays of the day's sun came through a notch in the western cliffs, to burn briefly on her face unnoticed.

Minutes later, with Camilla still at his side, Jake went plunging into the swift icy water of the river that ought to have been the Colorado.

At the last moment, right at the waterline, he seized a large piece of driftwood and dragged it with him. He wasn't a strong swimmer, but the wood allowed him some hope of keeping himself afloat. He tried to call to Camilla to take hold of the log as well, but she was already gone ahead of Jake, disappeared into the torrent.

The sun was now completely down.

The rocks on which the current tore itself to foam were black in the sky's last fading light. These were the deepest rocks of all the layers through which the Colorado cut.

The water was a shock of cold, followed immediately by a greater shock of impact. Lights whirled and flashed before Jake's eyes, and he saw, or imagined that he saw, first one white nodule protruding from a rock, and then a forest of them.

And Jake, in the few moments before the current slammed him even harder against more rocks, was sure that he could hear Tyrrell, released by sunset and howling like a windstorm, coming after him to make sure of his revenge.

But other hands than Tyrrell's caught at Jake first, and held him up. Bright light, like colored searchlights reflecting from the river, was all around him.

Whatever happened, Camilla was still with him. He could no longer see her face, but, whatever strange thing was happening to them now, he knew that she was near.

～ *19* ～

Maria on straying out of the cottage into the dusk followed the same call that had brought her down into the Deep Canyon. She went exploring, looking for the source of the attraction.

The call was voiceless and soundless, but somehow unmistakeable and almost irresistible, like the voices of friends, and—this struck Maria as very odd—of devoted pets. It led her past the workshop-cave, all dark and silent, and upstream along the little creek.

She walked on in the certainty that something—glorious—was waiting for her, just a little farther upstream. Something—she did not know what—but something truly glorious.

The afternoon of New Year's Eve had arrived on the South Rim. The last hours of 1991 were running out.

"All right," Joe Keogh said. "They're both gone. Cathy left a note, this time. Is anyone going to argue that Maria might have just wandered off by accident?"

No one of the group assembled in the main room of the Tyrrell House was going to defend that theory.

The gathering included Sarah, Bill, and John, as well as Joe himself, and Mr. Strangeways. Mounted predatory heads looked down with bared fangs from the log walls.

Curious stone animals, the work of Edgar Tyrrell, stared from shelves and tables.

Old Sarah looked at Mr. Strangeways. She said: "Cathy has gone down into the Deep Canyon again. Can you get her back this time? Somehow I doubt it."

Drakulya did not immediately respond. He was in a particularly dark mood. The signs were subtle, but to Joe, who had known him for years, they were unmistakeable.

John Southerland started to say: "Maria must have followed Cathy—"

The bearded man turned from the window, where he had been watching occasional snowflakes, with an outburst of anger. "No!"

"No?"

"No. The two young women may be together, but only accidentally. I ought to have recognized the hand that was on her!"

"On Maria?"

"Of course!"

Cathy, standing in the entrance to the workshop-cave and looking out, was astonished and frightened to see Maria approaching, in the company of a whirl of lights, a monstrous, glowing presence.

At first glance it had appeared to Cathy that the figure walking at Maria's side was a young man in work clothes. But amid a swirl of lights he disappeared, to be immediately replaced by the image of a young woman with red hair, similarly dressed.

Cathy retreated a step, reaching for Tyrrell's arm. "What is it, Father?"

Tyrrell's eyes were glowing, his voice was reverent. "It is the life of the planet, daughter. The light of the world."

For just a flash of time a new shape was visible among the lights: a saber-toothed tiger. Cathy thought she could not have been mistaken. Then all three figures reappeared in rapid succession, followed by a flurry of others, less distinct.

With the onset of this kaleidoscopic display, Maria seemed to pull free of whatever influence had made her walk so trustingly beside this incredible companion. Catching sight of Cathy and Tyrrell standing at the entrance to the workshop-cave, she ran toward them.

"I don't know where I am!" she cried. "Cathy, help me. I don't know what's happening!"

Cathy would have stepped forward to try to help, but her father's hand on her arm, immovable, held her back.

Maria looked desperately from one of them to the other. She made a choking noise, and in a moment had gone running off into the darkness.

Stalking slowly, unhurried, the thing of light began to follow her. Once more its shape was simply that of a young man, walking.

"Father, what is it?" This time Cathy made the question an intense demand.

"Your friend will not be harmed, girl. Perhaps she will be allowed to feel the embrace of the earth, of life itself. Perhaps she will even be granted a kind of immortality. What happier fate could any of us hope for?"

Cathy stared at her father. Then, suddenly terrified, she broke away and ran impulsively down-canyon, going in the opposite direction from that taken by Maria and her leisurely pursuer.

Cathy's father was shouting something after her. But he made no move to bring her back.

Up in the Tyrrell House on the South Rim, Drakulya was insisting that the rescue operation be methodically organized, even if they delayed the start a little.

He warned those who were going with him that they were volunteering for a perilous foray into a territory where none of them had ever been before: the territory of the vampire Edgar Tyrrell.

"More importantly, we are going into the domain of a unique creature. One that is stranger than any vampire I have ever known—and in some ways, at least, more dangerous."

Joe Keogh said: "One of my people is missing. We all understand it's dangerous; now how soon do we get started?"

"You do not get started, Joseph. You remain here, on the Rim."

"My ankle is all right."

"It is not. Great agility may be needed down below. More than two or three people will not be needed." Strangeways looked at John Southerland and Bill Burdon. "You two will come with me."

"The more people we have," said Joe, "the better we can search."

Bill, unconsciously ignoring the man who was still formally his employer, acknowledged the orders of the new leader with a businesslike nod. John, who had some idea of what he might be getting into, looked very thoughtful. But he nodded too.

"I've still got Brainard's gun," Joe said suddenly.

Drakulya looked at him again. "Then I think you should give it to whichever of these young men you think better able to use it. We may also face mundane perils below, against which firearms could be helpful."

"Once we get down there," Bill was volunteering, "I can probably find my way back to the place where I found Cathy's camp."

"That may be useful. We shall see."

Meanwhile Joe was pulling out the parts of the revolver. He had carried it, disassembled, in his coat pockets to this meeting, on the chance it might be wanted. "It'll just take me a minute to put this back together."

Drakulya viewed the pieces of firearm with innate distaste, but nodded. "No doubt it will be effective against certain creatures of the Miocene, who as I understand have no respect at all for humanity. I expect to be fully occupied with other matters."

At this point old Sarah emerged from the bedroom, where she had changed into trousers and a woolen shirt.

"Mr. Strangeways, I am going with you."

No one said anything. Everyone present looked at Sarah's aged, frail form.

But she persisted. "How will you find the cottage, and the cave, if I do not show you? I think Cathy will have gone there, this time, and I suppose the other one is with her."

Strangeways gave his little reptilian sigh. "Your suggestion has merit," he conceded.

Joe was outraged. "If an eighty-year-old woman is going—"

The bearded leader silenced him, for the moment, with a raised hand.

"If you do not take me with you," continued Sarah, "I shall go down by myself, if I die on the way. Two young lives are at stake."

Drakulya studied her for a long moment, then bowed lightly. "As you wish," he said. "In the face of such determination—" He looked at Joe. "Very well, both of you. Provided you follow my orders."

A few minutes later, Drakulya led his four followers out of the house. Old Sarah, jacketed and booted like the rest, walked beside him, leaning lightly on his arm. Her eyes were dreamy, as if in her mind she had already completed this journey into the past. The little procession passed into the snow-hazed light of midafternoon, moving unnoticed among tourists toward Bright Angel trailhead.

Joe now had Brainard's revolver, reassembled, loaded and tucked into an inside pocket of his winter jacket. Everyone but Sarah was carrying a canteen and some trail food.

Cathy, fleeing into darkness from the lighted work-shop-cave, turned to see her father apparently engaged in some kind of friendly discussion with the thing of lights and changing shapes—somehow, she thought, he must have called it back from following Maria.

But she, Cathy, could not go near the thing. Suppressing a sob, she turned and ran again. The night was not yet too dark for her to find a path. For whatever reason, she was not pursued.

The night, under a sky that held what looked like a million stars and an incredibly large crescent of a moon, never grew too dark for Cathy to find a place to walk. But the absence of familiar constellations was disconcerting, and the cacophony of unfamiliar animal noises even more so. Ignoring these oddities as best she could, she pushed on down the canyon. This was still her childhood home.

On the bank of the marvelous, starlit river she paused to rest, sitting on a boulder, thinking of what her father—she could not help still thinking of him as her real father—had told her about rapids in the flow of time.

Time passed. The sound of a footstep moving gravel jarred Cathy back to an awareness of her immediate surroundings.

It was only Maria, approaching in the starlight.

"Cathy? Thank God it's you. Help me. It—that thing—has stopped chasing me. But it wants me."

"Those people, moving in the light?"

"They're not really people, not any more. There are at least two of them in it now. They come out and talk sometimes, and I thought at first that they were real. But

I'm sure now that they're not really people any more. They're just in there, with all those—animals. All part of one great—thing."

Maria came close, and stood directly in front of Cathy.

Cathy said: "My father wouldn't—" But then she remembered her father's vague warnings about danger in the Deep Canyon, what he had said about Maria's fate not mattering.

"Cathy."

"What?"

"Stay with me. How long is it till dawn?"

"I don't know."

"What are we going to do?"

"When it's light again we'll go back to the house."

"And then?"

"And then I don't know."

The five people slowly descending Bright Angel Trail had left the late twentieth century and its swarming tourists well behind them. Drakulya and his four followers moved through a shrunken, adolescent Canyon, among the flora and fauna that flourished a million years before they were born.

It was still daylight, or it was daylight again, under clouds. There was light enough to see a snarling, furry nightmare approaching among the rocks and scanty brush, to see it before it became an immediate threat. Joe, aiming to kill, sent a revolver bullet close enough to discourage the approach of a saber-toothed tiger.

Studying the landscape warily, he observed how something that looked like a wolf—and yet was somehow different from any other wolf that he had ever seen—watched this demonstration intently from a little distance.

"What was that?" asked John, pointing in another direction. "I thought I saw an elephant."

"A hairy elephant," confirmed Bill's voice. "Those tusks, they looked like shovels."

Joe carried the heavy pistol ready in his right hand. The group pressed on, with Drakulya in the lead, a leader who paid no attention to such mundane matters as a few restless predators. To him they were simply animals, not worthy of much concern. Sarah was still at the leader's side, and now, more often than not, he was carrying the old woman, lifting her over obstacles as if she weighed no more than a glove.

Meanwhile she gave directions in a weak but eager voice.

They had reached the very dooryard of the little house before Cathy came out to greet them.

"Mother," she said at once, when her eyes fell on old Sarah.

Tears were running in Sarah's eyes. "A very old and feeble mother, dear. Can you ever forgive me, Cathy? I tried to hide you, to protect you, to save you, and perhaps there was no need."

"Where is Tyrrell?" Drakulya demanded.

"My father rests during the day."

"If I can face this clouded daylight, he can do as much. Where does he rest?"

The young woman in the doorway shook her head. "I don't know."

What Drakulya might have said or done next, Joe was never to learn.

Two voices were heard, coming from down canyon. In a moment Maria came into view in that direction. She was walking hand in hand with the glowing image of Edgar Tyrrell.

* * *

"He has given himself to it," Drakulya muttered. "Or it has taken him."

The walking, glowing man, guiding an apparently willing Maria by the hand, came within easy hailing distance, and called out: "Welcome, Prince of Wallachia."

"I do not come in peace, or in friendship."

"Then let your fate be on your own head, Drakulya." Tyrrell's image glowed and wavered. He dropped Maria's hand, and she began to edge away from him.

Tyrrell's voice boomed out. "You see, I need fear the sun no longer," he proclaimed. "I am no longer *nosferatu*." And with that he disappeared—

—to be replaced by a green-eyed young man. "I am no longer a mere breather," this one said. And in turn vanished—

—to be replaced by the red-haired young woman, whose lips moved but whose words could not be heard. And then replaced by one older human figure, and another, their faces and outlines blurred, so that no one could see what they might have looked like in full life.

—and, when his turn in the cycle came round again, Tyrrell was back.

He said: "This is our planet's life that dances before you, Drakulya. It was madness on my part to think that I could ever capture the essence of earth's life in a carved rock—"

Drakulya's voice rang out. "Tyrrell, if you have still enough of your mind left to understand, hear me. What you have done is madness. The madness of the artist is allowable, even necessary. But you have gone beyond that. Human lives, not only your own, have been destroyed. The damage you have done to the planet's spirit must be undone."

"Human lives?" The artist was scornful. "What are they? What is any human life, even yours or mine, compared to this?"

"Speaking as a human, I consider my own life a very great thing indeed."

Drakulya had done with arguing. He spread his arms, and murmured magic.

To Joe Keogh, standing by with Brainard's pistol ready, the language sounded something like simple German. But he knew it must be more than that.

Suddenly, the ground of the Deep Canyon quivered underneath Joe's feet. Others were feeling a great change too; uneasiness spread among the group.

"Hello. I'm Jake."

Tyrrell was gone again. Now the creature showed the face of the green-eyed young man, whoever he had been in life. It called itself by Jake's name, and then once more by Camilla's.

Camilla and Jake appeared in rapid alternation, each of them calling for the other. For a brief time their voices sounded desperate.

Then the young man, whose cheerfulness seemed to have been fully recovered, held the stage again. "This is Jake, everybody. We're going to be friends."

Maria had been slowly making her way to join her rescuers. Like most of them, she watched in awe and fear.

Drakulya's arms were still extended, his lips still murmured words.

The creature was visibly beginning to dissolve under the magical assault—the powers of the earth, Joe thought, were re-ordering themselves. Sequentially the thing of light disgorged a number of animals. Joe could recognize bears and deer. His mind recoiled from less familiar shapes.

Tyrrell had not yet been vanquished. He reappeared again, shouting something to Sarah—Joe could not understand the words. He called his daughter's name for a last time.

Cathy did not seem to hear. Her full attention was somewhere else.

"I need tools, physical tools," Drakulya cried to her, and to Sarah. "Where are they kept?"

"The workshop!"

Willing young feet dashed away. Young hands were soon back, laden with heavy, mundane miner's tools.

"Those are my tools!" screamed the wraith of Jake, looming amid boiling light.

Drakulya grabbed up a miner's pick.

The man who had been called Strangeways struck at the ground with iron, using all his strength. The tormented earth buckled up, sending people staggering, exposing a sharply demarcated seam between two layers of rock.

"The Great Unconformity," murmured Sarah.

The seam writhed in the earth, as if it sought to position itself below the creature. The being, the thing, the structure of light, was beginning to unravel. In a startlingly brief time it was gone.

The ground beneath the feet of the survivors ceased to heave convulsively. Instead it was bending, as if a hollowness were under it. The strata of rocks, no longer hard and dense, were stretching, changing uncontrollably.

"Back, get back!" Drakulya had abandoned magic and was shouting at his friends. "Withdraw, retreat uphill!"

Joe was still half-crippled, but with the adrenaline flowing and John Southerland's strong shoulder offering support he could force himself to run uphill, through a rapidly altering landscape, out of the Deep Canyon. Drakulya ran beside him, carrying Sarah, with Cathy hovering nearby. Others were running on their own power, under a sky that suddenly and repeatedly changed its cloud-configuration and modified its light.

Bill Burdon, feeling safe enough to turn for a look back, beheld a churning, upswelling mass of light and shadow, tones reversed as in a photographic negative, rapidly, silently, filling in the depths from which they had just climbed. He cried out in alarm: "Is that lava?"

Their leader grunted: "No, only energy, but quite as dangerous. Stay ahead of it!"

Rushing and scrambling, the visitors from the late twentieth century did their best to accomplish that.

At last the rocky ground regained stability. Around them, mundane snow began to fall.

~ 20 ~

The time on the South Rim was either shortly before, or shortly after midnight, on the last day of the old year—or else on the first of the new. After a day like the one he had just been through, Joe Keogh, now more or less collapsed in his room at El Tovar with his sore leg up on cushions, was not entirely sure which.

Nor could he convince himself that it really mattered.

Just across the room John Southerland was on the phone, completing a long-distance call to Angie back in Chicago, assuring her that the day's dangerous business had been brought to a conclusion that was, by and large, acceptable if not entirely satisfactory. Only minutes ago Joe himself had finished a similar call to his own wife.

Not very far outside the door of Joe's suite, no farther away than the hotel lounge, appropriate holiday music was being played—just now *Auld Lang Syne,* at holiday volume.

Tonight Mr. Strangeways and his companions were doing most of their celebrating within the solid log walls of El Tovar, but occasionally their party, or a strong contingent of it anyway, sallied forth onto the South Rim. Sometimes the strollers got as far as the Tyrrell House where Cathy and her mother were established, though they never strayed beyond shouting distance of the old hotel.

Whenever any celebrants from the hotel walked out on the Rim, to one of the places along the very brink where they could turn their backs on the streetlights along the tourist walk, they found themselves confronted by the full company of the wintry stars, and by the vast imperturbable black midnight that was the Canyon.

In the middle of one such sortie Maria Torres said to her nearest companion: "It's a little frightening." Then she almost laughed at herself. "It must sound silly to say that, after today. After what almost happened to us all. But I mean it anyway."

Maria was recovering very nicely. In fact, thanks to certain subtle ministrations performed by Mr. Strangeways, she no longer had any very clear memory of what had happened to her personally—or what had almost happened—only a few hours ago, down below.

Now she frowned lightly at the Canyon's darkness. "But . . . it's not like me to blank out."

"Might happen once to anyone. I wouldn't worry about it." John, who had been ready to walk outside after making his phone call, was being as reassuringly avuncular as possible, given the slight disparity in ages.

"I suppose you're right." Maria sounded doubtful.

"Take my word for it." John sipped from his can of beer. "What did you mean just now, when you said something is a little frightening?"

"I meant how the people come out here with their New Year's noisemakers, but all the noise that they can make is swallowed up. Like all the light we shine out over the brink. It all just disappears. There's not the trace of an echo or a reflection or an answer."

*   *   *

Presently it was time to look in once again on Mrs. Tyrrell and Cathy, in the family house.

A big tearful reunion had taken place between mother and daughter as soon as they were both safely out of the Deep Canyon.

For many years Sarah had been afraid to reveal her identity as Cathy's mother. But in fact the revelation had made the girl very happy.

"Now I have a real live mother."

"A very old one, I'm afraid."

"Mothers are supposed to be old. Experienced. That's what they're supposed to be."

Cathy, who tonight was remembering the day's events much more clearly than Maria, had mixed feelings about the loss of her original stepfather, that male figure of power remembered from her childhood.

"Who was my real father, then?" she asked her mother.

"Long dead, I'm afraid, my dear."

"I'm going to want a complete explanation, you know, of everything that's happened. As complete as you can make it. But that can wait."

With new and old pop music blaring alternately in the background, the survivors of the afternoon, except for Sarah and Cathy, gathered once more in Joe's suite.

It seemed to Joe that Bill Burdon was going somewhat out of his way to look after his young colleague Maria.

Strangeways, having gathered some old and now some new members of his trusted inner circle indoors where they could be comfortable, was explaining some of the afternoon's events.

"Around sixty years ago, Edgar Tyrrell, having used the special powers of the *nosferatu* to find his way for the first time into what he christened the Deep Canyon, encountered the . . . what shall we call it? An anomaly in the planet's life, a malformation, an artifact, perhaps, of the deep rock. Whatever it should be called, it had begun, ages before Tyrrell's arrival on the scene, to achieve sentience.

"His curiosity about the thing he had discovered caused him to nurture it, to feed it with new life—at first, no doubt, only with the lives of plants and animals. Service became devotion, and devotion eventually worship—I think that is not too strong a word. But it all began gradually, you must understand, in a spirit of intellectual inquiry. For years, for decades perhaps, he could still convince himself that he was only an investigator. An artist, with all that the word means, seeking to capture the essence of what he had discovered.

"When we began our own investigation I was not sure whether Tyrrell might not have come here as a breather, and been converted to vampirism by the entity he had discovered. But now we know enough to be sure that he had already passed beyond the breathing mode of life before he arrived at the Canyon."

Most of the audience seemed too timid to ask questions. But not Joe. "You don't think it was the thing itself that originally brought him to the Canyon."

"Almost certainly not. Rather he had somehow heard of the scientific possibilities—the first geological studies were made before 1860. The potential of such an incision into the secrets of the earth drew and fascinated him. What the fascinated seeker encountered in the deep rock was, by human standards, an alien kind of consciousness, though undeniably belonging to the earth as much as any human being does.

"A few days ago, in Tyrrell's native land, I spoke to one who gave me wise counsel—and even more than that. To destroy or slay this entity might well have been beyond my powers, and even beyond those of my borrowed magic. But by invoking the power of even deeper time, it became possible to release it—to undo the knot."

The phone rang in Joe's suite, and was duly answered, whereupon it became necessary to send a runner to fetch Cathy over from the phoneless Tyrrell House, and also someone to stay with Mrs. Tyrrell while Cathy came to talk. Her legally adoptive father was on the line, wishing everyone a happy New Year, cheerfully communicating the information that he was already somewhere in Nevada, that his luck had turned for the better. Brainard now seemed to think that his chances of surviving his current troubles were quite good.

When Cathy had finished her phone conversation, and had gone home to her mother again, Drakulya continued his exposition.

"Our friend—my compatriot, if you will, Tyrrell—had been, consciously or not, in a sense creating, defining, or giving substance to his own god—making it in the image of the god he wanted.

"But it was not in the nature of this creation to be benevolent toward its creator, or obedient to its self-proclaimed master."

"What'll happen to Cathy now?"

"I believe her to be what is now called a good survivor. Eventually she will be able to put all of these bizarre events behind her."

"And the rest of us," said Bill Burdon, "are going to have quite a story to tell." He looked hastily at Drakulya. "Someday," the young man amended. "Someday, when we can expect to be believed."

Saberhagen, Fred

A Question of Time